FORTUNE'S FOOL

A PSYCHIC SOCIALITE STORY

JANE SEVIER

ISBN-13: 978-1467978538
ISBN-10: 1467978531

Cover art and book design by April Martinez

Dedication

For my mother, Sue Paine Welch Johnson, MD,
who is and always has been an inspiration

CHAPTER 1

Memphis, 1933

For the longest time, Nell Marchand believed the happiest day of her life was the one on which she'd married dashing blueblood Daniel Ellis Overton Marchand IV. On the sun-washed Wednesday when she buried him next to I, II, and III under a magnolia in grand old Elmwood Cemetery with everybody who was anybody huddled in the March wind for the final send-off, she knew that she had been wrong all along.

Nell squeezed a fistful of rich West Tennessee dirt into the tightest clump she could manage and dropped it onto her husband's coffin. When it struck, the polished mahogany lid pealed for all the world like the Liberty Bell.

This, she said to herself, *this is it.*

A swell of thankfulness toward Ellis for dropping dead so completely unexpectedly and in apparently such resoundingly good health made her want to tear off her hat and veil and fling them into the air like a child celebrating the last day of school. Now, she really could do absolutely whatever she wanted whenever she wanted and wherever she wanted.

Paris, for example. She'd go back to that flat off Boulevard de La Tour-Maubourg where they had been so happy on their honeymoon. She would eat all the buttery croissants she could stuff in her mouth and wash them down with all the champagne she could swallow. The French had more sense that to put up with anything like Prohibition.

When the last mourner sprinkled the final handful over Ellis, the preacher closed his Bible with a gentle thump. Behind her black lace veil, Nell smiled.

Back at the house, all of Memphis society, Boss Crump, Mayor Overton, and even Senator Cordell Hull himself—come all the way from Washington—pressed her fingers in sympathy.

"Heart attack took his daddy, too, didn't it?," they murmured. "Still, he was awful young. What a shame."

"We sure are going to miss him."

"Bless your heart."

And then they passed into the double parlor, skirting General Oates's wooden leg in its burled walnut-and-glass case to get to the long tables on which her cook Hattie had piled mountains of food.

As was seemly for a fresh widow, from time to time Nell touched her handkerchief to her nose. A lady never wept in public. Even Bess Marchand was behaving tolerably, playing the grieving mother with quiet dignity rather than carrying on the way she could when she had a mind to.

All in all, it was a very good day.

—

ONCE THEY HAD ALL GONE, NELL WAS ABOUT TO FREE HER FEET FROM the torture of her stylishly somber shoes so she could stand barefoot on the cool floor at the sink and dry the dishes as Hattie washed them and talk over the wake and what everyone had brought and said and worn. A sudden shiver shook Nell so hard that she had to grab the edge of the table to steady herself.

"Somebody walking on your grave, honey?" Hattie said.

"Must have."

Nell hugged herself and wiggled her heel again. Just then, Anton Green, the Marchands' lanky family attorney and Ellis's godfather, poked his balding head into the kitchen. "I need you a minute, Nell," he said. He came to take her by the elbow and guided her into the sitting room that looked out on the back gardens.

"I probably shouldn't tell you this today, but I think you need to know before you get yourself into trouble."

"Anton, what on earth?"

Nell perched on the edge of old Judge Marchand's awful horsehair sofa.

Hands clasped behind his back, muttering, Anton took a couple of turns in front of the fireplace like a preoccupied stork. A definite unpleasantness stirred in Nell's middle. He stopped in front of her, and, Lord Almighty, if he didn't look as though he might bust loose and cry.

"Oh, my dear, I'm so sorry. There's nothing left."

"Nothing left. I don't understand. Nothing left of what?"

"Of your money. It's all gone."

It took a small eternity for that to sink in. Nell smoothed her handkerchief against her thigh, folded it in half, folded it again. "When you say 'nothing,' do you mean every bit of it?"

"Every last bit."

"I'm penniless?"

"I'm afraid so."

Choking back wild laughter that bubbled at the back of her throat, she looked up at Anton, who, now that he had delivered the death blow, seemed more composed.

"But how can that be? Ellis said he was too smart for the Crash to touch us."

"Well, now, Nell, you know Ellis sometimes found the truth disagreeable. I reckon he thought that if he didn't let on he was broke, he wouldn't be."

Nell twisted the handkerchief.

"What am I going to do?"

Anton sat beside her. "I'm sure we can find something for you."

"You mean go to some horrible little office all day?"

"There are worse things, Nell."

"Yes. Yes, I'm sure there must be, though for the life of me, I can't quite think what they might be just now." Nell unfurled the handkerchief and began to smooth it again. "What about Mother Marchand's money?"

"Gone, too."

Nell wiped her nose, feeling sincere but not particularly brave. "But this Depression they talk about. I thought that's why all those men show up at the kitchen door every day. I thought that's why there are such throngs when Miss Bess and I work at the soup kitchen downtown. I thought that's why we just elected Mr. Roosevelt. Because there aren't any jobs."

She slumped against the back of the sofa and draped her forearm across her eyes. "I don't know how to *do* anything."

"What about your folks in Mississippi?"

"Gone. The flu took most of them, just like Mama and Daddy. I haven't got anybody."

"You can learn to type or keep books."

"But I was going to Paris."

Even in her own ears, her voice was small. She thought several very unladylike things that would have made her mother speak sharply to her had she said them out loud and had her mother still been alive. For first time in she couldn't remember how long, Nell Marchand cried real tears.

—

ALONE IN HER ROOM, NELL STRIPPED OFF HER BLACK DRESS AND HUNG it in her closet. Belting the jade silk robe Ellis had bought her, she slid her feet into the matching slippers and settled at her vanity.

She reached for the cold cream, but her hand fell instead on the red tin box that her Welsh grandmother had given her on her sixth birthday, the box with the image of Tintern Abbey on the lid. A treasure box, Mared Blayney called it.

"This is to keep all your secrets in, pippin. This is where all the mysteries that the world lays at your feet are to go."

Nell poked through the contents. There was Mama's silver thimble. There was the bunch of violets Ellis had bought her from the basket on the little donkey's back their first night in Paris. There was the odd deck of cards her grandmother always used to tell Nell's fortune. She lifted the cards out and ran her thumb over the edge of the deck.

"This is the Tarot," her grandmother had said. "Look to it to know what your future holds, my darling. The cards will never fail you."

Nell shuffled them. Turned one over. The Queen of Cups, Mared Blayney's favorite. The scent of vanilla and soap, her grandmother's scent, enfolded her, so potent that Nell looked in the mirror at the empty room behind her to see if Mared had somehow materialized.

"I wish you were here to tell me my future now."

Nell kissed the Queen of Cups, returned the deck to the box, and closed the lid. She stared at herself in the vanity mirror. Thank goodness she didn't look nearly as ancient as she felt right then. What on earth was she going to do?

"I am too tired to think. Tomorrow is soon enough."

Nell picked up the cold cream and set to work on her face.

—

HATTIE TAYLOR DEPOSITED THE BREAKFAST TRAY ON NELL'S DRESSING table and opened the curtains. That girl sure could sleep. She shook Nell's shoulder.

"Time to get up, honey. Eat your breakfast before it gets cold."

Nell stretched luxuriously and pulled the covers up under her chin. Her eyes flew open, and she shot bolt upright.

"Oh, Lordy, Hattie, are we still broke?"

"Unless somebody dropped off a bag of money in the night, we are. I didn't see anything when I went out to get the milk."

Nell reached for the tray and settled it on her lap.

"I guess we'd better eat while we can, then. What did you bring me this morning?"

"Nothing but country ham, biscuits, and red-eye. A little preserves in case you want some on your biscuits, and a nice cup of tea."

"How did you know?"

"Don't I always? We've got to eat up all that food folks brought. The mayor sent over this ham straight from his smokehouse. I saved it back, and we can eat on it for a while."

Nell split open two biscuits and poured red-eye gravy over them. She chewed a great big old bite of ham and closed her eyes. "I hope we're never too poor to eat ham, Hattie. This one is just right."

No, sir, nothing spoiled that girl's appetite. Hattie took a biscuit herself. Nell poured her a cup of tea.

"Now, Hattie," Nell went on when she'd polished off the last crumb, "we've got to earn a living. Got any ideas?"

—

THE READING OF ELLIS'S WILL WAS ONE LONG HUMILIATION. ALL THE talk of bequests and little kindnesses when that sorry so-and-so had left nothing. And damn that pompous Franklin Bryant, nodding so gravely at each item that Anton read aloud. If he was any kind of banker, Franklin must know Ellis had squandered every dime.

Afterward, there was the task of telling Bess Marchand exactly what her darling son had done with his fortune and hers and Nell's. Mother Marchand did not take it well.

It was a performance that would have done Gloria Swanson proud, one of Bess Marchand's greatest. First the dramatic swoon, then the brief but effective where-am-I moment, and then a shriek so piercing that Anton Green actually put his fingers in his ears like a little boy waiting for the noon train's whistle to pass out of earshot. At some point, genuine hysteria had taken over, and Nell had called old Dr. Roberts to come give Bess something to make her sleep.

So, now Nell had to figure out a way to feed this crazy old woman and Hattie and the driver, Jenkins, when she didn't know how to keep even herself in grits and gravy.

At least they had the mansion on Poplar, if she could hold on to it, that is. If it would bring anything, she could sell it, but it had slept and birthed Marchands just about as long as there had been Marchands in Memphis. Bess Marchand was outraged at even the suggestion of it.

"If we have to go from this house," she said, "then we might as well rent ourselves out as sharecroppers and go live in a tarpaper shack or sit in the street in sackcloth and ashes. It'll be just like saying we're headed for the poor house."

Dadgummit, there was no help for it. Nell was going to find a way to support them. She couldn't do without her Hattie, who wouldn't go even if she told her to. And without Jenkins, who had been with them forever, they would have to traipse all over town on the trolley.

Nell put her arm around the old lady's shoulders.

"Don't worry, Mother. I'll take care of you."

—

FIRST, SHE TRIED TYPING FOR ANTON. THE KEYS STUCK, OR THE PAPER went in crooked as an old barn and couldn't be straightened. The keyboard made no sense. What in the world did QWERTY mean anyway? She was so slow that it took her hours to finish one letter. The other typists were forever snatching her work out of her hands to do it themselves and whispering about her without having the decency to do it behind her back. She wore out even Anton's patience, and he was Job incarnate.

At the end of the week, wild with frustration, she marched into his office to quit.

"Look, I'm disrupting this whole place, the other girls despise me, and I am sick to death of all of it. Isn't there anything else?"

Anton tipped his chair back, linked his fingers behind his head, and gnawed his lower lip.

"All right, then," he said. "I know an old boy over at the phone company I can call."

Her stint as a telephone operator lasted one day. The calls came in so fast that she never knew who was on the line, and she cut off every single one. Every one.

That evening, Nell dragged herself through the front door and down the hall into the kitchen, where Hattie was stirring something on the stove that smelled like heaven. With a groan, Nell pulled out a chair and tossed her hat and gloves on the table.

"Oh, Lord, Hattie," Nell said, her voice breaking, "I've tried everything. We really are going to end up in the poor house, just like Mother says." She blew her nose.

"Hush that squalling, now, Nell. I've been thinking about what we can do. I'll hire myself out to do baking and help with parties. That'll keep us going for a while."

Good old Hattie. Nell wiped her eyes, feeling a little better already. On the same day that Nell was born upstairs in the old Leyton house over on Park, Hattie came into the world in the room behind the kitchen. Except for the month of Nell's honeymoon, the girls had been together every day of their lives. When Nell moved to the Marchand house, it was simply understood that Hattie would go along to look after her.

"Nobody in Memphis can beat my ironing, and we've got enough wash pots to do half the city's dirty drawers," Hattie said. "You and Miss Bess can stir the pots if you need to and help me wring the wash."

Nell looked down at her elegant, much-admired hands. "I don't know, Hattie. Do you think it will be enough?"

"Well, we've got to fish or cut bait. Just like your daddy always said. 'We got to fish or cut bait, Hattie. No use wallowing around feeling sorry for ourselves.'"

Nell smiled at the memory. "You're right. I hope we can get Mother to help."

"You leave Miss Bess Marchand to me."

Hattie Taylor would have made a fine field general. By week's end, she had talked to every cook and maid in the grand mansions that lined Poplar all the way to downtown. Jenkins, who prided himself on keeping the Marchand's Duesenberg spotless inside and out, had a natural affinity for the laundry business. He took to stirring so well that Hattie told him he might make something of himself yet. He laughed.

Nell had sorting and folding duty. The steam from all the water wouldn't be good for one's complexion or coiffure, Bess said, but she didn't seem to mind hanging things out to dry. At least not too much at first.

Each night, Nell fell into her bed with every part of her body imaginable and unimaginable aching. And each night in the few seconds after she said her prayers and before she sank into that deep sleep of the dead and those who wished they were, she told herself that there had to be another way. If she didn't want to look as old as Bess Marchand by her fortieth birthday, there had to be an easier way.

CHAPTER 2

A week into their laundry adventure, Nell had just tasted her first spoonful of soup at supper when Bess turned to her, concern carving a tiny furrow between her brows.

"Nell, I've been pondering our situation, and I think it's time we sought guidance."

"Really, Mother?" Nell said. "Whom do you think best to guide us now?'

"Dr. Calendar."

Nell lost the battle not to roll her eyes. "You talk like a tree fell on you. We don't have the money to consult Dr. Calendar. But maybe we could offer him a share if he tells us where some Confederate gold is buried."

Bess thought a moment. "I do have $20 that I've been saving."

"You have $20." Nell dropped her spoon and gaped at Bess.

"Yes, Nell." Bess dipped back into her bowl. "I believe I just said I do, didn't I?"

It took Nell several breaths before she could trust herself to speak. "We've been working like dogs, and you've been hoarding a fortune?"

"I didn't really hoard it, dear. It was in my green handbag. I'd forgotten all about it until I got that bag down for church day before yesterday." Bess raised her spoon and swallowed the soup, smiling and unperturbed. "I can't think how on earth it got there unless it was from my last bridge game at the club."

"Nice Methodist ladies gamble?"

"We place a little wager from time to time, and I've done so well, you know, since I've been following Mr. Culbertson's method. Anyway, Dr. Calendar has always been such a comfort to me. I'm sure he'd offer some wonderful guidance for us in our present reduced circumstances."

"Well, if you're going to see Joseph Calendar, it had better not take that whole $20. I want some new drawers."

"Eleanor Leyton Marchand!" Bess clutched her napkin to her chest. "Ladies do not speak of their undergarments."

—

AND SO THEY VISITED JOSEPH CALENDAR, MEDIUM TO MEMPHIS society. Ever since the Judge died, Bess Marchand had consulted Calendar at least once a month to talk to her departed husband, who she claimed gave her better advice from the grave than he had in life. Nell suspected that this Dr. Calendar was simply a much more practical man than Judge Marchand.

Standing on the street in front of the medium's house in fashionable Central Gardens, Nell saw that hard times did not seem to have touched him. With its gold-domed turrets and bright azure-tiled steps, the house looked like something out of the Arabian Nights.

Calendar's elegant Negro butler answered the bell.

"Good afternoon, Simon," Bess said. "We're here to see Dr. Calendar, please."

"Yes, ma'am, Mrs. Marchand," he said. "Let me show you to the Spirit Room."

At the door to the room, Nell paused to take it in.

The windows were hung with velvet the green of cedar needles in the spring. Under their feet, Oriental carpets in fabulous hues promised to cushion each step, soft as down. A fantastic bronze gong ornamented with stars, moons, and odd symbols that Nell couldn't identify stood in a corner. The room's centerpiece was an Egyptian sarcophagus that served as a tea table. Nell and Bess seated themselves on a sofa covered in gold silk dupioni accented with crimson pillows and fringe.

"He must call this the Spirit Room because Mata Hari is obviously haunting it," Nell said. She swallowed an unseemly wave of envy at the opulence.

Simon returned with a tray. He poured each of the ladies a dainty crystal glass of sherry and set a plate of good old cheese straws on the sarcophagus. Nell's mouth watered. Breakfast had been a cold biscuit.

"I will tell the master that you have come."

"Thank you, Simon," Bess said.

The butler bowed deeply.

Nell waited only long enough for him to be out of sight before she stuffed two of the straws into her mouth and swallowed them almost whole. Lord, they were sharp and peppery and good. She summoned enough self-control to sip at the sherry rather than down it in one gulp. It was excellent, too. She sighed.

"Mrs. Marchand, what a delight to welcome you here again," came a cultured voice from the door.

Nell and Bess looked up to find Joseph Calendar standing there, cool and suave in a charcoal-gray suit that Nell would have bet good money he'd commissioned on Savile Row. She was sure she had seen his photograph in the paper, but Lord have mercy, it did not prepare her for the man in the flesh. He had the tall, manly-but-tender look of Gary Cooper, but Joseph Calendar was more elegance than aw shucks, not one hair of that perfect blond head out of place. Nell took another slug of sherry.

Bess rose to kiss Calendar on the cheek. "Nell, dear, I'd like you to meet Dr. Joseph Calendar. My daughter-in-law, Nell Marchand."

Nell stood. Calendar inclined his head in her direction, an Eastern potentate gracious in acknowledging a visiting dignitary. "I was quite saddened to hear of your husband's death, Miss Nell. He will be sorely missed in our city."

"Did you know Ellis?"

"No, but I have heard what a fine man he was."

Nell gave him an I-wouldn't-be-so-sure-if-I-were-you smirk.

Calendar cupped Bess's hands in his. "And Miss Bess, how greatly you must be grieving the loss of your son. Have you come to contact him on the other side?"

"Oh, do you think we could?"

"It is a little soon, perhaps, but with two of his loved ones here today, Mr. Marchand may be able to hear us. I will inquire of Imhotep."

"Imhotep?" Nell said. She cocked a derogatory eyebrow.

"Imhotep is Dr. Calendar's guide in the spirit world," Bess said. "He's very powerful."

Hand over his heart, Calendar bowed slightly to Bess. "I am fortunate in having so august a person as my guide."

"Imhotep, huh?" Nell said, crossing her arms. "My, that sounds awfully familiar. Didn't Boris Karloff play him in 'The Mummy' just last year? Where's your fez?"

"Imhotep has been my guide for many years." A smile both modest and patient curved his lips. "Why the movie depicted him as evil, I cannot imagine, for as I have known him always, he is the very soul of kindness. I did enjoy the film thoroughly, though. Karloff has such a talent for disappearing into whatever role he plays, don't you think?"

"So, you're a reincarnated pharaoh or something?"

Calendar laughed. He took up his post in an enormous leather armchair across from them. "Not precisely. I gather you're a skeptic."

"Not exactly. But I'm no sucker either."

"Nell!" Bess, who had been shooting Nell quelling looks, said. "Dr. Calendar has great abilities."

"I'm sure he does."

"It's all right, Miss Bess. We will let the spirits speak to her as they may. But come. Let's seat ourselves and begin."

Calendar led them to a round table by the window that was draped in layers of sheer, creamy organdy. Before he seated himself, he held out Bess's chair and then Nell's. "Your hands, please, ladies."

At the touch of Calendar's fingers, a jolt of something indescribable that was neither pain nor pleasure but somehow both burned and froze shot up Nell's arm and up the back of her neck. A flash of brilliant white scalded her eyes. She could have sworn that a voice whispered, "I'm sorry."

Squeezing her eyes shut against the blinding light, she jerked her hand away and gasped. When she opened them, Calendar was watching her, keen-eyed and puzzled.

"Nell?" Bess said. "Are you all right, child?"

Lord, let her voice not shake, please. "Why wouldn't I be?"

"Well, you just jumped as though you'd been shot."

"Can you tell me what happened, Miss Nell? Did you see something?" He leaned toward her.

Nell shook her head.

"Are you sure there was nothing?"

"Absolutely nothing."

"Ah," he said.

The crease of his brow and the downturn of his lips told her that he did not believe her, that he somehow knew exactly what had happened to her and was troubled, even sad. She was about to look away before he could reach into her soul again when he turned to Bess. "I believe Miss Nell may be a sensitive."

Bess's hands fluttered to her mouth before she grasped Nell's forearm with both hands. "Nell, how marvelous!"

"Don't be silly. It was one of those sneezes that never happens. That's all."

Calendar still watched her, grave-eyed. "Have you had any contact with the spirit world? Felt that perhaps you have lived before?"

Nell made a wry face. "My grandmother used to tell my fortune on my birthdays, but that was it."

"And she was a believer?"

"She used her Tarot cards to tell fortunes at parties. Everyone loved it."

"I see."

"You know, I've always felt Nell had an otherworldly air about her, Doctor," Bess said.

"Oh, Mother, for goodness sake. You've never said any such thing before."

Calendar reached carefully for Nell's hand again.

She wanted to draw back but let him take it. This time, nothing. No jolt. No light. Just his fingers enclosing hers, gentle and strong. Tender.

"On such short acquaintance, it's impossible to know what her powers may be," he said. "They are not a matter to be taken lightly. If you wish, Miss Nell, it would honor me to work with you to explore your abilities. Most sensitives are aware from childhood, though. I wonder that you should not have not felt anything before now."

Nell's hand was growing decidedly warm in his grasp. She pulled it free. "No, thank you."

"But, Nell–"

"That's enough, Mother. I said no. And both of you stop looking at me as though I just rolled into town with the carnival. Let's get on with the séance or whatever you're calling it."

Calendar gazed at Nell as though he'd read her heart, deciphered every last one of her secrets there, and found them discouraging. She wished for a second glass of sherry.

"Very well," he said. "Your hands again, please, ladies."

—

AN HOUR LATER, JENKINS TURNED THE DUESENBERG INTO THE PARKING lot of the Piggly Wiggly.

"Oh, Piggly Wiggly," Bess said.

Nell smiled at her mother-in-law, who just now looked like a six-year-old presented with her first pony. Before the day Anton Green had informed them of their destitution, Bess had never set foot in a grocery store. All of her life had been one of tradesmen eager for the privilege of doing business with the Oateses and the Marchands. When she was a young wife, there'd been no such thing as a self-service grocery. If she wanted something, she simply rang up Seessel's, and a delivery boy brought it right to the kitchen door. Clarence Saunders changed all that when he opened the first Piggly Wiggly on Jefferson.

Being able to go down the aisles and take groceries from the shelves herself wasn't something Nell had learned to enjoy yet, but it fascinated Bess.

"Yes, Mother. And if you're very, very good, I bet Jenkins will let you carry the basket, won't you, Jenkins?"

"Yes, ma'am, Miss Nell."

Bess flapped a playful hand at her daughter-in-law. "Oh, stop it. I like the Piggly Wiggly. You just never know what you're going to find next."

Jenkins helped the ladies from the car and then hurried to open the door of the market for them. Once inside, he secured a basket for Bess, who rewarded him with a beatific smile before she slipped her arm through Nell's and pulled her down the first aisle.

"I was hoping we could speak with my Ellis today. I so wanted to know that he is content on the other side."

Consulting Hattie's shopping list, Nell refrained from telling Bess just what she would have said to him, given the opportunity. "Well, they say you can't take it with you, so I was just hoping he would tell us that there was a mattress full of money hidden somewhere in the house. Maybe Imhotep didn't feel like crawling out of the crypt today."

Lips pursed, Bess faced Nell. "Nell, I must speak to you about the lack of respect you showed Dr. Calendar. I was quite shocked. You should be more open minded. He is a learned and accomplished man, and he displayed a great deal of interest in you."

"Yes, Mother. I imagine he thought I was the wealthy Widow Marchand and his interest was in my bank account. I guess we set him straight about that, didn't we? How much did our visit to the learned doctor cost us?"

"How can you be so ugly about it? Dr. Calendar is very generous. Because he felt he was in the presence of a fellow adept today, he told me that he couldn't accept anything for our session. A professional courtesy, he said."

And a good way to ensure we keep coming back, Nell thought. Meanwhile, she had Bess's entire $20 to spend.

"We'll stop by the butcher's on the way home. Perhaps if we pay him a little of what we owe, he'll let us have some chops for supper. Or some nice, thick steaks. I suppose I can thank Joseph Calendar for that. I am so tired of soup."

CHAPTER 3

For several minutes after Bess Marchand and her intriguing, flame-haired daughter-in-law drove away, Joseph Calendar stood looking out at the street without seeing, his eye turned inward. There should be only one like her in a lifetime, and that one had already flared bright across the sky, only to fall to earth and be extinguished.

Nell Marchand had the kind of power many would give the world to possess. That one touch, and he had known her. Could she be truly so unaware when it radiated from her in such waves that it left him dizzy and unsettled? Had she no idea what harm such power could do unchecked? Deny it she might, but today he was sure she had felt it. A pity she had come in determined that he was a fraud. Or perhaps not such a pity after all. He was not sure he could bear to risk such a one again. Not this time.

Calendar never thought of himself as a charlatan—not in the sense that she obviously did—nor after so many years did he pretend that he had any sort of real gift. Neither priest nor healer in his own right, his fate was to be ever the acolyte. If along the way he helped those who consulted him to find peace, hope, comfort, or whatever it was that they sought, he was content.

"Simon," Calendar said, coming to himself again.

The butler appeared in the front hall. "Yes, Dr. Calendar?"

"Bring my cloak, please. I'm going out."

"Yes, sir. Will you want the car?"

"No, Simon, I need to walk."

"Then I'll fetch your cane, too, Dr. Calendar."

The air at dusk was still crisp, spring arriving slowly in Memphis this year. Calendar missed the cool evenings and sweet warm summers of Vienna. Now, with Mr. Hitler spreading his shadow across the face of Europe, he might never be able to go back to Austria. Better to let memory of it go.

Turning left out of his front door, he strode to Madison and headed west toward the shops and restaurants there. Moving among the throngs of people hustling from shop to shop or simply out to take the evening air, as he was, it was somehow easier to think.

Just ahead, Phoebe Brooks, his companion of late, emerged from a bakery, holding her mother by her elbow to guide her across the threshold. She carried a box of what must be fresh pastries, judging by their aroma. Calendar stopped and swept off his hat to greet them.

"Joseph, I'm going home to supper with Mama," Phoebe said. She drew close and rested her hand on his arm. "Why don't you come along? I'm not sure what the cook has planned, but we have just bought a treat for dessert, so you're assured of getting something good for your trouble. We'd love for you to share it. Mama, help me persuade Dr. Calendar."

"I do regret refusing a repast with two such charming ladies, but I must think," he said before the old lady could speak. "A walk at twilight clears the mind and refreshes the spirit."

Phoebe masked what he felt must be her disappointment with a broad smile. "Another time, then."

"Delighted. Now, if you will excuse me, ladies."

The Brooks women waved him on.

And what he said was true. Walking was a lifelong diversion. When he'd been too impoverished for any other type of amusement, he'd wandered the streets of Chicago or San Francisco or Paris or whatever city or town he was in and studied the faces of those he passed. He thirsted to decipher when they were exultant or morose or irate and what made them so. To see written there when their lovers had abandoned them or their husbands had beaten them or they had stolen from their employers.

"You read people's faces, boy, and you will know everything you need to know about them," the Great Otto, his mentor, had said more than once. "Their faces and their hands and how they hold themselves. You see those things, and they won't be able to keep their secrets from you.

"You notice the bank teller with the fancy watch, and you have to ask yourself, how does this man who makes $20 a week have such a timepiece? Or a woman with a beautiful gown and her hair just so but her hands red and rough. That woman may dress like a lady, but you can be assured she makes her living scrubbing floors. You watch, boy, and you will know everything."

This evening, there seemed a multitude of faces to explore. The people too poor to afford a nickel for a cup of coffee or a movie were out walking, too. Even the ones who had drudged all day and might have been home with their feet up were out in the street, savoring the crisp nights that would too soon fade into the swelter of summer.

He would like to study Nell Marchand's face. Save for that flash when the recognition or current or whatever it was had passed through her and rendered it incandescent, that fine-boned structure with its remarkable sea-green eyes had been illegible to him. She'd opened those eyes, and he'd seen wonder and joy give way to confusion and something close to terror. Then, in an instant they were shuttered again, and Nell's countenance had taken on the carefully schooled porcelain poise that a lifetime in polite society had given her.

Unsure how long or how far or in what direction he had walked, Calendar looked around him and realized that he had left the bustle of Madison behind and ended up somehow on Poplar where it pointed toward downtown and the Mississippi River just beyond. It was black night now, but the street lamps cast enough light for him to find his way. Among the majestic residences that lined the avenue here like grand duchesses awaiting the queen's arrival for tea, he recognized the

Federal-style façade of the Marchand house, the casements facing the street dark, and all seeming still within.

Should he knock and say he'd been out for his evening stroll and stopped by to see that the ladies had reached home safely? He paused by the front gate, gazing up the drive and wondering if behind those windows Nell Marchand's face were as closed now in the shelter of her own house as it had been in his and if she thought at all of what had passed between them. Yes, perhaps it would be better for them both if she did not.

He tapped his cane on the sidewalk and turned back toward home.

—

AS JOSEPH CALENDAR TURNED AWAY FROM HER HOUSE UNNOTICED, Nell was keeping Hattie company in the kitchen, wiping the good silver while the cook extracted the Limoges from the pantry and rooted in the ice box for some ingredient or another. Bess was somewhere in the front of the house, dusting. It was about the only household chore they had decided they could trust her with, and she hadn't broken anything much so far. To celebrate having meat again, Hattie had poured over her cookbooks and was preparing béarnaise sauce for the Delmonico steaks and fixing potatoes Lyonnaise as only she knew how.

Hattie asked her about their visit to Joseph Calendar, and Nell told her as little as possible about anything but Bess's apparent conversation with her husband, which had ranged from his thoughts on Mr. Roosevelt in the White House to whether or not it would be a good year for cotton. Imhotep had failed to encounter Ellis among the shades of his acquaintance, perhaps not venturing far enough south to find him.

"Miss Bess never has had the sense God gave a goose," Hattie said, "but I guess if pretending to talk to the Judge and now to her no-account dead son makes her feel better, we ought to let her have that much. At least that Dr. Calendar hasn't told her anything dangerous."

"He did seem decent enough," Nell said. "I was expecting someone much more flamboyant and affected, but Joseph Calendar acts and talks like a gentleman. His house was lavish, but it wasn't in bad taste. Even that Spirit Room of his was stylish in its own way."

"Seems like everybody and his dog is setting himself up as some kind of swami or psychic these days. Most of them will tell you anything just to separate you from your money." Hattie sampled the béarnaise to see if it was ready and nodded to herself before she offered Nell a taste. It as music on Nell's tongue. "Now, come on and help me get this supper on the table. Thank the sweet Lord Jesus and his heavenly love for sending us these pretty steaks."

"I think Ely Culbertson and his bridge book are whom we ought to thank."

"Bless you, Mr. Culbertson," Hattie said, casting her eyes heavenward.

She pushed the door leading to the dining room open with her hip and passed through with the platter of steaks.

"Think we might be able to turn Miss Bess into a card sharp?" Nell said, following with the potatoes, the butter, and some of Hattie's yeast rolls.

"Might be worth a try."

CHAPTER 4

Como, Mississippi

Quick as you could say Jack Robinson, Memphis could swallow you up. 'Tweren't no place for a decent girl, but even a plain farmer like Luther Evans who loved his children and tried to teach them how to do right had to admit that maybe his Ginny wasn't always a decent girl. Not by Como standards, anyway.

When she left home in the fall after they'd brought the crops in, Luther knew she must have high-tailed it to Memphis. Good riddance if she was that big a ninny, filling her head with the moving pictures and Hollywood. He had torn down the photographs of Myrna Loy and Jean Harlow and all those other movie stars she'd tacked up on the wall. The girl didn't have good sense.

"Maybe it'll do that fool girl good to have a taste of what city folks are like," Luther had said when Kate told him that their Ginny had run off. "Always prissin' around thinking about pretty dresses and doin' her hair up when what she ought to be doing is minding her chores and finding her a good man to work alongside. Get all that dreaming about singing out of her head. Never should have let her go up to Memphis in the first place. That sister of yours is the one gave her all those fancy ideas."

Kate had simply cried, having first-hand experience of what life beside such a man could mean. Not that she didn't love Luther, but he didn't understand Ginny. Couldn't understand that a girl could dream about something more.

After six months of Kate being all tore up because there was no word and him feeling more than a little worried what had happened to the fool girl, Luther saddled his old mare Sal.

"Where you going, Daddy?" Little Luther asked.

"I'm going after your sister," Big Luther said.

"Can't I come along? I always wanted to see Memphis."

Luther squeezed the boy's shoulder. "Now, who's going to look after your mama and all your brothers and sisters if we both go? You know your mama can't chop the stove wood no more since she's had the misery in her back, and your brothers is all too little. I need you home. Besides, Sal can't hardly carry me, and she sure can't take the both of us. You do your work and look after everything, and we can talk about getting up to Memphis come fall."

"Yessir, Daddy. Don't you worry about anything. I'll look after Mama while you're gone."

"There you go," Big Luther said. He dug a quarter out of his pocket and gave it to the boy. "You take everybody into town on Saturday and buy them some candy. Don't you spend it all, though. And anything happens, you go to the general store and ask Mr. Drucker to let you use the phone to call your Aunt Sadie. She'll know where I am."

Luther slung a leg over Sal and settled his hat on his head. The roan mare was a little long in the tooth for the trip to Memphis, but she rode better than the mule, which wasn't much younger than Sal anyway. He'd take it slow to go easy on both of them.

Kate grabbed his knee. "You call soon as you hear anything, Luther. I got to know my girl's all right."

"Don't worry, Mama. I already talked to Mr. Drucker. He'll send his boy to the house to fetch you soon as we know anything."

"And don't be too hard on Ginny. I didn't have much sense when I was 15 either."

"You had enough sense to marry me. But I'll go easy on her. If she's got a job up in Memphis and she's living a decent life, then I'll leave her be. If not, I'll bring her home if I have to hogtie her to Old Sal and lead her home."

Kate and the children watched Luther ride down the road until long after he was out of sight. She wiped her eyes with her apron. "All right, chilluns. Get to your chores. Daddy'll be back before we've done had time to know he's gone. I'm going to catch us a chicken for supper." Kate pulled the ax loose from the chopping block and went to look for the old red hen, who hadn't laid an egg in at least a week. That hen was Ginny's pet, but Ginny wasn't there to see.

CHAPTER 5

Not long after their encounter outside the bakery, Joseph Calendar phoned Phoebe Brooks and asked to make up for missing supper with her by taking her dancing at the Peabody. She invited him around to her apartment for cocktails first. He offered to take her mother along, too, but Phoebe assured him that her mother preferred reading a good book to what she referred to as those fast crowds and that jivey music.

Now, Calendar heard Phoebe in her kitchen opening a bottle of Edouard Besserat that a friend had smuggled back from a trip to Montreal.

"You're distracted this evening, Joseph," she said.

Startled, Calendar looked up to find her standing over him, holding out a glass of the champagne. He took it from her, and she settled on the sofa next to him.

"Is something wrong?"

"I'm sorry, Phoebe. I'm afraid my mind was somewhere else."

"That much is obvious. And where might it have wandered off to, this brilliant mind of yours?"

"I had a new client the other day. Nell Marchand. Bess Marchand's daughter-in-law. Not really a client, though. She came in for a consultation with Miss Bess—or I should say that Miss Bess dragged her in to see me—and was quite resistant. But there was something about her, a rare power. I think she may be an adept."

Phoebe laughed, but there was the tiniest sharp edge to the sound. "There are no such things, darling. And even if there were, I doubt she is one. I know Nell Marchand, and believe me, there's not even an inkling of any special talent there."

"You may never have encountered an adept, but I have known them, including an exceptionally sensitive young woman in Vienna who was unimaginably gifted."

Calendar sipped his champagne absently before he placed the glass on the smart, mirror-topped side table at his elbow, new since his last visit. Phoebe changed her apartment's decor as often as she changed her gowns. The flavor of the day was silver and white. Tonight, her costume was a snowy silk as well, rich and supple in the way it molded itself to her form. With it she wore a single strand of pearls only a whisper darker than the silk. It was the sort of style that might have looked too studied on a less-elegant woman, but on her, it was as natural as moonlight on a garden.

"I like to keep an open mind about such things," he went on. "After all, it's belief in them that keeps me afloat, isn't it?"

Phoebe scooted much closer and slid her arm through his before she gave him a playful kiss on the cheek. "And I suppose there are unicorns, too."

"Who knows?"

"Be careful, Joseph. Maidens were used to capture unicorns. I'd hate to see you enslaved."

Calendar smiled at Phoebe. "Don't worry, Phoebe. Freedom is my most prized possession. It is not something I would ever choose to give up for anyone or anything. You understand that." He took her hand. "You're not jealous, are you?"

"No, Joseph. Not jealous." Phoebe smiled with her teeth but not with her eyes. "I'm simply concerned. I've never seen you troubled like this before."

"I'm sorry. It seems I'm not very good company tonight. Here I am with one of the most beautiful, cultivated women in Memphis, and my mind wanders. Perhaps I need a reading myself." He kissed her hand. Calendar stood and pulled Phoebe to her feet. "Come on. I've got reservations for us at the Skyway. We won't talk any more of Nell Marchand or anyone else but you."

But even guiding Phoebe cheek-to-cheek around the dance floor, he found that Nell nagged at the back of his mind the entire evening.

—

IT TOOK LUTHER AND SAL THREE DAYS TO RIDE TO MEMPHIS, WHICH was dang good for a mare her age. When they finally got to Kate's sister's house, Luther tied Sal to the fence and dusted himself off a bit before he walked up on the porch to knock.

Sadie didn't seem at all surprised to see Luther at her door. They led Sal into the back yard. The mare plunged her muzzle up to the nostrils in the bucket they filled for her and drank deep. Sadie poured the wash tub on the back porch full of hot water so Luther could scrub off the road dirt that covered his clothes and had crept up under his hat and into his hair. He usually made do with his Saturday night bath and didn't think that much of skipping it every now and then in cold weather, but now he settled back into the tub and let the heat seep into his muscles and reach down to the ache in his bones.

When he was clean and dressed in the Sunday shirt and pants he'd brought with him in his knapsack, Sadie set a plate of ham and beans and hot cornbread in front of Luther with a big glass of cold buttermilk. She waited until he was sopping up the last of the bean drippings before she asked him why he'd come to Memphis, not that she ought to need to ask.

"I reckon you're here after Ginny," she said. "If you'd told me you were coming, I could have saved you the trip. She's gone. Haven't seen her since not long after she showed up on my stoop six months ago, just like you."

"You could of called to let us know where she was."

Sadie crossed her arms across her chest and leaned back in her chair. "She begged me not to. Said she couldn't stand another day shelling peas and plucking chickens. I never could tolerate farm work myself, so I understood. I figured I'd give her a month to see if she could find a job or go back to school before I told you where she was. Anyway, if you hadn't been too damn ornery and proud to call yourself, I would have told you."

"She ain't here?"

"No, I already said she ain't. She told me she had a job in a restaurant, but when I asked her which one, she wouldn't let on. I finally followed her to one of those speakeasies, told her she ought to be ashamed of herself working with a rough bunch of men like that. She said I couldn't tell her what to do. I said, fine, I'm going to call your daddy, then.

"That night, she took her clothes and lit out. I went back to that bar looking for her, and they told me she left. Got a job singing somewhere else, but they didn't know where."

"And you still didn't call?"

"What was I going to tell you then? That I let her run loose in Memphis? I kept thinking one day she'd get tired of all those low-down, hard-drinking folks and come home. Then I was going to bring her back on the train myself."

"But she never did come."

"No, she never did. I'm real sorry, Luther."

Staring down into his plate, Luther worked his jaw and clenched and unclenched his fists. Much as he might want to knock Sadie into the middle of next week, that wouldn't do nobody no good now. Wasn't nothing for it but to let it go. If he was going to have a hope in hell of finding Ginny, Sadie had to help him.

"How on earth am I supposed to know where to start looking?" he said. "There's too many people here. Too many places she could be."

Across the table, Sadie relaxed. "We'll go to every speakeasy on every street until she turns up. Or we find somebody who can tell us where she is."

Luther couldn't begin to figure how long that would take in a place like Memphis.

—

BY THE END OF THE SECOND WEEK AS HATTIE'S LAUNDRY HELP, BESS Marchand flopped down amid the clotheslines and declared that she could not hang another thing, not even a lady's handkerchief.

"I was not born to work like a field hand, and you cannot force me to it. No, you most certainly cannot."

Nell sighed, refrained from saying that she hadn't been born to it either, and helped Bess to her feet. She settled her on the parlor divan with a cool washrag across her eyes and went to the kitchen. The tin of Fortnum & Mason was running low. Nell added a defiant extra spoonful of tea to the pot.

She strained Bess's tea and fixed herself some as well. Extra cream and sugar for comfort.

Bess sat up to take the cup.

"Feeling better?" Nell said.

"Much better. You know I don't mean to be a burden, but at my age, that work is just too much for me."

Nell found herself wondering how many of the women who had sharecropped Marchand land expected to pick and chop and plow until they dropped in the row behind the mule. Not that Nell blamed Bess or had herself ever before given those women more than a passing thought. She hated every minute of working with the laundry. But Nell wasn't about to stop when Hattie was at it from before sunup until after dark.

In the kitchen, she fixed two glasses of water, chipped a couple of slivers off the block in the ice box, and took them out to Hattie and Jenkins, who sweated over the kettles of boiling laundry.

"Thank you, ma'am," said Jenkins.

He reached up to touch the brim of the cap that wasn't there. Nell smiled at him, and he nodded to her before he drained his glass. Hattie drained hers, too.

"Hattie, I think we've gotten everything we're going to get out of Mother Marchand," Nell said. "I'm just about to give out myself."

"Huh. Don't sull up on me now, Nell. Your daddy should have made you work at least one summer, just to know what it was like to haul a 100-pound tow sack of cotton over to the scales and maybe get 40 cents for it."

"Oh, hush, Hattie. You never had to work in the fields either."

"Well, maybe not, but soon as we got home from school, you know Mama had me sweeping the kitchen and washing pans."

Nell stretched a kink out of her spine. "Yes, you've had an awfully hard row to hoe always."

"Compared to you, I did. "

"All right. Hand me that basket, please, Jenkins."

"Let me carry it into the house for you, Miss Nell." Jenkins started to lift the hamper of clean, dry shirts, but Nell put a hand on his arm.

"Thank you, but it's my job."

"Yes, ma'am."

Nell propped the basket against her hip. There'd be the wet things to hang, too, now that Bess had dug in her heels. In the house, she left the shirts with Hattie's other ironing and went back out.

"You know, Hattie, you could probably do even better if you didn't have Bess Marchand and me to worry about."

Hattie dropped the petticoat that she had just run through the wringer onto the mound at her feet. She mopped her face with her sleeve, wiped her hands on her apron, and handed Nell the basket.

"Uh-huh. These are ready to hang."

Hattie waited, hands on her hips. Nell picked up two clothespins to secure the petticoat to the line, put them in her mouth, and grabbed the wet garment from the pile. Hattie started another shirt through the wringer. There was no end to all the mountains of washing that Nell could see.

CHAPTER 6

That evening, Hattie and Jenkins were late from their rounds of delivering laundry, and Nell's stomach grumbled like a field hand's at quitting time. Bess must be able to hear it clear across the kitchen.

The old lady's nattering was not helping her mood either.

"Mother," Nell said, "I believe if you mention Joseph Calendar to me one more time, I will turn wrong side out and jump out the window."

Nell was rolling out the biscuits the way Hattie had taught her, enjoying the give of the dough under her hands, but she put down the wooden rolling pin, afraid she might succumb to the urge to do Bess harm with it or at least fling it across the kitchen. "I am not a sensitive or a seer or a swami or whatever you want to call it," she said. "I was simply tired the other day and hadn't eaten enough. Anything I thought I felt or saw was because of that."

"There's no need to snap at me, Nell," Bess said. "I simply observed again what a fine, handsome man Dr. Calendar is. And, of course, he's quite wealthy, too."

"Mother–"

"All right, my dear."

Nell picked up Hattie's old tin cutter and stood over the biscuit board, studying the dough and deciding where best to start and how to get as many biscuits as possible with the fewest cuts.

"I wish they would come on," she said. "I'm telling you, I am some kind of hungry."

She punched the cutter into the dough. What was the point of being so angry about Calendar? She never had to see him again, and that was that.

There was an explanation for what she'd felt and seen when he touched her. She was worn out from working dusk 'til dawn, that was all. He'd seen it and tried to take advantage of a weak moment. That was how he made his living, wasn't it? Watching people for their soft spots and telling them what they wanted to hear?

And a fine living it was, too. He'd probably never even set foot in his kitchen, let alone stretched dough for more biscuits. There was no telling how much that house had cost him. And the rugs in his silly Spirit Room—each one of them was probably worth a considerable fortune.

The kitchen door opened, and Hattie hustled in with a bag of groceries. Jenkins followed with an enormous sack of potatoes.

"Well, thank goodness," Nell said. "Mother and I were just about to fall out from starvation."

—

AFTER SUPPER, NELL LEFT BESS SITTING BY THE RADIO LISTENING TO "The Voice of Firestone" and excused herself, claiming that she was too tired to stay up for the program. She went upstairs, closed the door to her room, and went to her vanity. There, she opened her treasure box, drew out the cards, and spread them before her, thinking. She chose first one and then another, studying them and asking them to speak to her the way they'd spoken for her grandmother.

What she'd felt when she touched Calendar's hand still disturbed her. Lord, he was handsome as a picture, but she was no ninny to give in to a crush. After heaven or whoever it was had freed her from Ellis, she couldn't imagine looking at a man that way ever again. You never could tell what a man might do, not even when you thought you had them safely in the grave.

And she couldn't possibly have heard Ellis's voice speaking to her. He'd never said he was sorry about anything in all his life, at least not to her.

Nell came to the Queen of Cups and ran her fingers over the surface of the card.

"I wish you were here, Grandmother. I need someone to guide me. I don't know what to do."

Then, there it was, plain as day, as though her grandmother had whispered it in her ear. Nell's breath caught. If anyone in the world could set herself up as a medium, why couldn't she, Nell Marchand, do it? She could use her Grandmother Blayney's cards. At least she knew enough about them to start, to make people believe that she was reading them. And she knew just about everybody in Memphis. Enough people were bound to come to her out of friendship or pity or curiosity to have their fortunes told. And it had to beat baking pies and folding laundry.

For the first time since Anton had told her that she was broke, Nell felt a wave of hope and laughed out loud. She ran to her closet and pawed through her scarves, looking for something exotic. She unearthed a scarlet silk wrap that was between a scarf and a shawl and wound it around her head into a turban, the fabric a caress to her fingers. Add some dark eye makeup and lip rouge and, voilà, she was a gypsy.

Nell tore open the door to her room and called down the stairs. "Hattie! Come quick."

Back at her vanity, Nell studied herself. She poured out her costume jewelry, picking through the riot of earrings, rings, and necklaces now spread before her and holding up first one piece and then another.

She heard Hattie thunder up the stairs and burst into the room.

"What on earth is it, honey?"

"Hattie, I know how to save us."

"You're not sick?"

"No, I'm fine."

"Child, you scared me half to death." Hattie sighed and sat down hard on Nell's bed. "When you hollered like that, I thought something awful had happened. What are you doing with that rag wrapped around your head? Lord, if you don't look just like Aunt Jemima."

Nell rolled her eyes at Hattie. "I'm supposed to be a gypsy. I'm going to be a fortuneteller. What do you think?"

Hattie's mouth opened, shut, and opened again before any sound came out. "I think you have finally run clean jab out of your mind."

"No, it's perfect." Nell spun around to face her. "Oh, Hattie, don't you see? It's going to save us, and it's something I can really do. It'll be just like performing in a play. All I have to do is get a few people I know to come, then they'll tell everybody else about it, and before long, we'll have so much cash we won't know what to do with it. Who knows? Maybe I'll give Joseph Calendar a run for his money."

Nell danced back to the closet, pulled out her silk dressing gown, and belted it high up under her bust. She rolled the sleeves up to just below her elbows and studied herself in the mirror.

"Hmm, I wonder if I can get Oz Sherman to put something in the paper about me?"

"Miss Bess is going to throw a pure-dee fit."

"Well, let her, then. Besides, she ought to be happy. Now she's going to have her fortune told right here at home whenever she wants it."

Nell turned this way and that. She liked the headdress, but the robe just wasn't right. "How much of Mother's money do we have left, Hattie?"

"About five dollars."

"Tomorrow, we're going shopping. We're going to turn me into a gypsy."

—

THE EFFECT WAS ALTOGETHER SATISFACTORY, IF NELL DID SAY SO

herself. Emmie, her usual salesgirl at Lowenstein's downtown, had outdone herself in transforming Nell into a gypsy fortuneteller. Amazing what a practiced hand could do with a bright dressing gown, a scarf, and well-chosen jewelry. The voluptuous dangle of the earrings against her neck made her feel as exotic as she looked. She rehearsed a few theatrical poses in her bedroom mirror and was pleased with what she saw.

"What do you think, Hattie?"

"You're just about the best-looking gypsy I've ever laid eyes on."

"Do you think I should dye my hair black? For the authentic effect?"

"I am not about to let you mess up your pretty hair like that. There's folks all over town would give their eye teeth for that hair."

"I suppose you're right. I'll just tell people that I'm a redheaded gypsy stepchild." Nell sat at her writing desk and pulled out a sheet of paper. "Now, I need a name. Madame Something, don't you think, Hattie?"

"Just use your name. What's wrong with Madame Eleanor?"

"Not mysterious enough. It makes me sound like a seamstress or a milliner. I need something foreign. Glamorous. Intriguing."

Nell waved her hand in the air to punctuate each word. Hattie snorted.

With a flourish, Nell wrote "Eleanor" on the paper and began rearranging the letters. "Noralee. No, that sounds like somebody's cook. Sorry, Hattie. Lee-a-nor. Nelora. Hmmm. Nelora. I think that's it, Hattie. Madame Nelora. What do you think?"

Hattie pondered for a moment. "That's good. All you need now, honey, is the crystal ball."

"No, I'm not going to use a crystal ball. That is nothing but tacky. Too much like the carnival." Nell lifted the red tin box from her vanity and removed the Tarot cards. She spread them out before her. "I'm going to use my grandmother's cards. She would have liked that."

Turning up the Queen of Cups, Nell laughed over at Hattie. "You see. She approves."

"But what you know about using those cards, honey?"

"It doesn't really matter, does it? I don't know anything about crystal balls, either. As long as my clients believe I know what I'm doing, that's just as good. I watched Grandmother often enough. And you know I had plenty of practice telling people what they wanted to hear when I was a debutante. I'll learn as I go. Anyway, women will always want to know about love, and men will always want to know about money. See? I'm good at this already."

Hattie moved to stand behind Nell and locked eyes with her in the mirror. "Uh-huh. You better be careful with Miss Mared's cards. Respect the power they've got. This may be a game for you and for some of them that come to see you, but the rest of those people, they are going to be looking for help. People who have hurt in their hearts they don't know how to fix. People who are lost and don't know how to find their way again. Have you been thinking about those people at all, Nell Marchand?"

"Oh, for goodness sake. You know I'm not going to hurt anybody."

"Not on purpose, but you know how you are, Nell. All I'm saying is you need to be studying on this a little bit before you get yourself into some mess that isn't what you thought you were getting."

Nell looked down at the cards. She returned the Queen of Cups to the deck and shuffled slowly. "Maybe you're right. Maybe I haven't thought about this enough."

"Ain't no maybe about it. I'm going to study on what you need to do to get right with the cards."

CHAPTER 7

Bess Marchand took to Nell's scheme like a hog to slop. When Nell appeared before her in her gypsy dress and told her what she planned, Bess squeaked with glee. She dropped her sewing and flung her arms around her daughter-in-law.

"Oh, my dear child, how exciting," Bess said. "You know Dr. Calendar feels that you're a sensitive, but I never expected you to take to his suggestion, at least not so quickly. He'll be thrilled. I can't wait to see what wonders you discover." She patted the table in front of her. "You must do a reading for me first. Right now."

Bess settled back onto the Judge's sofa beside Nell, all eager anticipation. Nell shot a glance at Hattie, who gave her a knock-me-over-with-a-feather smile. Nell handed Bess the Tarot deck.

"Shuffle these until I tell you to stop, please."

Nell wasn't sure how to begin the reading, but she remembered her grandmother sometimes laying three cards out on the bedside table at night to tell her what the next day would bring. Past, present, and future, Mared Blayney had said. "Think of a question."

"That's easy. Will we always be poor?"

Nell wanted to know the answer to that one herself. "Now, pick three cards, and place them face up on the table in a row."

To the left, Bess laid out the Nine of Cups upside down. In the center, the Six of Swords. To the right, the Two of Swords, also upside down.

Bess looked expectantly at Nell, who blinked back at her. No time like the present to practice pretending she knew what she was doing. Nell put her hand on the Nine of Cups.

"This is the past," Nell said. "The cups are inverted, so everything they once held has flowed out of them and away. This is the wealth and comfort that you once knew that is now gone."

Bess clapped her hands and clasped them at her throat. "You see, Hattie, she is gifted."

Hattie said nothing.

"And here, the knight is on a boat, making his way out to sea or perhaps crossing a river," Nell said, moving on to the Six of Swords. "This is the present. It's a journey, a search for new opportunity." Nell tapped her fingers on the last card, thinking. "The Two of Swords, the future. The card is inverted, and lady is blindfolded, so the way is unclear. Difficult. We'll have to be careful, Mother."

Nell sat back, disconcerted that she was suddenly more spent than she could have imagined possible. Bess hugged her again.

"That was marvelous, Nell. You answered my question beautifully. You're going to be a very great success."

It was true. She really hadn't sounded half bad. Nell wondered if she still had the old book that her grandmother had consulted sometimes when she did the birthday readings. It couldn't hurt to have a little help, especially if she was going to read for anyone who knew more about the Tarot than Bess Marchand did. Or than Nell Marchand did, for that matter.

"Now, do Hattie," Bess said. "Hattie, think of a question."

Hattie shook her head. "I think you already wore Madame Nelora out. I'm going to wash the dishes."

"Yes, well, I suppose she should start slowly, conserve her strength. But, Nell, you know you can practice on us as much as you want."

"Thank you, Mother. That's a great comfort."

Bess sprang up and paced around the room. "Oh, wait until I tell the ladies at bridge club on Tuesday. They'll be beside themselves. You know, this room would be perfect for your readings. We'll need to get a better table for you, of course, but I'm sure there's something suitable in the attic."

No, not here. Of that, Nell was sure. She wanted an office, a place that was strictly Madame Nelora's, just like a real business. Otherwise, how would anyone take her seriously?

"Do you really want people traipsing in and out of here all day? I know I don't. I want to open a small salon somewhere. Something intimate. I think it's important to have a place that's just for my readings and not mess around here like an amateur at a grade school fair.

"I'm going to call Anton. He'll help me find the perfect place."

—

CONJURER, ROOT DOCTOR, HOODOO WOMAN—AUNT MARY RUDOLPH was all these things. From a tiny shop off Beale Street, the Main Street of black America and the soul of black Memphis, she practiced her art. The daughter of an Arkansas former slave woman renowned for her healing gifts, from birth Mary Rudolph had known what her task in life would be. When she learned everything her mother had to teach her and then some, she began her own practice. She fell in love with a young man from the place just one over from hers who was determined to leave the dirt and sweat of the fields behind him forever and set off to find his fortune in the city perched on the bluffs above the Mississippi River, and she left the farm and her mother to go with him.

It was toward Beale Street and Aunt Mary's shop that Hattie Taylor made her way on the morning after Nell Marchand announced that she intended to take up telling fortunes. Hattie believed in always hedging her bets. If Nell was determined to pursue that ancient practice, Hattie was calling on every aid she could to help her and keep her safe, including the supernatural. She was going to see the hoodoo doctor.

At Beale, Hattie stepped off the street car. She ignored the catcalls of more than one too-full-of-himself shooter in a zoot suit shaking his capped dice and offering to buy her a drink at 10 o'clock in the morning,

Jesus help them. Once, Beale had been an exclusive neighborhood for the moneyed of Memphis, and there were still plenty of businesses for decent folks mixed in among the dives and boarding houses. Hattie passed cafes and drugstores and tailors and Schwab's Dry Goods.

Aunt Mary's shop was tucked on a side street between a second-hand store touting the finest gently worn spring fashions and a beauty parlor that advertised Madame C. J. Walker Beauty Culture. Hattie entered and breathed in the scent of herbs and ancient earth. At the sound of the bell over the front door jingling, sprightly, diminutive Aunt Mary emerged from the back.

"Come in, Hattie Taylor. Come in. What can I do for you today?"

"I need a charm for Nell Marchand."

"What's that girl up to now? I'm not about to make her up a love spell yet. No, sir. No matter how no count that first man was, looks like she'd let him at least get cold in the grave before she gets herself another one."

"Setting herself up to tell fortunes," Hattie said. "Another husband is just about the last thing she's studying right now. That one she had didn't leave her anything, and she's trying to find a way to make some money. At least she's onto something I think she can actually do besides plan dinner parties. She's got sense, and she's stood up pretty well ever since we found out we were broke, but I need something that's going to ease her along in the right direction."

Both women laughed.

"Lord, that child. Think she's going to be any good at it?"

"Hard to tell so far, but I think she might. Everybody said her grandmama had the sight."

"What you want from me, then? A money charm?"

"Something that will help her find what she's looking for."

"I can't bring the power to her 'less it's already there. She got it, I can make it stronger, but if she don't, ain't nothing going to make it so."

"I know that. I'm just asking you to help her with whatever she's got."

"All right, then. Come on in, and let me see what I can find. I'll make her up a mojo sack, but you got to fetch me some of her hair and fingernails for the conjuring. You bring her with you when I make it, the magic will be stronger."

"Even if she doesn't believe?"

"She don't have to believe. The magic will show her, find the power and fetch it to her. One day, then, when it comes down on her, she'll believe."

—

NELL SET A BASKET OF DRY CLOTHES NEXT TO HATTIE WHERE SHE stood ironing. She picked up the copy of "Ladies Home Journal" that Miss Bess had brought home from her bridge game and flipped it open to the Eleanor Mercein story she'd been waiting all day to read.

"A mojo sack, Hattie?" she said. "You talk like a tree fell on you."

"Well, you're about to be telling fortunes with a deck of cards. How is a mojo sack any different from that? Of course, if you're just planning to tell white folks' fortunes, I guess you don't need it. But if you're going to have coloreds coming to you, too, a little mojo might help. Unless, of course, you're too good for us black folks."

Nell dropped the magazine to her lap. "Oh, good Lord. You know better than anybody I don't think that way."

"Well, come on then."

"I am a little surprised though. Good Baptist that you are, I didn't think you believed in any of that hoodoo mess."

"That doesn't have anything to do with how I feel about Jesus, Nell Marchand, and He knows it. The hoodoo woman goes to Beale Street Baptist, just like me. She loves Jesus as much as anybody else does and more than a lot of folks do. Who am I to turn my back on thousands of years of African tradition? After all, your daddy used a mojo sack to get your mama, didn't he?"

"Well, yes, he did."

"All right, then. It was Aunt Mary Rudolph made him that mojo sack, and we're going back to her to get yours. Now, stick out your hand so I can get some fingernail."

Hattie pulled a clean white handkerchief out of her pocket and spread it out beside Nell. Nell put out her right hand as she was told. Hattie trimmed a sliver of nail from her pinkie and snipped an auburn curl from the back of her head. She wrapped them in the handkerchief and slipped them in her purse.

"Now, I've already got the dollar for Mrs. Rudolph, so we have everything we need."

"I can't believe you're making me do this."

"More white folks than you would think go to Mrs. Rudolph, so don't go sticking your nose in the air about it," Hattie said. "You think your mama would even have given your daddy the time of day without that mojo sack? He wasn't nearly as pretty as she was, honey."

"I know, and I'm not sticking my nose in the air. I just feel a little foolish is all. And maybe a little disrespectful to Aunt Mary Rudolph. I mean, she's sincere. I know I can't really tell people's fortunes. I'm going to make it all up."

"That's why you've really got to go see Mrs. Rudolph, then. I know you want to do right by folks, and she'll help you see how to do that. You don't want to go just tricking people when you could be helping them, do you? You just won't be doing it the way they think you are."

CHAPTER 8

After all this time eating the good oats and hay down at the Keck Livery Stable on Second, old Sal was fat and sleek and glossier than she'd been since she was a filly. If they stayed much longer, she'd eat clean through the rest of the money that Luther had brought with him. In exchange for her board, he asked the owner to let him muck out stalls and groom the teams of mules that farmers brought in to trade. The liveryman had a girl about Ginny's age himself. A good girl, but you never could tell what might happen.

Each day, Luther and Sadie went out to look for Ginny. Seemed like Memphis had a speakeasy for every two people in town, and they tried to visit every one of them. They knocked on so many doors that their knuckles were raw and Luther wore a new hole in one of his shoes.

Nobody wanted to own up to knowing her. Nobody knew anything. The Memphis police, who had seen too many farm girls come to hide from their families just like Ginny, weren't much help either.

"Any chance your girl was kidnapped, mister?" the police sergeant name of Acker down at headquarters on Adams Avenue asked.

"You mean, like they run off with that Lindberg baby?" Luther scratched his chin. "What fer? Unless they want my old mare or that broke-down old mule, we ain't got nothing nobody could take."

The sergeant nodded and made a note. He slid Ginny's picture back across the desk to Luther. "Mighty pretty little girl, Mr. . . .uh–"

"Evans. Luther Evans. My girl's name is Ginny." He tapped the photograph. "She weren't but 10 when this was took, but that's the only picture we got. You get a fair idea of what she looks like."

"Yessir, Mr. Evans. Now, you hold on to that picture so you can show it to other folks. We'll call you as soon as we find her."

Luther looked at Ginny's photograph again before he put it back in his shirt pocket. He tried not to notice when the sergeant slipped Ginny's paperwork into a drawer.

"Lost daughter?" Officer Murphy asked Sergeant Acker after Luther had shuffled out, head down.

"Yes, poor bastard."

"What did you tell him?" On Murphy's lips, the question came out as "Whud ja tell 'im?"

"Same thing I tell all of them. We'll keep an eye out. Your daughter's probably safe working in a shop or taking in washing. Anything that lets them go on hoping."

"'Poor bastard' is right," Murphy said.

"Yeah, and this was a nice-looking girl."

"Well, then, did you tell him to check the whore houses on Gayoso? Not that all them girls is good-looking."

"No, I thought I'd check those out myself. I don't suppose you would want to come along, would you now, Murphy?"

Murphy pulled the chair in front of Acker's desk out and sat. He slicked back his hair with both hands, a grin all but splitting his face in two. "Sure, Acker. It's our duty, ain't it? Besides, there's this high-yella girl I got my eye on down there. It's about time to see how generous she feels about the boys who serve and protect."

"You are just about no count, Murphy."

"Oh, now don't tell me you never visit one of them houses a little more often than your duty demands, Sergeant."

"I've been married for a long time, Murphy. Even if I wanted to, Marta would kill me if she found out. I don't go down there unless there's trouble. Last time was back in the fall when old Belle and some of her girls got roughed up for saying they were voting Republican."

"I heard about that. Busted her nose, didn't they?"

"I thought it looked better afterwards, but she didn't agree." Acker stopped to chuckle over his own joke. "She was lucky, though, considering what happened to some of the others. Those thugs put one of the girls in the hospital for a month."

"Holy Mother!" Murphy let out a low whistle.

Acker pointed at him. "You think about that if you're ever tempted to go against what the ward boss tells you. I don't want to be fishing you out of the river. Speaking of Belle, she owes me a favor, so we can start with her place. Come on, Murphy. Maybe we'll get lucky and find the old corncob's daughter."

"Maybe," Murphy said. "Even if we don't, I bet I can find something good down there." He winked and scooted the chair back with a screech.

CHAPTER 9

Aunt Mary Rudolph was not the tall, willowy, dramatic woman Nell imagined a hoodoo doctor would be. With a flush of shame, Nell realized that she'd half expected a necklace of shrunken heads from Borneo and some outlandish headgear. Instead, Aunt Mary was short and round and sweet-faced. Her bright, black eyes that were just beginning to show the first clouds of age fairly snapped with good will. In her simple cotton-print dress, she looked more like a school teacher than someone who dealt in the occult.

The shop itself was a wild jumble of herbs and roots and mysterious items in baskets and glass jars that covered every surface, including the tall shelves behind the counter. A diminutive brass scale sat on the counter, a mortar and pestle beside it. It was a place that felt timeless and magical, and it smelled like a spice bazaar.

"Come on in here, Miss Nell," Aunt Mary said, turning to greet them. "Let me get a good look at you. I knew your mama and your daddy, and I'm glad to know you, too. I can't believe Hattie Taylor hasn't brought you to see me before now."

Aunt Mary took Nell by the hand and turned her this way and that before she walked around her in a slow circle like a horse trader looking for spavins or turned hocks. She pulled her into a quick hug and held her back out at arm's length.

"You sure turned out to be a fine, pretty girl," she said. "I'm right proud."

Nell glanced at Hattie for guidance but got none. "Thank you,

Mrs. Rudolph."

"Call me Aunt Mary. Everybody does. If you count all the love charms I've done over the years, I bet I brought on half the babies born in Memphis, at least. I take credit for you, too." Aunt Mary stepped back and studied Nell, her head cocked to one side. "Now, tell me, Miss Eleanor Leyton Marchand, what do you want from me?"

"I thought Hattie had already talked to you."

"She did, but I need to know what *you* want. Can't make the charm unless I've got your wishes in it."

In Aunt Mary's benevolent presence, a swell of goodwill toward all humanity washed over Nell, a sentiment familiar to her childhood but so long mourned that she'd thought it forgotten. Grateful, she drank it in.

"Well, I, um . . . I'm going to work as a fortuneteller, and I want to be a good one, Aunt Mary. I want to tell people things that will help them, not just anything that comes into my head."

Aunt Mary pressed her palm over Nell's sternum. "You want to see what's inside they hearts."

"Yes, I suppose that's exactly it. If I'm going to do this thing, I want to do it the way it ought to be done."

"Good, Miss Nell. That's just what Aunt Mary likes to hear. I don't do charms for people who got evil in they minds. I got to help you all keep on the path of righteousness, no matter how narrow and stony it may be. That's what the Lord Jesus teaches us."

Aunt Mary guided Nell and Hattie to a rough wooden table where she had laid out colored stones, feathers, and small bones from some kind of bird, maybe a chicken. She stretched out her hand to Hattie, who placed the handkerchief with its relics in it. These the hoodoo woman dropped onto the center of a square of clean sky-blue calico before her. Muttering under her breath, she poked at them with a fingertip. She looked over the treasures on the table and chose a small blue stone, a milky white marble that made Nell think of a blind man's eyeball, a teal blue feather, and the tiniest bird bone. Last, she added a dry sprig sweet with the perfume of chamomile. Aunt Mary took Nell's hand and placed it palm down over the items collected. Then she launched into the 23rd Psalm, which Nell had memorized in Sunday school.

"The Lord is my Shepherd . . . . Come on, Miss Nell, you got to speak the words with me. You, too, Hattie."

When they had finished the psalm, Aunt Mary released Nell's hand. She twisted the calico into a bundle that she tied with a snip of plain, white string. "These things are going to help you see, Miss Nell. They going to keep your heart true and your feet on the path. If you put this mojo sack around your neck on a string so it hangs over your heart, that's the strongest. When you set down to read your fortunes, you put your hand on it and remember what it is you want to do. Let me know what happens. And if you ever need Aunt Mary, you know where she is."

The old woman pressed the bundle into Nell's hand and closed the other one over it. Then she placed her own hands over Nell's and murmured a prayer, her eyes closed. Aunt Mary opened her eyes and smiled at Nell. She patted her hand over her own heart.

"You going to be just fine. Aunt Mary can feel it in here. Now, you come see old Aunt Mary some time, girl, just to say hello."

"I will. Thank you, Aunt Mary." Nell stood tall. "I feel stronger already, knowing you're here."

Leaving the shop, Nell and Hattie walked along Beale toward Hernando where Jenkins and the car waited in front of Pantaze Drug Store. Nell was quiet for a block or two.

"Well," Hattie said at last, "we got you all fixed up now."

Nell swung around to face Hattie, walking backward up the street for a few paces. "She was wonderful, you know. I had no idea what she'd be like, but she was just wonderful. Do you think we can find a place for my salon down here, close to her? I think I'd like that. There's something spiritual about this street."

"I told you."

"Thank you, Hattie. I think I can do this, I mean, make it something good for people."

"Always knew you could, long as you keep your eye on what's right."

CHAPTER 10

For Nell Marchand even to consider putting her shop anywhere on Beale Street simply wasn't fitting, and Anton Green was doing what he could to talk her out of it while she dragged him the length of the street and back again. When he could get a word in edgewise, that is.

"Anton, you can't imagine the energy, the spirit the place has," Nell said. "I felt it with Aunt Mary. And aren't Mr. Church and Boss Crump always going on about how safe and respectable it is now? For goodness sake, Hattie goes to the Beale Street Baptist Church every Sunday. Do you think I'd let her set so much as her big toe down here if it weren't all right?"

They stopped in front of a particularly shabby spot with cracks in the plate glass window, peeling turquoise paint, and a front door that seemed to have been kicked in more that once. Up the alley alongside the building drifted faint cries of "Come on, now!" and "Six holes and three pins!" from what Anton decided was a crap game in progress. But from the rapt expression on Nell's face, you would have thought she stood before the Pink Palace itself.

"Nell, you don't think any of your society clientele would want to come down to Beale, now do you? You think their husbands would let them?"

"Plenty of those husbands come to Beale for lunch. Plenty more of them probably come down here to go to nightclubs and gamble and do Lord knows what else. And, yes, I realize what I just said. Their wives might enjoy the disreputable allure of it, Anton. The venture into the dark heart of the city, if you want to think about it that way. Don't you think that would appeal to them even more? Now, there's another place up the street I want to see."

Nell was off like a greyhound after a rabbit, with Anton hustling to catch up. They turned in the direction of the One Minute Lunch, where the aroma of onions frying on a griddle wafted out the door. He did love the One Minute and had just suggested they go inside for a big old mess of fried catfish, hushpuppies, and slaw when, three doors down, he could swear he saw Franklin Bryant's distinctive gray homburg emerging from a bar with Franklin under it. Why, the old rascal. Sneaking down in the middle of the day for a snort. Anton wasn't about to let him get away with it.

At the door, Franklin looked both ways as though assuring himself that his wife, Margaret, wasn't waiting on the street with an ax handle to whale the tar out of him. He headed toward downtown and his office.

Anton grabbed Nell's wrist and whispered, "Franklin Bryant is trying to tiptoe out of that bar up ahead of us. Let's go embarrass him." He started to pull her along, and they fell into hot pursuit. "Franklin Bryant, you drunken old reprobate, what are you doing coming out of a Beale Street bar at this hour?" he hollered. "Have you already emptied the decanter on your desk?"

Franklin didn't respond or glance back, but he quickened his pace until he was just short of running.

"Franklin! Hey! Hang on. Franklin Bryant!"

At the corner, a truck from Schwab's Dry Goods cut off Franklin's progress, and he stopped, looking right and left for an escape route. Anton and Nell caught up with him, a little out of breath. Franklin turned to meet them, pasting on a puny, abashed smile.

"What were you running for, boy?" Anton said. "Are Margaret and the WCTU after you?"

At the sight of Nell, Bryant swept off his homburg and nodded to her. "Miss Nell. What on earth are y'all doing down here?"

"I'm thinking of opening a salon, Franklin. Anton came along to protect me and talk me out of Beale Street as the spot for it, if he can."

"Now where is it?" Anton said. He held out his hand palm up and waggled his fingers. "Or don't you plan to share?"

Sullen as an old bulldog with a cucklebur stuck in its paw, Franklin turned to him. "Where is what? I have no idea what you're talking about."

Anton held up both hands, placating. "Now, hold on, old son. I can't blame you for sneaking down here to fill your flask. I would have to do it myself if I didn't have my connections for a more palatable product from Canada. I could have arranged for a couple of bottles for you. And you know I'm not going to tell Margaret. You think I want the furies of the WCTU descending me?"

Franklin relaxed, his smile sly now. "I arranged to have it delivered." He took one of Nell's hands in both his own. "But Miss Nell, you do need to listen to Mr. Green. I don't think Beale Street is an appropriate place for a lady's shop. It's downright rough in the evenings, and some of the ne'er-do-wells loiter in the back alleys even after sunup. I just wouldn't like to think of someone as fragile and sheltered as you being exposed to that sort of trash. I'm sure we can find you something much more suitable. What sort of shop do you plan to open? A woman with your style could make a real success of ladies' wear."

"It's not really going to be a shop because I won't be selling anything but the Wisdom of the East. It will be a salon of enlightenment."

Brow furrowed, Bryant glanced at Anton.

"Miss Nell is going to tell fortunes," Anton said.

Franklin threw his head back and laughed.

"I have to make my way in the world somehow, Franklin Bryant," Nell said. She snatched her hand away and looked as though she wanted to make him eat his homburg. "You of all people know that. I still haven't forgiven you."

That sobered the old hound up. "I'm truly sorry that you've been left in this state, Miss Nell," he said. "If there were anything I could have done to prevent it, believe me, I would have. If your situation is so desperate, I wish you had come to me."

"For what? A loan? Based on what? You know the house is all I have, and I'm not about to risk that."

"Based on my respect and affection for your family."

"Affection?" Nell said. The chill in her voice wasn't directed at Anton, but it still froze him to the bone. "Then you should have come to see me when Ellis died and explained why that affection didn't keep my husband from leaving me poor as Job's turkey. I think you owed me that at least."

Franklin had the decency to color at that. "I wish there had been some way to make Ellis listen to me."

"We're managing, and if there's anything I don't need, it's to be more in debt," Nell said. "But you send Margaret along to my salon when it's open. Or come yourself. Maybe I can help you predict the next bankruptcy ahead of time."

She turned on her heel and marched back up the street. Anton did not follow her right away but stood with Franklin gaping after her.

"Come on, Anton," she said over her shoulder. "I thought you were hungry for some catfish."

With the slightest of shrugs to the banker, Anton started after her.

Watching them go, Franklin Bryant cursed his luck for letting himself be seen on Beale Street.

CHAPTER 11

With the Depression on, there were more empty storefronts than anybody knew what to do with scattered around Memphis. Anton felt sure they must have visited every vacant shop in the city. As skeptical as he was about Nell's new undertaking, he had finally talked her into using a place he owned on Madison free of charge. Because that fit her budget better than anything else they'd seen, she had agreed. The spot had the advantages of being not too far from her house in an area that was fashionable enough for the well-to-do without being intimidating to clients of more modest means who might seek her services.

Now, Nell wandered around the place, peering at the molding, looking through the window from both the street and inside. At last, she turned to Anton, glowing, and pronounced herself satisfied.

"If you start to get rich from all this foolishness, Nell, I'm going to charge you top dollar, so there will be no use haggling," he said. "If you start to make a bundle, I might have to come see you myself so you can tell me how I can get rich, too."

"Thank you, Anton," Nell said. "I'll remember that. And, of course, I'll start paying rent as soon as I have my first clients. I feel bad that I can't give you anything now."

"Never thump a free watermelon. If you need a loan to decorate, I can help."

"We're not going to do much, but thank you. I want to keep things simple, elegant. It should feel mysterious, yes, but I don't want it to look like the set of 'The Sheik' or 'Dracula.' I'm going to use the desk Daddy had in his office and a couple of suitable chairs that I've found." She took him by the hand and guided him around the space, pointing out where things would go as she spoke. "There will be a little waiting area out front, and Hattie's going to make lemonade and cookies. I want people to feel welcome, relaxed."

"What about the gypsy garb?"

"Oh, I'm going to keep that. I think it's important to dress the part, but I'm going to be the classiest, most refined fortuneteller anybody in Memphis has ever seen. No moaning. No trances. No accents. No histrionics. Elegant, simple. That's how my grandmother would have done it."

"I'm sure she would approve."

"I hope so. And I hope she'll be beside me for every session. Are you sure you wouldn't like me to do a reading for you, Anton?"

"Oh, no, my dear. I'm too afraid of what you might see."

"I can't image that you have any deep, dark secrets. You're such a sweet man."

No. No dark secrets but plenty deep. She was free now, but it was too soon. With time, he hoped she would discover it for herself, naturally.

"Is something the matter, Anton? You look all down in the mouth all of a sudden."

"No, Nell. Not really. It's just that I'm so sorry to see you come to this."

"To being a gypsy?"

"No. To such reduced circumstances. Having to work so hard. Ellis should have taken better care of you."

"You're right about that. But he's gone now, and good riddance. Besides, this is going to be fun." Breaking into a grin, she grasped both his hands and swung them like a happy child. "And you know, you can spread the word about Madame Nelora. She knows all, sees all. You know what to say."

"All right, my dear. I wish you all the luck and good fortune you deserve. If you need anything . . . ."

"You've always steered me in the right direction."

"That's what Dutch uncles are for." Anton eased his hands free, afraid he might succumb to the urge to pull her into an embrace not the least bit avuncular. She was too precious to him, and he could be patient. "I tell you what. Why don't I take you out for supper tonight? We can celebrate your finding a place that suits you finally."

"Only if you promise to take me to the Galindo." She hugged him. "You know I love their veal chops, and I'm sure I'll be starving half to death tonight."

"We'll put on the dog. And I'll see if the maitre d' can dig up a bottle of champagne to have on ice for you."

"Heaven."

"Good luck, Nell. I hope this turns out to be everything you want it to be."

"I'm counting on it, Anton."

THE BOOK WAS IN A BOX OF MARED BLAYNEY'S THINGS THAT NELL HAD tucked away in her closet after her grandmother died. "*The Tarot: Its Occult Significance, Use in Fortune-Telling, and Method of Play, Etc.* by Samuel Little MacGregor Mathers," the cover read. A wordy and portentous title for such an enormously slim volume. The author's biography explained that Mathers was the founder of the Hermetic Order of the Golden Dawn, whatever that was. An inscription on the title page proclaimed, "For the glorious and beautiful Mared Blayney, whose eyes see into man's very soul and whose smile captivates every heart. From her humble and devoted servant MacGregor Mathers."

"Grandmother, I do believe there's story to this book," Nell said aloud. "If only you were here to tell it."

Tarot deck in hand, Nell sat down at her writing table and opened the book. The Tarot, Mathers said, was perfectly suited to fortunetelling.

"That's lucky," Nell said, "since that's exactly what I want it for."

She spread the deck out in front of her, the cards as familiar to her in their own way as her grandmother's smile. Plenty of evenings beside the fire, she had watched her grandmother count them out, study them, and muse or frown to herself over what she found there.

When she'd been 5 or 6, Nell asked Mared Blayney why she played with the funny cards so much.

"You see, pippin, these cards are my guides. I ask them a question, and they give me the answer. If ever I'm sad or frightened about something, I ask the Tarot what I should do, and the cards tell me. Before I know it, I've forgotten all my troubles."

"What if the cards tell you something bad? Don't they ever do that?"

"Well, yes, sometimes they do, my sweet little Nell. But sadness is part of life, too, and all of us know it some time or another. The cards help me understand that and show me the way past the bad things."

"In Sunday school, Miss Bertha Chapman told us that Jesus is the Way and the Light. She said He's the path to eternal salvation. Does he know about the Tarot?"

Grandmother laughed and pulled her close, raining kisses on the top of her head. "That He is, my precious girl. That He is. But there's room in every Christian's heart for other ways of seeing, too, because sometimes God chooses the church to show us, and sometimes He chooses the Tarot. It's all one truth, though."

"Will you teach me to read the cards like you one day?"

"Yes, pippin. When you're ready."

But her grandmother never did get around to teaching her, time having run out before Nell was ready. Nell ran her hands over the cards spread before her on the desk. Then she opened the book and read a page or two. It might as well have been Greek, what little of it there was. Apparently, Mr. Mathers was long-winded only in his dedications.

"I wish you could teach me now, Grandmother. But I'll learn. You'll be proud."

CHAPTER 12

Osgood Sherman had been one of Nell's admirers since she was old enough to begin breaking hearts, which was in the first grade. Before she'd married Ellis Marchand, he'd never had a chance with her. Now, she was more beautiful than ever, and she'd called the Press-Scimitar to ask him to lunch at the Peabody. On his way to meet her, he got a shoeshine.

When she told him that she wanted him to write about her new venture as a fortuneteller, he forgot his romantic aspirations for a moment.

"Dadgum, Nell, if there's anyone in Memphis who can pull this off, it's you," he said, slapping the table and making the silverware and the two elderly ladies at the next booth jump. "Oh, I can see it now. We'll play it up big. Pack it with mystery. Why, they'll be eating out of your hand. You'll be the greatest thing to hit Memphis since the Cotton Carnival."

"Keep it tasteful, Oz." Nell straightened her knife and fork and then Oz's. "It would be too easy to make what I'll be doing come across as tacky."

"Don't you worry, honey. You haven't got a tacky bone in your body. Old Oz knows just how to put Madame Nelora across."

Two days later, the story he wrote for the Press-Scimitar about Nell and her sudden calling to the mystical ways of the Ancient East, as he put it, ran with a quarter-page photo of Nell in full gypsy regalia, gazing inscrutably toward that very Ancient East, although she'd really been staring past the photographer in bewilderment at Oz, who had waved and beamed at her like some lunatic newly escaped from the asylum in Bolivar.

The story read, "The charming, beautiful, aristocratic Mrs. Marchand, it should be remembered, is the granddaughter of Welshwoman-turned-Memphian Mared Blayney Leyton, herself an accomplished psychic and member of the inner circle of MacGregor Mathers, founder of the storied Order of the Golden Dawn, who was a firm believer that it was possible to communicate with loved ones even after they have crossed over to the other side. At social gatherings and charity benefits, Mrs. Leyton often entertained with her readings from the mysterious Tarot, a source of ancient wisdom. No doubt her granddaughter will prove as talented. She has begun receiving clients at her new salon on Madison."

First through the door of the salon the day after the story ran was Miss Frankie Dobbs, Nell's girlhood piano teacher, who had always rapped her on the knuckles during lessons and admonished her to keep her nail joints curved. A few people wandered in, some with questions and some obviously wanting only to get a look at the fabulous Madame Nelora.

The girl sitting before Nell now couldn't have been more than 15. By the fresh, prim, saddle-oxford-wearing look of her, she was a St. Mary's girl. Probably sneaked out of the house with her allowance money to consult the Madame Nelora. Nell did her best to muster an inscrutable-but-encouraging smile.

"So you, see, Madam Nelora," the girl said after an interminable preamble, "the minute I turned my back, Susie stole Andrew right from under my nose. I couldn't believe she was low down enough to do that. I mean, we've been best friends since kindergarten, Susie and me, for heaven's sake. She batted her lashes and promised him who knows what, and the fool trotted off after her like a little dog."

The girl dabbed at her eyes.

"I haven't slept a wink since. Honestly, Madame Nelora, I love

Andrew despite everything he has done. I don't think I can go on living without him. Besides, the cotillion is coming up in May, and it's too terrible to think of seeing him there with Susie, especially if I have to go with my brother, which is what Mama says I have to because she won't let me go without an escort. You've got to tell me what I should do. Please."

Nell thought about how desperate she had felt when she was 15 and was sure that Ellis Marchand would never give her the time of day. "Give me your hands," Nell said, stretching out her own palm to the girl.

"Aren't you going to look at the cards and see what they say?"

"The message I'm receiving is so strong that I don't need the cards this time. Now, give me your hands and close your eyes."

"Yes, ma'am."

Nell clasped the child's hands. "I want you to think about being at the cotillion. Are you concentrating?"

"Yes, ma'am."

"Here's what you're going to do. Who's the handsomest boy at St. Mark's?"

"Andrew."

"Aside from Andrew, then."

"Um, Herbie, I guess. A lot of the girls think he's a real dream."

Oh, Lord. It would have to be someone named Herbie. "All right. You're going to call Herbie on the telephone. No, wait. Better than that. You're going to march over to Herbie's house and tell him that you want him to go to the cotillion with you."

The girl's eyes flew open. "I can't ask a boy to the dance! Mama says nice young ladies don't ever call boys."

Nell squeezed her hands. "Yes, you can."

"What if he says no?"

"He won't. And you don't have to tell your mother anything. Now, close your eyes again. Good."

Nell dug deep into her own observations of girls' tactics for what came next. "When you get to the dance with Herbie, you're going to laugh at all his jokes. You're going to make him dance every dance, no matter how tired either of you gets. And you are not going to look at Andrew once. Not even one little time out of the corner of your eye. That's the most important part of all."

"But won't that hurt Andrew's feelings?"

"That's the idea. If Andrew comes up to talk to you, you don't have to ignore him because that would be rude. Just don't notice him until he notices you. And if he asks you to dance, be sure you talk about Herbie the whole time. Do you understand?"

"Yes, ma'am. If you think that will work. But what about Herbie?"

"Well, you just might find out that you like Herbie better, especially if Andrew is stupid enough to go off with that Susie. Oh, and be sure you wear a pink dress."

"We have to wear white."

"A pink ribbon in your hair, then."

The girl looked so grateful that Nell felt a pang for all the joy and suffering of young love. "Thank you, Madame Nelora."

"You're welcome, sweetheart. Come back and tell me what happens."

"Yes, ma'am. I will."

The girl scooted out, and Nell looked up to find Hattie standing over her.

"What was all that about? Wear a pink dress."

"I was hoping you weren't out there listening. Is anybody waiting?"

"No, she was the last one."

Nell pulled off her scarf and took the earrings out of her ears. "Thank goodness. I think I would have to climb a slick pole if I got another question even half that silly. Bless her heart."

"You want me to go next door and get you a co-cola?"

"Please. That is just exactly what I need."

Hattie was back in a moment with two small green glass bottles so cold that they were already sweating in the moist Memphis air. She handed one to Nell, and they both took swigs.

"I am telling you, that is some kind of good," Hattie said. She wiped her mouth with one of the paper napkins that she had brought from the bakery along with the Cokes and put the bottle on the desk. "You want me to tell you what I think, Nell Marchand?"

"I don't know why you're asking my permission. Would it stop you if I said no?"

"Uh-uh."

"Well, you might as well go on then." Nell drained her own Coke and braced herself.

"What you told that girl just in here was good. Real good. Remember what you said to Aunt Mary about wanting to do right? Well, you're doing it."

Nell sat back and closed her eyes. "I know, but I'd give my eye teeth for something even a little serious and interesting."

Hattie stood up and picked up the Coke bottles. "Now, come on. We're going to turn off the lights, take these back to the man next door, and go on home. Hattie is going to fix you a great big old mess of fried chicken and biscuits and chess pie. Then we are going to kneel down and ask the Lord to prop you up."

Hattie held out her hand to Nell, pulled her to her feet, and walked her out the door.

OZ WAS RIGHT. NELL WAS AN OVERNIGHT SENSATION.

The next day, three ladies from Miss Frankie's bible study group arrived together. Then, Bess Marchand's entire garden club. By the end of the week, the waiting area was jammed, and Hattie began turning people away.

Nell wondered why it had taken her so long to understand just what her grandmother had been on to all those years.

CHAPTER 13

Down on Beale Street, it was going to be a good night at Kelly's. Hell, Blackjack Kelly could practically count the take in his head already.

Al had been right. When Chicago got too uncomfortable for the old gang, Memphis was just the place. Blackjack figured he'd stick around permanently, maybe even get married. These Southern broads were all right.

Oh, jeez, not that damn Bryant kid again. Not tonight. He couldn't count the times they'd tossed him out, but here the kid came through the door, big as life. Twice as hard-headed as his old man, the moron. If Bryant didn't get the hint and stay away this time, maybe he'd think about asking Little Nick to take him aside and explain how things were to him. That goon wouldn't be nearly so genteel about the warning, but he got the point across. Once Little Nick told these cut-rate Casanovas to scram, they scrammed and stayed scrammed.

Blackjack pushed away from the bar to head Gaylord Bryant off before he had a chance to bug any of the dames. He was already making his way toward a busty blonde wearing a barely decent dress and laughing too loud at a table with some big moose, a real gorilla, the kind who didn't like it much when someone messed with his girl. Always went for the blondes, this kid did. Blackjack was a leg man himself. Show him a nice pair of pins, and he didn't care what color a dame decided to make her hair that morning.

He grabbed the boy by the elbow and spun him toward the door.

"Now look, kid, find a new dame somewheres else. I told you to stop coming around here. Next time you show up, I may not be so friendly."

The kid jerked his elbow away and leaned into Blackjack's face. He had balls, you had to give him that. Three sheets to the wind already, too. Even more reason to get him out of here.

"Give me a break. I just came to listen to the music. I'm not hurting anybody."

"Yeah? Scram so we keep it that way."

Blackjack took hold of his arm and started dragging him toward the door. The kid pulled free and threw a punch that missed by a mile. The blow not landing carried Bryant forward. He fell across the gorilla's table, sending glasses flying.

The blonde let out a real ear-splitter. On his feet in a flash, the gorilla grabbed Bryant by the collar. "Hey, what's the big idea spilling hooch all over my girl's dress, you lousy jerk?"

The gorilla dangled Gaylord Bryant from one fist and drew back his other, which was the size of a ham. Oh, jeez, here we go. Next thing Blackjack knew, the kid sailed backward across the room into another table, knocking it over. A new chorus of loud what-gives rose up from the crowd. Somebody yelled, "ye-haw, mammy," then punches were flying everywhere, and Bryant disappeared under a pile of flailing arms and legs.

Dammit! Blackjack peeled off his jacket—it was brand new, and there was no way in hell he was about to get blood on it. He hoped he wasn't going to have to hit any women. He dove into the pile to pull the kid out while there was still something left to pull.

"Little Nick!" he yelled on the way in.

"Right here, Blackjack."

Once Little Nick waded in, it didn't take long to break up the fight. He cracked a couple skulls together good and knuckle-punched the gorilla in the throat so hard that he might not ever be able to holler again. The rest of the boys who'd been so ready to brawl before scrambled away, looking back over their shoulders to make sure Little Nick wasn't coming after them.

Blackjack picked up the overturned tables and signaled for the band to start playing again. He shrugged back into his jacket and held up his hands to quiet the crowd. "Sorry about that, folks. How about a round on the house to make up for all the trouble?"

There was a stampede to the bar, the fight already forgotten. With the tables cleared, Blackjack found the Bryant kid at the bottom of a pile by the back wall, out cold with a whopping shiner coming up on his left eye. Little Nick stood over him, hands in his pockets.

"What do you want I should do with him?"

"Throw him on the sofa in my office. When he comes to, clean him up and drive him home."

"You want me to have a little talk with him when he wakes up?"

"No, I'll talk to his old man again and tell him he'd better straighten the little punk out this time. He ain't going to be too happy about this either. Now get him out of here."

"OK, Blackjack. Whatever you say."

Little Nick pushed up his sleeves, grabbed the kid under the arms, and hoisted him across his shoulder. Watching them disappear into the office, Blackjack shook his head. Jeez, the kind of trouble some mugs got themselves into over a broad. He just couldn't figure it.

—

JOSEPH CALENDAR LOOKED UP WHEN SIMON APPEARED AT THE DOOR. Before the butler could open his mouth, Hilda Ledbetter bustled into the Spirit Room and flopped on the sofa across from Calendar with the breathless air of a woman hurtling from one absolutely crucial appointment to the next.

"Have you heard the news, Dr. Calendar?" she said, pulling off her gloves and removing her hat as she spoke. She laid them on the sarcophagus. "Nell Marchand . . . . Do you know the Marchands? Well, of course, you do. Nell Marchand has set herself up as a fortuneteller. You must have seen the story in the paper about it. She's drawing quite a crowd. In fact, I've been to seek advice from her myself."

She picked her hat back up to fan herself. "Oh, dear, I hope you don't mind that. You don't, do you? My daughter was *so* eager to witness how the mighty have fallen, she said. Nell was always so snooty to her at school. You know, always so standoffish with all the other girls, really. I'm afraid my Beulah wanted to see poor Mrs. Marchand just to lord it over her."

Mrs. Ledbetter was a good client, but she did natter on. Calendar reflected for a long moment before he answered her. "Yes, I have met Nell Marchand. Her late husband's mother, Miss Bess, is a good friend. She has consulted with me for years."

Mrs. Ledbetter put her hands over her mouth in a show of girlish dismay. "My goodness, I hope I haven't offended you, then. I've known the Marchands forever myself. Forever. We move in the same circle, you know. Nell is a lovely girl. Astonishingly beautiful, of course—why, I didn't have skin like that even when I was young—but a little cold for my tastes. Still, one can't help feeling for her, you know. I just can't imagine being brought so low, but I suppose one must make one's way somehow."

"I hear Nell Marchand is doing quite well, that she has a rare talent, in fact." Poor, silly Hilda could never grasp just how talented Nell was.

"It was the eeriest thing." As though about to divulge the secret of the ages, Mrs. Ledbetter looked over her shoulder and leaned forward. "I went in prepared to be amused. Ordinarily, I'm not interested in such foolishness." She gasped, and her fingers flew to her mouth again. "Oh, I didn't mean that the way it sounded. Goodness, I seem to be saying all the wrong things today. Of course, you're the exception, Dr. Calendar. I have every faith in our consultations. They have meant the world to me."

Hilda fluttered her fingers across the sarcophagus at Calendar. He squeezed them briefly but reassuringly. "You know what I mean, though," she said. "I've never put any faith in these sideshow psychics who travel with carnivals and spout any nonsense that pops into their heads. And all those gullible sharecroppers and coloreds and little secretaries who soak up every word as though it were gospel. I have no time for those people at all, you know. Not at all."

She drew in her chin, compressed her lips, and looked over her nose at him in a way that reminded Calendar remarkably of an aging buzzard on its nest.

"I can see that," he said. "But Mrs. Marchand . . . you said you had an impression altogether different from the one you expected."

"Oh, yes, Dr. Calendar." Mrs. Ledbetter, who always punctuated her conversation with her hands, now clasped them at her sternum. "It was quite marvelous. Even Beulah was impressed. More than that. Why, the poor, dear girl was in tears by the time Madame Nelora—that's what Nell Marchand calls herself now when she reads fortunes—by the time Madame Nelora had finished her reading. She told Beulah that she's destined to marry a great man, a renowned healer, and that she must prepare herself to meet him and be worthy of his love. Beulah is to do volunteer work among the poor. She said he would find Beulah there, see her soul for the shining star of goodness that it is, and sweep her away to live and work at his side."

Hilda sighed and shook her head.

"I tell you, it was quite remarkable," she went on. "My Beulah is a changed girl, Dr. Calendar. Positively changed. There's a light that shines from her face now. A purpose. She told me that as soon as she can find an appropriate charity, she's going to work there at once. That very minute."

It took every iota of Calendar's professional training to suppress the smile that tugged at his lips. "Remarkable. It sounds like a profound transformation."

"Oh, yes. Yes, it was. Truly remarkable. You should see Madame Nelora at work, Dr. Calendar. It's quite, quite extraordinary."

Calendar agreed. It was high time he paid her a visit.

Chapter 14

A dry cleaners and a Japanese bakery flanked the storefront on Madison. Had he not known the street address and been searching for it, Calendar might never have noticed it. Only a simple sign that read "Madame Nelora, Spiritual Guidance and Divination" identified Nell's salon.

Underneath the lettering, there was a tasteful depiction of the Eye of Providence, the same all-seeing eye found on the reverse of the Great Seal of the United States. He wondered if Nell remembered anything of the eye's history, which dated back at least to the Eye of Horus in Egypt, or if she had chosen it simply because it looked mysterious.

When he entered, he found the anteroom was decorated with three Egyptian-themed chairs complete with lion feet and hieroglyphic markings on the backs, a simple carved stool, a replica of a cat-headed canopic urn, and a wall-hanging depicting the jackal-headed god Anubis weighing a heart against the feather of truth on the scale of Ma'at. A small gong that was not even vaguely Egyptian but not unlike the one in his Spirit Room stood before the window. Where she had found such items in Memphis was a mystery, and Calendar smiled over it. The effect was an oddly occult elegance.

A tall, sturdily built Negro woman dressed in a plain, good-quality dress distinctly out of keeping with her exotic surroundings bustled forward to greet Calendar. Before she could speak, he put a finger to his lips.

"Is anyone with Madam Nelora?" Calendar said, his voice low. "I am Joseph Calendar. I'd like to surprise her."

The Negress nodded, seeming to recognize his name, and ushered him toward the curtained-off area at the rear, where he assumed the readings took place. She drew back the sheer panel and stepped aside to let him pass through.

Seated at a handsome antique walnut writing desk, Nell studied a deck of cards fanned out in front of her. She was much too fair for a gypsy—and he had known many from the various groups that term encompassed—but the kohl lining her deep-set eyes and the wanton auburn curls escaping from under her headscarf gave her a sage-yet-raffish air that any fortuneteller would have envied.

She looked up and, seeing him, grimaced, fierce in her displeasure.

"Well, I'll be dog," she said. "Joseph Calendar. I would think that you'd be the last person who needs spiritual guidance. Doesn't your good buddy Imhotep take care of that for you?"

"He and I are dedicated to the service of others. I do not confer with Imhotep for myself."

"Such noble self-sacrifice."

Hand across his waist, Calendar bowed his acknowledgment. "We do what we can. I hear you're becoming quite prosperous, Miss Nell. In fact, I'm surprised to find you unoccupied. By all accounts, there should be a line of supplicants clamoring at your door."

"I'm doing all right so far."

"I've heard you have quite a flair for seeing into the future."

"You know better than anybody else how that works, Dr. Calendar. I offer comfort, and most people hear what they want to hear. It's pretty easy to figure that out. After all, I did it all my life on the Memphis society circuit. You can't beat a solid foundation as a debutante."

Calendar pulled back the chair that faced Nell and raised an eyebrow. She nodded for him to sit. "That is a great insight in itself," he said.

"What do you want?"

"Will you read the cards for me?"

Nell hesitated, her eyes on Calendar's face. She bit back some retort. He found himself regretting the loss of an opportunity to parry it.

"Why not?" she said. Nell set the cards in front of him and tapped the top of the deck. "Concentrate on your question. When you're ready, shuffle these."

Calendar turned the deck over and spread them before him, face up.

"Afraid I stacked the deck?" Nell said.

"Not at all. I'm simply admiring the cards. They're quite beautiful. I don't think I've seen a Tarot like this before."

"It's called the *Jeu de la Princesse*, the Game of the Princess. These cards belonged to my grandmother Leyton. Everyone called her by her maiden name, Mared Blayney. She used to read them for me on each of my birthdays."

"I recall your saying so. You come from a family of sensitives."

Nell made a face halfway between distaste and wistfulness. "Please don't start that hogwash again. In a way, though, I suppose it's possible. She came from Wales, and she said the Welsh are a very mystical people. I know she was. She was part of a spiritualist circle in London for a while, before my grandfather married her and brought her to Memphis."

"He was Welsh as well?"

"No. From right here in Memphis. He went to London on business—something about cotton commodities trading there—and he met my *nain*. Love at first sight for both of them, it seems. He always said he would have had to move to London if she hadn't agreed to come home with him."

"Your nain?"

Calendar pronounced it as "nine," which is how it sounded to an English-speaker's ear.

"Nain, spelled n-a-i-n. It's Welsh for grandmother. She used to speak Welsh to me when I was little. She wanted to teach me, but I wouldn't apply myself. I learned a bit, but after she died . . . ."

Nell fell quiet. She reached for the cards where Calendar had spread them on the table before him, gathered them back into a deck that she clasped almost like a prayer book in her elegant, long-fingered hands, and set it in front of him again.

"It was her language, and with her gone, it didn't seem right to speak it anymore," Calendar said. "It was part of what made her special."

Nell smiled, but the corners of her perfect lips turned down ever so slightly, remembering something both sweet and sad. "Yes, it was. I guess you can read minds after all. Anyway, these are her cards."

"Did she use them for others? In public, I mean."

"Sometimes, she read at parties. Her friends saw it as a kind of parlor game, I suppose, part of her charming eccentricity. But mostly she kept them for herself. And for me."

He shuffled the cards and divided them into three stacks.

Nell gave him a sharp look. "Do you know the Tarot?"

Calendar paused, shook his head. "I am not a reader, but I have seen others work with them with great skill."

She considered him as though weighing the truth of his statement. "Choose the stack that speaks to you and put it on top," she said.

He picked up the stack to the left.

Nell took the cards from him and shuffled them all once. "We'll do a five-card spread. Think of the question you want to ask."

"Thinking."

"Now, deal them out." She tapped the table to show him the order for placing the cards. "Have you had a reading before?"

"No, I've merely observed. I've never felt the need for guidance from without."

She shot him another sharp look. "Then tell me. How come I am the lucky one?"

"There are so many ways that one might use abilities such as yours, and I wonder that you've taken up this particular craft after you refused my help so adamantly. And, of course, I hear on good authority that you are quite brilliant in your readings. I am curious."

"I'm still learning."

"The truly gifted never stop learning."

Nell ignored him and pointed to card in the center of the spread. "Now turn over the center card, which shows us the present."

The Queen of Cups. She gasped.

"What is it?" he said.

"Nothing. It's just that this card keeps turning up. It was my grandmother's favorite. Every time I see it, it reminds me so much of her. She always said the Cups meant love and abundance."

The second card, which Calendar knew represented past influences, was the Three of Swords reversed.

"You've had your heart broken, haven't you, Dr. Calendar?"

"Perhaps the cards will tell you."

He motioned for her to go on. The third card, the card for the future, was the Ace of Cups. Nell's brows drew together. She tried not to look at him, but he could see her thinking fast.

"A new beginning or a new love," he said when she did not speak right away.

"I thought you weren't a reader."

The fourth card, the reason card, was the Lovers. Now, she blushed, but it was clear she was also beginning to be enthralled.

The fifth card, the card of potential, was the Two of Cups. Then Calendar knew, whether she did or not. A sweet, sad pang squeezed at his heart. They were bound to each other, fated, no matter that neither of them wanted it now. There would be no point in resisting. One day, they would be together, as they had been lifetime after lifetime.

He had known it that first day, felt it when he took her hand, felt the fear and fascination. Please the Lord, let it not end as the last one had done, in madness and despair. This time, he would find a way to protect her. This time, he would be able to keep them both safe.

"So many Cups," Nell murmured in rapt attention. Studying the spread, she reached for the Two of Cups but snatched her hand away as though the card had seared her fingers.

"Are you all right, Nell?" Calendar said.

"It's hot." She stared at the card, clutching her fingers to her throat.

"What are you talking about?"

"The card. It burned me."

He put a tentative finger on the Two of Cups. Picked it up.

"Don't!" Nell said, her voice trembling. She grabbed at his wrist the way a mother grabs at an infant to stop it from trying to catch hold of a flame.

"Nell, it's fine. Perfectly cool. I don't know what you mean, hot." He held the card out to her on his palm.

She touched it again quickly once and then took it from him. "I don't understand it. The card was burning when I touched it, so hot it scorched my fingers. See?" She held her hand out toward him, palm up.

He ran his thumb over the fingertips, fingers, and palm, searching for any injury before he closed his hand over hers to keep himself from kissing it. "There's nothing here, Miss Nell. There are no burns."

"I'm telling you, it blistered my fingers." She tried to sit back. "You may release my hand now, Dr. Calendar."

But he did not let go. Rather, he covered it with his free hand and leaned closer, grave. "Miss Nell, I want you to listen to me. Promise me that you will be very careful. Something is happening here that you don't understand. I truly believe you have a powerful gift, a gift more dangerous than you can imagine if you do not respect it."

Nell pulled free, looked at her fingers, and seemed astonished that the skin of her hand had not bubbled and peeled away, all blackened and crisp. She hid the hand under the table. "And I suppose you want to teach me just how to do that."

"I can work with you, if you wish."

"That's very generous, but one of us manipulating the truth here is enough."

Calendar forced a smile to his lips. "One day, if you need my help, I am at your service."

"I'll remember that. Now, if you'll excuse me, I believe there are other people waiting for me."

"Are we not to continue with my reading?"

"No, I . . . I don't feel like going on. I've lost my concentration."

"May I come again? I hardly feel I've gotten my money's worth."

"Since you've paid nothing yet, I think you have. Now, please. Others must be waiting."

At the door, Calendar turned to look back at her. "Remember what I said, Miss Nell. Have a care."

On his way through the still-empty salon, Calendar gave his calling card to Nell's black gatekeeper. "If she ever needs me for anything, come to me at once."

"Yes, sir, Dr. Calendar. I will."

He slipped quietly out the door, turning over in his mind the expression of shock and confusion on Nell's face as she touched the card. Whether she wanted it or not, he would watch over her.

—

STILL AT HER DESK, NELL SHIVERED AND EXAMINED HER FINGERS AGAIN for burns. She studied Calendar's cards, picked up the Two of Cups again. Nothing this time. She started to puzzle out what the cards might mean, thought better of it, and swept them back into the deck. Sometimes not knowing was wisest. She shuffled them again and again until she was sure his cards were lost in the deck.

CHAPTER 15

In his years as a lowly loan officer before he'd reached the dizzying heights of investment banker at the Union Planters Bank, Franklin Bryant learned that, should he wish to do so, the best way to intimidate a loan applicant or business associate was to leave him standing while he, Franklin, sat behind his desk looking stern or indifferent or whatever way suited his wishes in the matter they discussed. The young man now on the other side of the desk, head down with hands shoved deep in his pockets, was his first-born and only child, Gaylord. Franklin did not offer him a seat.

"Son, are you bound and determined to ruin your life?" Franklin asked. "I heard about your latest brawl in some disreputable Beale Street bar. I have told you that I am not going to put up with that kind of carrying on. Do you want to humiliate your mother, have all her friends talking about what a reprobate her boy is?'

"I just wanted to have a little fun, Pop, that was all." The boy shifted his weight, eyes fixed on the carpet. "Benny and I were at the Peabody, and he met a girl. They left, but I wasn't ready to go home, so I went to Kelly's."

Franklin drew the silence out, let the rascal sweat before he spoke again.

"One of these days your cousin Benny is going to get you into some kind of trouble that I can't get you out of. That boy is as wild as a peach-orchard boar. I'm going to speak to his father about this. Perhaps he can do something to control that scoundrel before he becomes an irredeemable degenerate. Your mother and I have indulged you too much, I'm sure, but Benny, he's another case altogether."

"Benny's not bad, Pop. He just likes to have a good time. And he likes girls. All of us like girls. You can't expect a fellow to live like a monk in this day and age."

At that, Franklin came around the end of his desk to look his son in the eye. At least the damned young fool had the courage to meet his gaze this time.

"If I hear that you've been doing anything but exactly that again, Gaylord Bryant, I will cast you out of my house, cut you off without a penny, and never allow your name to be spoken in my presence again. That is not the kind of man I have brought you up to be. I would think with all the trouble you had with that last girl, you would have learned a lesson."

"Pop, not that again."

The stricken look on the boy's face almost made Franklin relent in his lecture. Almost. "I will not have you besmirching the Bryant name and breaking your mother's heart. Remember who you are. And you might suggest to Benny the next time you see him that he remember as much, too. Your uncle won't put up with such shenanigans either."

"Yes, sir."

Franklin considered his next words carefully. "And if you have already indulged yourself in such carryings-on, son, I don't want to know about it. But you get yourself right down to see Dr. Roberts and have him examine you. You can't be too careful if you've been consorting with some cheap cocktail waitress. These things can have serious implications if they're not dealt with promptly. You understand what I mean, don't you, Gaylord?"

The boy had the good grace to blush. "Yes, sir."

"Of course, if Dr. Roberts should find something that does need to be dealt with, you are to come to me at once, do you understand?"

Now, Gaylord was a satisfying shade of beet. It was good enough for him. "Yes, sir."

"There are special sanitariums to deal with such . . . ailments. I'd hate for you to be the first Bryant to shame our name in such a way, but if it must be done, well, we will address it. Remind your cousin of that, too."

The boy shifted uncomfortably. "Yes, sir."

"Very well, then. I assume you'll be home for Sunday dinner as usual?"

"Yes, sir."

"Good. We've allowed you to live in the dormitory, but unless you can show us that you know how to comport yourself like a true gentlemen, you will lose that privilege. Do I make myself clear?"

"Enough, Pop, please." Gaylord jammed his hands back in his pockets. "Pop, if it's all right, I'd like to move home anyway. It's too hard to study at the dorm."

"I'm glad to hear you're taking your studies seriously, son." Franklin put his arm around the boy's shoulders. "You understand that I have your best interests at heart, don't you, Gaylord? You're a fine boy, and I don't want to see you throw your life and everything we've worked so hard for away like this."

CHAPTER 16

It was the inevitable day that Phoebe Brooks had dreaded from the moment she'd first set eyes on Joseph Calendar. Denying that it would ever come had not kept it from doing so. All her life, she had been accustomed to getting just what she wanted, but not this time.

He came in the door of her apartment, bearing a bouquet of Michaelmas daisies that he presented in his usual gallant fashion. He did not, however, kiss her on the cheek as was his custom.

"Where did you find these at this time of year?" she asked. The flowers of farewell. She appreciated the irony. With a deep breath, Phoebe looked up into his eyes. "I'm ready."

"Phoebe, you are an intelligent, fine woman, and I have enjoyed our time together."

Oh, sweet Jesus, she wasn't ready after all. The pain was worse than she could have imagined, sharp and cold and as bitter as a green persimmon. Biting down on her lower lip, Phoebe squeezed her eyes shut and turned her face away. Afraid her knees would give way, she leaned back against the door for support.

Calendar waited quietly for her to master her emotions, and she was grateful to him for that. Crying would humiliate her. After a long, shuddering breath, she regarded him, struggling to smile.

"You don't need to say anything else, Joseph. I knew from the beginning that there would be no strings. I thought I would be ready when the end came. Funny how that works, isn't it?"

"Phoebe–"

She put her fingers over his lips to stop him. Phoebe Brooks endured pity from no one. “No, I’m all right. I can take my medicine like a big girl.” There. She managed a smile at last. “If you have a new companion, though, I’d just like to know who she is so I can prepare myself to see you with her.”

Calendar kissed her hand. “There is no new companion. I just don’t feel that we should see each anymore.”

Was there something almost bowed and beaten about the way he stood, still holding her hand? He did feel something at leaving her after all, it seemed. She was touched. Hope began to raise its head and breathe within her again. She was about to throw her arms around him, say that she understood, that she could give him time, as much time as he needed, that they could go on as they had been after all. But then she saw that it wasn’t for her, this ineffable sadness. It was for someone else . . . and for himself.

“Oh, my Lord, Joseph. You’ve fallen in love, haven’t you? Surely it’s not for the first time.”

“No, not the first. I had hoped there would never be another, though.”

“Oh, darling, I’m so sorry. Who is it?”

He didn’t answer, but she knew anyway, and it broke her heart. “Tell me it’s not Nell Marchand.”

He looked like a man who has just been stood up against a wall to face a firing squad without a cigarette or a blindfold. “Yes.”

—

THE LAST PERSON ON EARTH NELL EVER EXPECTED TO SEE COME through the door of her salon was Mildred Epps, the bottle-blonde who was with Ellis when he died. She might never have been face to face with Mildred before, but Nell knew who she was.

If you liked her sort, the hussy was pretty enough, but her features were pinched together in the middle of her face. Nell doubted, however, that it was her face that men looked at. Mildred had enormous breasts that gave her a banty-rooster strut, and she kept them on display for all to admire or envy. Nell hoped that at least the effort of holding them up made her back ache at night.

"I don't know why I should be surprised that you would dare to come here," Nell said.

"I wanted to see what you looked like in person. I saw your picture in the paper. You're better looking than I thought, you know, Mrs. Marchand. That gypsy getup suits you. Besides, I want my fortune told."

Mildred stretched her hand across the table, palm up. Nell looked at it as though she'd been offered a fresh cow pie.

"I don't think you'll like the one I have for you, Miss Epps. It ends with you in the gutter where you belong."

A hint of a smile on her lips, Mildred interlaced her fingers and leaned across the table toward Nell. "You shouldn't be sore like that. So I was Ellis Marchand's sheba."

Sheba. Oh, good Lord, what tacky magazine had she gotten that out of? If she called Ellis her sheik, Nell was going to vomit.

"So what?" Mildred went on. "He was good to me, and I was good to him. We had a swell time together. It's not like you loved him or anything, so who did it hurt? You and me, I think we ought to be friends."

"What makes you think I'd ever want anything to do with you?"

"Maybe you don't know everything there was to know about Ellis. Maybe there's a few things I could tell you. "

"The kinds of things you knew about Ellis, I wouldn't want to hear. There is absolutely nothing you could possibly say that would be of any interest to me ever."

A look of anger—or was it worry?—flashed across Mildred's face, but then she shrugged. "OK, but you're making a big mistake. Maybe we could help each other."

"Why would you want to help me?"

Mildred contemplated Nell's question. "Maybe it tickles me. Maybe I want to find out things that people you know could help me with. Besides, I got nothing against you. We've got a lot in common. It's not like I was stuck on Ellis either. He was fun, but mostly, he was convenient."

There almost wasn't enough debutante training the in the world, the tradition of Southern female gentility almost wasn't deep enough, and the memory of her mother's voice telling her to consider the source and rise above it almost wasn't vivid enough to keep Nell from knocking Mildred's teeth down her stinking, trashy throat. She swallowed against a fury that threatened to choke her.

"I think you'd better leave."

"Don't I get my fortune told?" Mildred said, holding her palm out again.

"If you don't get out of here right now, your future is going to be so brief that you won't have time to notice it." Nell leapt from her chair and shouted past Mildred. "Hattie!"

"All right. All right. I'm going." Mildred gave a sniff as she rose. "But if you ever change your mind, you can find me at the Peabody Grill most days. I'm the hostess there."

"I must remember never to go there again."

Hattie appeared, scowling. Mildred sauntered past her, each step a blend of impudence and nonchalance that made Nell want to hurl something very heavy or very sharp after her.

"Who was that?" Hattie said.

"Ellis's floozy," Nell said.

"Lordy mercy. What in the world did she want?"

"To humiliate me, I'm sure. I can't think of any other reason for her to come here." Nell collapsed back into her chair. "Is there anyone else in the waiting room, Hattie?"

"A couple of folks from Miss Bess's bridge club. You sure you're all right, honey?"

Nell nodded, heaved a deep, shuddering sigh. "Show someone in.

I'm not going to waste any more time thinking about that woman."

With this, Nell shuffled the cards again and tamped them into a neat pile in front of her. In the outer room, she heard Hattie say, "Madame Nelora will see you now," and she pasted on a welcoming smile.

—

MILDRED EPPS AND NELL MARCHAND. NOW, THE TWO OF THEM broads would be some combination, wouldn't they? What the hell Mildred was doing coming out of the Marchand dame's saloon or whatever it was called, Little Nick couldn't figure. Them two getting chummy would have been something he'd like to see if it wouldn't have been so inconvenient for so many people, him included. He'd keep an eye on the Epps skirt a little bit longer. The boss might think he had her in his back pocket, but you never could tell with Mildred Epps. Kinda crazy, if you asked him. Cute though. Real cute.

He pulled at his tie, which all of a sudden seemed too tight. Good thing, too. Like a rope around his neck to remind him that hanging wouldn't be much of a laugh if they caught him. The trick was to see that they never did catch him. He wasn't too keen on the idea of getting his neck stretched. Except they didn't hang you anymore, did they? These days, they gave you the chair. He didn't like to think about getting the juice, either.

Yep, he'd better keep an eye on Mildred Epps. She could be trouble, lots of trouble for all of them, and Blackjack, he didn't like no trouble.

He walked away, flipping a quarter in his hand, like George Raft in "Scarface." Little Nick had practiced until he got it just right. He could roll it over his knuckles and between his fingers, too, like that old rummy magician at the speak back home taught him, and he bet George Raft couldn't do that.

Still, that George Raft, he was good. And he'd heard Raft liked to hang out with some of the gang who went to California when things got a little too hot in New York or Chicago. That Raft was all right.

Little Nick stopped to look at his reflection in the bakery window and ran his fingers along the brim of his hat in front, getting the angle just right. Dressing good was part of the game. You had to let 'em know you weren't some cheap hood. You were a businessman, a man of the world. You had class, and any dope who said different got his face pushed in.

He stuck the quarter back in his pocket and went into the bakery to see if they had cannoli.

Chapter 17

It was a shame for any man this beautiful to go to waste.

Looking across the table at Joseph Calendar in his Spirit Room as he closed his deep sapphire eyes to summon Imhotep, Bess Marchand thought that if she were a younger woman, she could quite lose her head over him.

Bess's matchmaker's instinct was stirring. A man like Dr. Calendar should not be doomed to a life alone. He would do quite nicely for Nell, who, after all, deserved happiness after everything the poor dear had endured.

"Phoebe Brooks is a lovely girl."

"Why, yes, she is, Miss Bess," he said, his eyes opening.

A man couldn't take a woman dancing at the Peabody and expect no one to notice.

"And a good dancer."

"That, too."

"Have you never thought of marrying, Dr. Calendar?" Bess said.

Lips pursed, Calendar seemed to consider before he answered. "I am wed to my calling, Miss Bess," he said. "Rather like a priest who marries the church. My work doesn't leave much room for romantic love, nor can I afford to be distracted from my mission."

Calendar then gave Bess a lazy, amused smile full of good humor and more than a tinge of wickedness. "Are you thinking of remarrying, Miss Bess?"

She giggled like a school girl looking at her first naughty picture.

"Oh, good heavens, Dr. Calendar. Not me. Of course, not me. Why, I'm old enough to be your mother, and I will never marry again. I had one husband whom I loved very dearly. That was enough." She opened the locket she wore around her neck and looked at her Daniel's picture. "No, I simply wondered why a handsome, accomplished man like you—a cultured gentleman—would be alone. I'm glad you and Phoebe are keeping company."

"Miss Phoebe and I are no longer keeping company, as you so charmingly put it."

"I'm sure more than one woman has set her cap for you."

He inclined his head. "Thank you, Miss Bess, for your interest. If women have set their caps, as you say, I find it diplomatic not to understand their intentions. The last thing I would wish would be to wound a tender female heart. If they believe me ignorant of their interest, then we can remain friends.

"And I am anything but alone. As I said, I have my work and the spirits I commune with. They are company enough for any man. I would not wish to dilute my gifts with worldly distractions. Home and hearth are noble pursuits, but they are better suited to other men than they are to me."

What a shame, Bess thought, closing the locket. But, then, a man, like a woman, could always change his mind. As long as a dog was still ranging the field, the Judge used to say, you could hope that eventually he would point the right bird.

—

BLACKJACK KELLY WAS AT HIS DESK COUNTING THE TAKE FROM THE night before. Little Nick knocked on the door.

"This better be good," Blackjack said, not looking up from the stack of bills in front of him. "You make me lose count so's I have to start over again, I'm making you pay for it in a way you're not going to like."

"There's some rube out front asking about Ginny Evans," Little

Nick said.

"Tell him we never heard of her."

"I tried that, but he says he's not leaving until he speaks to the pro-pri-e-tor. The old broad who was here asking for her before is with him. I think he might be Ginny's old pappy."

"All right. Pour them a couple of drinks and tell them I'll be out there in a minute."

"You got it."

Cursing above his breath, Blackjack stashed the pile of bills in his desk drawer, which he made sure to lock. He dropped the desk key in his vest pocket and put on his best, most-unaffected smile.

Geez, rube was right. The old man at the bar was dressed in worn overalls and a rough cotton work shirt that was frayed at the collar and cuffs. Too many hours in the hot sun had creased his face, and the skin on his forehead was white from where his hat usually covered it. Dirt farmer. That hat sat on the counter next to him, ringed with the kind of stain around the band that a guy didn't get unless he was sweating hard outside day after day. Farming was too much work, if you asked Blackjack.

There were no liquor glasses in front of the man or the woman who sat with him. Teetotalers, he'd bet. Well, on second thought, the dame might be the type to cut loose every now and then, but the old man had that church-going look.

"How can I help you folks?" Blackjack said.

The man smoothed a photograph on the bar. "This is my girl Ginny Evans. She used to work here."

"Oh, yes. I remember Ginny. Nice kid. She sang with the boys for a while."

"She ain't but just turned 16 years old. Would have made her 15 when you had her working here. I come to find her and take her back home to her mama."

"Well, now, Mr. Evans, your daughter seemed a lot older than 15." Blackjack tugged at his cuffs. "We didn't ask her age. She said she wanted to sing more than anything, she looked like a nice kid, so we gave her a job. These days, most people are grateful for a chance like that."

"I wish we could help you." Blackjack handed the picture back.

"You still say you don't know where she went after she left out of here?" the farmer said.

Pretending to think, Blackjack rubbed the back of his neck. "No, sir, I really don't. Like I told this lady before, I don't believe we asked her. She wanted her pay, we gave it to her, and she left. That was it. Little Nick, you know anything about where Ginny Evans went?"

"No." Little Nick stopped flipping his coin in the air for a moment. "No idea. She said she wanted to be a canary out in Hollywood. You know, sing in the pictures. We just figured she hopped a train for the coast after she had enough dough saved up." Up the coin went again. Little Nick caught it and gave them an innocent look.

Blackjack turned to the old man, looking as sorry as he knew how to. "You see, Mr. Evans, we can't help you. I wish we could. Why don't you ask around at some of the restaurants downtown?"

The man put the picture carefully back into the pocket of his overalls and fastened the button over it. He picked his hat up from the bar and stood holding it between his hands. "If you see my Ginny, please tell her she needs to come home," he said. "Her mama misses her."

"I'll do that," Blackjack said.

Evans nodded. He took the woman's elbow, and the two of them passed through the door into the street beyond.

"You think he'll find her?" Little Nick said.

"Not in a million years, Little Nick. Not in a million years. Pour me a glass of that rye, will you?"

"Sure. Coming right up."

Blackjack took the whiskey and downed it in one gulp. He wiped his mouth with the back of his hand. "All right," he said. "That dough ain't going to count itself."

He stuck a finger in Little Nick's face.

"And this time, don't interrupt me. I don't care if Franklin D. Roosevelt himself comes in. You tell him he's got to wait until I'm done counting."

CHAPTER 18

The counting done, Blackjack dropped two packets wrapped in brown paper on the table in front of Little Nick where he sat scanning the Commercial Appeal. Blackjack lifted the paper from his fingers and dropped it on the table.

"Hey, I'm reading here," Little Nick said.

"It's time for a visit to our banker friend," Blackjack said.

"Aw, I'm in the middle of an in-ter-esting story. Anyways, you know he don't like it when I show up at his office. Can't you go?"

"No, I got better things to do, and I went last time. We don't want the same guy showing up asking for loans every week, do we?" Blackjack kicked the leg of Little Nick's chair. "Come on. Come on. Get a move on. I'm the boss here, and I'm telling you, it's your turn to go."

Little Nick sighed and smoothed out the paper. "I liked it better when he came down here to pay us his little visits."

"Yeah? Well, me, too. Is it my fault he decided it was too hot for a respectable member of the community like him to be showing up in a joint like this?"

"Blackjack, I gotta tell you, I don't like the guy. Every time he sees me, he acts like I'm something he wants to scrape off the bottom of his shoe. Like I stink or something. Can't we find somebody else to do business with, somebody a little, you know, friendlier?"

"Maybe you ought to try going easy on that cologne you wear and stop acting like you think you're Jimmy Cagney. We ain't in Chicago anymore, and you could try for a little class. Sophistication. One of these days, I might grab that stinking quarter of yours in midair and shove it down your throat. Besides, I don't feel like breaking in a new banker to handle our . . . uh . . . investments. Now shut your yap and go."

Little Nick squinted at the story he'd been reading and put a check next to the headline so he'd remember where he was when he came back. He slid both the packets into his inside jacket pocket. "All right, all ready. I'm going. What's my sob story this time?"

"Sick mother, and you want to talk to him about a personal loan. Your Uncle Al from Chicago said he might be able to help you."

Little Nick wheezed out a sound like someone sitting on an accordion and slapped Blackjack on the arm. "My Uncle Al. That's a good one, Boss. But, hey, the old stuffed shirt ain't never met Al for real has he?"

Blackjack sighed. "Yeah, they used to play golf together after church on Sundays. Come on." He kicked the chair again.

"OK. I'm going." Little Nick held up his hands. "I'm going."

One step out onto Beale, and he was digging for his lucky quarter. He tossed it as high as he could and caught it before he rolled it over his knuckles and slipped it back into his pocket. A jut of his jaw and a quick so's-your-old-man sneer back at the door of the joint, and he turned toward downtown. Blackjack Kelly was getting to be a real wise guy, but that was better than some stiff who had no sense of humor at all. Playing golf with his Uncle Al. Jeez, that was rich.

Little Nick decided he would walk to the bank. He could cut through the lobby of the Peabody on the way back from Madison Avenue and see if they had those ducks out. Talk about a sense of humor. He'd like to shake the hand of the guy who came up with the idea of walking a bunch of damn ducks from the penthouse down to the lobby fountain every day. Ducks. Now, that was really rich.

The stuffed shirt had his office on the third floor of the Union Planters Bank Building. There was a real cute number out front—the shirt's new secretary, he guessed—a real doll, but she looked down her nose the minute he came through the door flipping his quarter. He whirled and caught it in midair to impress her, but she didn't bat an eye. He stuck it back in his pocket. Who needed an iceberg like that anyway?

"May I help you?" the iceberg said in a tone that meant, "Why don't you drop dead?"

The accent, though. These Southern dames got him every time.

"Yeah, I'm here to see Mr. Bryant."

"Do you have an appointment?"

Maybe he'd give it another try. He was a sucker for a brunette, and this one was a looker. She had style, too. The glamour girl hair and that red lipstick were a little too racy for a dame pretending to all proper like. Little Nick sat on the edge of her desk, peeled a piece of gum, and popped it in his mouth. He held out the gum package to her, but she shook her head.

"No, thank you. I don't chew gum. Even if I did, I wouldn't do it in public."

Little Nick returned the package to his pocket. Yeah, a real iceberg. "No? Well, maybe you ought to try having a little fun some time, sister. You might like it. So, ring the old guy. Tell him Mr. Jones, who knows his Uncle Al from Chicago, is here. I bet he'll want to see me right away."

She looked up at him through her lashes with almost a smirk and pressed the button on her desk to buzz her boss. "There's a Mr. Jones here to see you, Mr. Bryant. He asked me to tell you that Al sent him."

He grinned. Maybe she was more fun than she looked.

The shirt's voice crackled from the other end. "Ask Mr. Jones to come in."

"This way, please."

She led him to a door off to the right, and, brother, there was enough swing in those hips to keep a guy thinking about what else they could do. He hitched up his pants. Maybe they'd have a little chat on his way out. Meanwhile, she was opening the door. The shirt was standing behind his desk waiting with something that wasn't exactly no welcoming look on his mug.

"Come in, please, Mr. Jones. Thank you, Shirley. That will be all."

"Catch you later, Shirley," Little Nick said out of the side of his mouth.

This time—ha, ha!—she smiled.

—

ANTON HELD THE DOOR TO FRANKLIN'S SUITE OPEN FOR NELL, followed her in, and with a wave to Franklin's secretary, steered Nell toward the banker's office door.

"Good morning, Shirley," he said. "Is he in?"

"Good morning, Mrs. Marchand, Mr. Green. There's someone with him. Would you like to wait?"

"Every moment in your company does a man nothing but good, Shirley."

"May I get y'all some coffee?"

"No, thank you," Nell said.

"Please," Anton said.

The secretary disappeared down a small hallway.

"Nice girl, Shirley," Anton said. He pulled out a chair for Nell. "How she puts up with someone as stiff-necked as Franklin Bryant, I don't know. More stars in her crown, but maybe Franklin is less of a sourpuss with her. Pretty girl like that."

Nell was about to tease Anton about his rogue's eye, when the door to Franklin's office opened and out stepped the hulking caricature of a Hollywood gangster down to the suit with its just-too-wide pinstripes and the oversized fedora. Good Lord, he was even tossing a coin into the air and catching it.

"See you around, Pops," the ersatz Raft paused at the door long enough to say. He walked to Shirley's desk, glanced around for her. Spotting Nell, he directed a knowing leer at her that made her reach to see if her blouse had come unbuttoned and sauntered out.

"Oh, Franklin couldn't have liked being called Pops like that," Anton said, grinning. He knocked on the office door and peeked in. Nell came up behind him just as Franklin, startled, looked up from the drawer he was digging through. "Got a minute for an old friend, Pops?"

"Very funny, Anton," he said. "Oh, Miss Nell. What a pleasure. Please, come in."

Franklin settled Nell in a chair across from his desk and pointed to another for Anton. A knock sounded behind him.

"I've brought Mr. Green's coffee." Shirley stopped in the doorway.

"Yes, yes, come on in," Franklin said.

"Would you like a cup, Mr. Bryant?"

"No, thank you. I've had my two for the morning. You may go to lunch now if you like, Shirley."

Anton watched her exit and shut the office door quietly. Nell gave him an I-caught-you smirk, and he blushed.

"Who was that character we just saw coming out of here, Franklin?" Nell said. "I hope that's not a style that's going to catch on in Memphis."

"From Chicago. No manners at all, but I suppose I have to overlook that in a client."

"That's not the kind of old boy you usually handle, is he?" Anton said. "Don't tell me he has wagonloads of money to invest. Or does he have something on you that you don't want Margaret to know?"

The look Franklin turned on Anton would have curdled milk. "No. He's a referral from a business associate, and I feel I must help him if I can. He was looking for a loan." He turned to Nell. "What can I do for you, Miss Nell?"

"I'm starting to make a little money with my new venture, and I want to put it somewhere safe. Thing is, though, I don't know that anywhere is safe these days. After what happened with Ellis's money—and mine—I'm not sure that would necessarily be here."

Speechless, Franklin blinked at her.

In the silence that followed, Anton went to the cabinet behind the banker's desk, extracted a decanter and glass, poured a drink, and offered it to Nell. She shook her head. He waggled the glass toward Franklin, who also declined. Anton took a sip and perched on the edge of the desk.

"Perhaps it is time for a change for all parties concerned," Franklin said. He turned to Anton, a smug smile quirking his lips. "Young Blankenship is a good man. Good-looking and single, too. I imagine he would suit Mrs. Marchand just right."

Nell started to retort, but Anton held up a peace-making hand to silence her. He took another sip of his whisky and put the glass down on the desk.

"You always did have a mean streak a mile wide, Franklin Bryant," Anton said. He looked at Nell. "I think you're right. A change is just exactly what Miss Nell needs. But what will Claude Beaumont have to say when he finds out that the Marchands have left his bank after all these years?"

He gave Nell his hand and led her out of the office without a backward glance.

"Anton, I could have defended my own honor, but you were sweet to do it for me," she said when the door had closed behind them.

"Franklin has a mighty high opinion of himself these days. 'Bout time somebody took him down a notch or two. Come on. The folks at the Central Bank always treated your daddy right, and I bet they'll be glad to see you."

—

"I DON'T RECKON WE'RE EVER GOING TO FIND HER, KATE," LUTHER SAID into the phone. "I'm just about ready to give up and come home. For all we know, she ain't even in Memphis any more. Wherever Ginny is, we got to believe she's fine. Probably got the world by the tail. Why, she could be out in California all this time. You keep an eye on the moving pictures. She might be in one by now."

Kate didn't laugh. Luther didn't blame her.

"We're getting by all right here, Luther," Kate said. "Give it another week. Please. I just know you'll find Ginny if you keep looking."

"All right, hon. One more week." He hung up and rubbed the back of his hand across his eyes. He leaned against the wall, every bit of hope gone out of him, but straightened when he heard Sadie's step behind him.

"Are you heading back?"

"I done promised Kate one more week, but then I've got to hand Ginny over to the Lord and go back home. I don't know what else to do. There's just too many places to look. I can't keep going on forever. Not forever."

Sadie studied on him like she was trying to make up her mind about something. "There's one more thing we can try, Luther. If you're willing, I think there's one more thing we can try."

CHAPTER 19

An old farmer approached Nell's table, humble, earnest, dignified. Or maybe not so old when he drew closer as he first seemed. He held himself erect, but the way he clutched his hat in his hand and the down-turned corners of his mouth bespoke sorrow. With him was a city woman wearing a sad blue dress that told of being resewn each year but carrying its wearer's history in the fading robin's-egg fabric.

The woman spoke first.

"Madame Nelora, I'm Sadie Rainey, and this is my sister's husband, Luther Evans. Six months ago, Luther's girl ran off. We've been all over Memphis looking for her, but she's nowhere to be found. The police ain't no help either." She clutched at the purse in her hands until the leather squeaked in protest. "We've heard so much about you, and we've got nowhere else to turn. Can you help us?"

Lord, a missing child. Nell swallowed, and her heart began to work its way closer to her toes than she liked it to be. She should turn them away, not fill them with false hope. Nell opened her mouth to say it, to tell them that she was sorry, but she couldn't help them. The flicker of pleading in the old man's eyes stopped her, made her want to weep. Maybe she could try a reading, offer him a little comfort somehow.

"Please sit down, Mrs. Rainey, Mr. Evans. I understand how frantic you must be, thinking no one can help you. Of course, I can't be sure I'll be able to discover anything, but let's see what the cards say."

"Thank you, ma'am," Luther said.

"Have you consulted a seer before, Mr. Evans?"

"No, ma'am. Sadie was the one told me about you. We been everwhere else. She thought you might be able to find out something can't no one else tell us."

"Are you from Mississippi, Mr. Evans?"

"Yes, ma'am. Como, just south of here."

"My mother's people came from Oxford. You sound a lot like home."

The old man smiled, and some of the stiffness went out of him. He nodded, his look saying, "I know you, and I'm glad to have some kind of kin helping me."

"Do you have something that belonged to your daughter, Mr. Evans? Or a picture of her, perhaps, that you can show me, please?"

Luther pulled a beginning-to-tatter photograph from the pocket of his overalls and pushed it across the table to her.

"That's my Ginny."

Nell picked it up to study it. Out of nowhere, a flash and a rush of image and sensation flung her upright and pressed her hard against the back of her chair, squeezing every bit of breath from her lungs.

The world was heat and sun and the smell of freshly turned earth. One step and then another, stooping low along the row to drop the seeds. A foot encased in a worn shoe covering every one over with the loose dirt. Sinking into that soft, just-plowed soil with each step until the dirt worked its way into both shoes and down the collar of her sacking dress and even got into her mouth. She felt the flop of her straw bonnet on her cheek, not quite keeping the sun from her eyes, out of her face. She knew it was a pretty face—everybody said so—but it was already too freckled. Never mind. One day, she'd have silks and fine, feathered, smart hats just like the ones Myrna Loy wore.

Lordy, her back ached. Her lips were so dry that she didn't move them for fear they'd crack. No matter how much lard she rubbed into them, they would peel again tonight. Peel and crack and bleed. She worked her tongue against her teeth to try to get up enough spit to swallow and wash a little of the taste of Mississippi dirt out of her mouth.

"Daddy, can't I stop and get a drink, please?"

"Don't think about being thirsty, Ginny. Your mama'll be here with the water pail in a minute, and you can have a dipper then. We all want a drink. Now, move on, girl. I know it's hot, but your brothers and sisters ain't complaining. We're almost to the end of the row, and we got to finish this field afore sundown."

"Yessir."

Moving on up the row, not thinking of anything now but that dipper and the water cool from the well washing over her tongue and easing her throat all the way down. Tonight after supper, maybe Mama would let her fill the tub and bathe herself. It was so much easier to sleep on these hot nights without the dirt from the field getting down in the sheets with her. So sweet to feel cool and clean herself for a little while, anyway, even if Ruthie and Lizzie didn't do anything but wipe their necks and wash their faces and hands before supper and still smelled like sweat and the fields there in the bed beside her.

One day, she'd bathe whenever she felt like it, spend hours in one of those fancy bathtubs in its own room with all the bubbles and a maid in a uniform to wait on her. She'd soak for days if she wanted. She'd have her own soft bed. And fingernails. She'd grow long nails that she'd paint red, and her hands would be soft and clean and white, not brown and rough, the nails ragged and broken.

Gasping in a lungful of air, Nell opened her eyes. Have mercy, what was that? She was in her salon, still pressed up against the back of her chair. The old farmer and the woman watched her, their faces squinted with concern. It was his face she'd seen in the vision, his voice she'd heard. Luther's. The photograph of Ginny Evans was on the table in front of her.

"How old is your daughter, Mr. Evans?" Nell said when she could trust herself to speak. It took all her strength to form the words, but her voice sounded like itself, thank goodness.

"This here's an old picture, ma'am. She turned 16 last month. Old enough to have better sense than to run off."

"Was she seeing anyone? Do you think she might have left with a beau?"

"You mean did she have a feller? No, I wisht she had, but she wouldn't have no truck with any of the boys back home. Had it in her head that she wanted some fancy feller that didn't farm and always smelled nice."

Always smelling nice didn't seem an unreasonable ambition, but Nell refrained from saying so. "And how long since you've heard anything from Ginny?"

"She stayed with me for a month in September," Sadie said. "Then she left in the night one night. Not a sign of her since."

Nell took another minute to breathe and think and hope that some feeling would come back into her hands and feet, which right now felt like dead things at the ends of her arms and legs. Luther Evans and Sadie Rainey waited for her to speak again. Keep going. Keep going as though whatever it was that just happened to her were perfectly normal.

"Because you were the last to talk with your niece, Mrs. Rainey, I want you to shuffle the cards, please. Then give them to Mr. Evans, who will divide them into three stacks. We'll start by consulting one card for inspiration. If we don't see anything, then I'll ask him to choose and arrange the five cards for the reading. Both of you must think about Ginny. In your minds, ask her where she is. I'll do the same. Mr. Evans, take a card, please."

Luther pulled a card from the top of the middle stack. The World, inverted.

"Interesting," Nell said. She reached for the card. Before she could think about resisting or accepting it, another rush of sensation and images flooded her.

A dark bar full of laughing people, their voices shrill from too much drink. Cigarette smoke like a fog over the dance floor. The lights too bright in her face. The smell of gin and sweat and lust everywhere.

But this wasn't how it should be. Where were the elegant women in silks and diamonds? The men in tuxedoes and top hats? Where was the sleek band leader like Paul Whiteman to introduce her and the full orchestra to back her up instead of these four coloreds in their cheap suits and slicked-down hair? She could hardly follow their playing. No one listened anyway.

No one was listening.

Nell was back again.

"You seen something, ain't you, ma'am?" Luther said. He leaned across the table, straining toward her, desperate. "I know you seen my Ginny. Where is she?"

"I don't know, Mr. Evans, but I think I did see her. No, I'm sure I did see her."

"She's all right then," Sadie said. She collapsed against Luther's shoulder. "I told you, Luther. I told you she's all right."

"You got to tell me where she is, ma'am. Where is she?"

"I don't know, Mr. Evans. That wasn't clear."

Luther pushed the cards toward Nell, patted his anxious hand over them. "Then look again. Please, you got to look again, see where she is."

"She is all right, isn't she, Madame Nelora?" Sadie said.

"I can't be sure." Nell gathered the cards into a pile, straightening them deliberately and trying to think of how to answer without flying all to pieces in front of these people who looked at her with such eager trust. "The truth is, I've never had such a . . . such a powerful reading before, but the images aren't completely clear. I need a little time to consider what I saw."

"Can't you tell us anything?" Sadie said.

"All I can say is that I felt that Ginny had been singing in a nightclub."

This time, Luther and Sadie both leaned forward.

"I don't know which one or where, but I felt that it was here in Memphis."

"We been to ever night club in Memphis there is, ma'am," Luther said. "Ain't nobody will allow as how they know where Ginny got to."

"I'm sorry, Mr. Evans. I can tell you only what I see. We'll have to decipher what it means. I need to think. Can you give me some time, let me sort things out a little more clearly?"

Luther Evans looked like a drowning man who couldn't quite reach the lifeline thrown out for him. "How come you–"

"I'm sorry I can't be more definite, Mr. Evans," Nell said to stop him before he pressed her further. "It's just that . . . well, I'm terribly tired all of a sudden. But at least we have something to work with."

"Come on, Luther," Sadie said. She stood, took him by the elbow, and eased him up from his chair. "Madame Nelora's going to help us, and that's more than we've had up to now. We'll call Kate when we get home."

"Well, I reckon if I come this far, I can wait another day." Luther ducked his head at Nell. "Thank you, ma'am."

"Thank you, Mr. Evans. Mrs. Rainey." Nell pulled aside the curtain that covered the entrance. "I promise you'll hear from me soon. Be sure to leave your number with Hattie out front, Mrs. Rainey."

She began to shake, and her legs gave way beneath her. Just how she was going to keep that promise—or if she wanted to try—Nell had no idea.

CHAPTER 20

At the knock on his library door, Joseph Calendar tore himself away from Halliburton's *The Flying Carpet*, which had absorbed him since supper.

"Enter."

"Mrs. Marchand is here, Doctor," Simon said, stepping into the room.

Calendar glanced at the clock on the mantel. It was 9 o'clock. "I'm not expecting Miss Bess until tomorrow, Simon. I can't imagine what she wants at this hour."

"It's the young Mrs. Marchand. Miss Nell. She says she's got to talk to you."

"Even more peculiar." Calendar held himself still, breathed in slowly and out again. "All right, Simon. Show her in, please. And start some coffee, will you? See if we have some little cakes or something to serve with it."

"Yes, sir."

A heartbeat later, Nell hurtled into the room as though the hounds of hell were after her. Calendar leapt from his chair to meet her. She stopped short of running into his arms.

"Miss Nell, what has happened? Are you ill?"

"I don't know. Today . . . I think perhaps I'm insane or heading that way."

He took her gently by the hand, felt her trembling. He guided her to the chair across from his.

"Here, sit by the fire. Simon is bringing coffee, but I think perhaps a bit of brandy is what you need. Have that first, and then you can tell me what's upset you so."

"Thank you."

Nell gulped the brandy and held out the glass for more. Calendar poured it. She tossed that back as well and handed him the empty glass. He took an afghan from the back of the chair and spread it across her knees.

"Better?"

"Yes, thank you."

"When you're ready." He returned to his chair.

All the bones in her hands stood out in relief where Nell gripped the arms of the chair. "Today a man, a poor Mississippi farmer, came to me looking for his lost daughter." She drew in a shuddering breath.

"A child?" Calendar prompted when she didn't continue.

"A girl. Sixteen"

"A runaway, then."

"Yes, this man—Luther Evans—said the girl, Ginny, came to Memphis in the fall. She has ambitions to be a singer."

"And she knew no one, and he fears she's dead."

"Something like that, except that she has an aunt, the mother's sister, who looked after her for a while before the girl disappeared. They've asked everywhere for her, even talked to the police, but no one had seen Ginny. So, they came to me."

Nell seemed to run out of words. Calendar gave her time to find them again.

"Doctor Calendar, I saw her today," she finally went on.

"At your salon? She appeared to you?"

"No, it wasn't like that. I mean, I didn't see her there. It was as though I *were* the girl for an instant. Mr. Evans showed me a photograph of Ginny taken on the farm. When I touched it, I was there. I was Ginny working in the field, the sun hot on my back and the sweat in my eyes. I was her, thinking her thoughts. And then it was gone."

Simon came in with a tray and poured coffee for Nell and for Calendar.

"Anything else, sir?" he said.

"A glass of water, please," Nell said.

"Yes, ma'am. Some cool Memphis water coming right up. Dr. Calendar?"

"No, thank you, Simon. Just the water for Mrs. Marchand."

Simon bowed and left for the kitchen.

Nell spooned sugar into her cup and poured a generous drop of cream. She stirred it carefully, thinking, before she took a sip and then another. Calendar neglected his own cup on the table.

"Were you able to talk to this man about what you saw? What did you tell him?"

"Nothing much at first. I was so shocked, all I could think was that I'd had some kind of spell or waking dream. That I'd fainted, perhaps."

"But you hadn't?"

"No, I was still sitting in my chair with the photograph there in front of me. They looked a little worried, but they made no sign that anything dramatic had happened. I did the only thing I could think of. I tried to go on with the reading."

Nell gulped at the water that Simon had placed quietly beside her.

"Did the reading tell you anything?"

"I didn't finish it. I hardly began. Another flash, and I saw Ginny in a nightclub, a cheap, dingy place full of sad drunks. I could feel her despair, Joseph. Everything she'd wanted but played out as a cruel parody of it. It was terrible." Nell rubbed a hand across her eyes.

"You didn't recognize the place?"

"Well, I don't exactly frequent speakeasies, but there wasn't enough to identify it." Her eyes shut, and she clutched at the arms of the chair again. "Just impressions, flashes of emotion. Nothing was well-defined, but it was a speakeasy. I felt it more than I saw it, but while it was happening, it all seemed real." She opened her eyes. "With everything that has happened, I could have invented it all out of my own disappointments." She shook her head. "I told Luther Evans I needed time to think about what I'd seen. I've been going over it all day, but I didn't know what to believe, what to do. I . . . ."

"So you came to me."

"I thought, with your background, you might . . . . You said–"

"Yes, I said if you ever needed me."

"Am I losing my mind?"

Calendar pulled his chair closer to Nell's so that their knees almost touched. "No, Nell. It's what I suspected from the first. When it mattered, when there was something important at stake, you allowed yourself to see."

"How can I be sure? How can you?"

"Somehow, this girl reached out to you. I've known true sensitives before, among them an astonishingly gifted woman I studied with in Vienna. A dear friend."

"But you've never had visions yourself."

"No, not like yours. I've never been blessed in that way."

"If this is a blessing, I'd sure hate to find out what a curse would be."

Calendar reached across for her hand. "It is, Nell. Accept it as such, and learn how to guide it. How to channel it. You've been given a great responsibility."

"I don't want it." She crossed her arms and tucked both hands out of sight under them.

He sat back. "It's natural to feel that way. Something astonishing has happened to you. You don't understand it, so you are frightened. But resisting this power will prove impossible, and you can do yourself terrible harm if you do. Trust me, you must accept it for your own sake."

"No, because I'm quitting. Now. I'm not going to tell any more fortunes. No more Madame Nelora. I'm going back to being plain Eleanor Leyton Marchand. I can still learn to type or do something. Even the poor house looks pretty good right now. Anything but this.

You don't know what it was like."

But he did know, had seen what visions could do, especially when they were denied. "This is much more for you now than a way to make money."

"I didn't count on any of this mess from the spirit world. There are plenty of other ways to help people."

"What about this girl? What about her mother and father?"

"I have no idea how to find her."

"I think you do. We can find the way. You can find the way."

"No. I'm going to call the aunt, tell her I was wrong. That I was making it all up. That I'm a fraud who bilks people."

What he knew he must say next broke his heart because it would break hers.

"It's too late to turn back, Nell. You can't hide from this."

"Watch me."

As quickly as Nell had rushed into his study, she was gone again, slamming the front door behind her in her flight.

"Anything wrong, Dr. Calendar?" Simon asked, coming into the front hall at the sound of the door, a fresh glass of water in his hand.

"No, Simon. It's all right. Mrs. Marchand is distressed, but that will pass. It must. You may clear away the coffee things now. I won't need you anymore this evening after that."

Calendar poured himself a glass of brandy. He stood by the grate, looking into the fire. That the universe was capricious in the gifts it bestowed, he'd never doubted. Nell Marchand had a lot to learn, and all he could do was try to help her learn it. The universe wasn't going to give her any choice in the matter.

CHAPTER 21

The man sitting at Nell's kitchen table in the tatters of what might once have been a good suit gathered up the last crumbs of pie, mashing each precious morsel onto the back of his fork to make sure he didn't miss any of them. His plate scoured, he leaned back with a sigh.

"Would you like another cup of coffee?" Nell said

"Yes, ma'am, I would love another cup. Thank you. Best coffee I've had in months."

Hattie was about to get up from her spot where she was shelling peas, but Nell motioned to her to stay put and went to the stove herself to fetch the coffee pot. She filled her guest's cup—George Baxter, he'd said his name was—took his plate and, without asking, served up another sizeable wedge and set it in front of him. When he'd arrived at the kitchen door at dinner time offering to do some chores in exchange for a little food, she thought he was the hungriest-looking man she ever seen.

Staring down at the plate, Baxter blushed, and for a moment, she thought he was going to refuse it. But he put his napkin back in his lap, took a polite bite, and savored it as though it were ambrosia brought down from Olympus itself.

"Thank you. I've never had pie quite like this before."

"Don't they make chess pie up in Chicago, mister?" Hattie said.

"Is that what you call it? Chess pie? I've never heard of it."

"Y'all don't know what's good, then." Hattie took the notepad on which she wrote her grocery lists and turned to a new page. "Here, I'll copy down the recipe so you can make yourself as many chess pies as you want once you get where you're going."

Baxter blinked at Hattie, his throat working. He took a deep breath before he could answer her. "That would be very kind."

"You know, Mr. Baxter, I think you're about my late husband's height," Nell said. "Would you accept some of his clothes? I'd like to get a few of his shirts and pants for you if you'd take them. I haven't been able to go through his things yet, and I'd like to put them to good use."

"I...," Baxter swallowed hard again. "Thank you. Traveling the way I do, I can't carry much, but a pair of pants and a couple of shirts would be very welcome. Anything plain will do. I, uh...I don't want to attract thieves who might think handsome garments mean I have money." Baxter smiled, his face drawn with regret and the shadow of hardship.

"Of course. I'll be back in just a minute."

Upstairs in Ellis's closet, Nell ran her hand down the rack of fine suits. Time to swallow her distaste over touching any of his belongings. She and Hattie should go through everything and take it all down to the mission. The waste of it was shameful. She chose two shirts and a pair of plain trousers, folded them, and secured them with a belt to replace the piece of rope that the man wore in place of one.

In the kitchen 5 minutes later, Nell found a diffident George Baxter standing by the back door. Hattie was wrapping a sandwich and the last piece of chess pie in wax paper for him.

"I hope these will do, Mr. Baxter." Nell offered him the makeshift bundle, which he took reverently. "Would you like to wash up and change before you're on your way? There's a bathroom down the hall."

"Oh, I couldn't use your washroom, ma'am, the state I'm in, but thank you. I saw a bucket by the back door, and if you wouldn't mind my filling it from your tap, I could wash there."

"But you're welcome–"

Polite but resolute, Baxter held up a hand to stop her protest. Nell caught a glimpse of the man of authority he must once have been. "I know, but I'm really not decent to set foot beyond this kitchen. I felt bad enough about coming in here, clean and nice as it is. I've been on the road for a long time, and too much of the road is on me."

"Of course. If you're more comfortable. There's a bar of soap on the shelf above the bucket."

"Thank you, ma'am." Baxter tucked the bundle of clothes under his arm, accepted the sandwich and pie from Hattie, and was gone.

Hattie closed the screen behind him and sat down at the kitchen table to finish the peas. Nell picked up a pod and pretended to help. Hattie watched her over the bowl into which the shelled peas dropped.

"You keep giving everything away the way you're doing," Hattie said, "and you're going to have to go back to fortunetelling no matter what. These tramps are eating us out of house and home. I never saw a man could eat as much as this last one."

"I don't care. Let's feed them as long as we can. I don't want to send anyone away without some dinner and a little something to take with him. It could be us out there standing in the breadlines or trying to sell off all the silverware for next to nothing. We've got to do what we can long as we can."

"Talking about doing what you can, you planning to help that poor old man find his girl? You know you're fretting about it. Feeding everybody in creation isn't going to get her home to her folks."

Nell put her hands over her ears. For two days, she had tried to think of anything but Ginny Evans, but it was no use. Everything reminded her of the smiling girl in the gunnysack dress. Every man in overalls who showed up at the back door looking for a handout might as well be Luther Evans, asking Nell to look for her.

"Please, ma'am. Any little thing you can spare," they said, but it was Luther's voice she heard.

"I can't do it, Hattie. You don't know what it was like. I couldn't breathe."

"Well, you asked for, and you got it. God has set you a mission. You can't turn back now. That girl is out there, and if you ask me, you're the one who's got to help find her."

"Hush, Hattie. I don't want to hear any more."

Hattie gave a little grunt of disapproval at the back of her throat but got up to rinse the peas at the sink. She emptied them into a pot, filled it with water, and placed it on the stove to cook. Nell slumped across the table. Hands on her hips, Hattie came to stand over her.

"Sit up and look at me."

Nell did as she was told.

"There never was a Leyton who gave up on a fight," Hattie said. "Nor a Taylor either. Even all that time that Ellis Marchand was running around acting like a fool, lot of women would have been crying and going on about how hard it was and how embarrassing it was with everybody knowing and feeling sorry for you. But not my Nell. No matter how bad it got, you held your head up."

"I don't see how not wanting to risk going crazy is the same thing."

"You've got to remember to take the good with the bad. You've finally found something you can do. Maybe Dr. Calendar is right, and it's going to be worse if you don't try. Why don't you let him help you?"

Nell groaned. "Hellfire and damnation." She got up from her chair, straggled to the ice box, and took out the last bit of ham hock for Hattie to add to the peas. "I guess I'll invite Joseph Calendar to supper."

Hattie turned a glorious smile on her. "I'm going to fix him something special."

—

WAITING IN THE MARCHAND'S PARLOR FOR HATTIE TO ALERT THE ladies that he had arrived, Calendar found himself studying a wooden leg in its case, where it resided like the relic of some obscure saint. "General Augustus Washburn Oates," the tasteful bronze plaque adorning the case read.

General Oates was Bess Marchand's one-legged grandfather and the originator of the Oates fortune in livestock. Unable himself to fight in the War between the States, the General had made a fine living selling horses to the Confederate cavalry before Memphis surrendered to Union naval forces under the command of Captain Charles H. Davis on June 6, 1862. Thereafter, Grant and Sherman headquartered in Memphis, preparing for their campaigns against Vicksburg, and General Oates made an even better living selling mules and cattle to the Yankees. He was nothing if not pragmatic.

Calendar looked up as Bess hurried in.

"Oh, Dr. Calendar, we've neglected you shamefully," she said, fluttering to his side. "Forgive me for not being ready to receive you when you arrived."

"Not at all, dear lady. I was absorbed in observing this remarkable artifact."

"My grandfather's," Bess said. She smiled fondly down into the case. "General Oates lived with us when I was a child and told the most thrilling stories about the battle in which a cannon ball took his best gelding and his right leg out from under him." She sighed. "In his dotage, I'm afraid he sometimes thought he was fighting the Mexican War all over again. My parents finally had to send him to Bolivar where there was no risk of his running guests through with his cavalry saber. I used to visit him at the hospital there."

"And the leg?"

"Oh, when he died, I asked to keep it. The General was adamant it should not be buried with him least someone else in the family needed it. For a while, we kept it by the hat rack in the front hall so people could appreciate it when they entered, but after Ellis was born, the Judge and I put it out of reach on the top shelf of our closet for fear the baby would chew on it when he began to teethe."

"Most wise." Calendar smothered a smile.

"Yes," Bess murmured, lost in a reverie. "Ellis was always quite taken with the General's leg. On his eighteenth birthday, he found it when he was exploring my closet for gifts he thought I might have hidden there. I was so happy that he was interested in family history that I couldn't be angry with him for going through my things. He had this case built for it."

Calendar caught a whiff of lilac, and Nell appeared beside them. He resisted the impulse to buy his nose in her hair.

"It was all I could to do to persuade Ellis not to take that leg to Paris with us on our honeymoon. I wanted to bury it with him, but Miss Bess insisted that it would be a shame to let such a priceless heirloom pass out of the family." She shot Calendar an amused glance. "It makes her feel close to the General, so I gave her the job of dusting the case each day."

Nell kissed Bess on the cheek. "If anyone is hungry, Hattie says supper is ready."

Calendar offered each of the ladies an arm, and they went in to supper.

—

DURING THE MEAL, NELL ENJOYED WATCHING THE TINIEST CRACKS appear in Joseph Calendar's sang-froid as he scraped and sopped up the last morsel and drop of his supper in a manner just short of unseemly. Hattie now appeared at his right to take his plate. With the look of profound sorrow that a hungry boy gives his empty ice cream dish, he watched it go.

"Hattie, if I were the marrying kind, I'd take to courting you," he said. "That was the most delicious veal I have ever put in my mouth. There's not a cook in Memphis who is your equal. Or in Paris or London. Escoffier himself would fling himself at your feet in worship."

Accustomed to such accolades but not immune to them, Hattie smiled her pleasure. "Thank you, Dr. Calendar. I like to feed an elegant gentleman who still knows how to eat." She collected Bess's plate and then Nell's.

"A man would be fool not to consume every bite of yours that he could get his mouth on."

"We got Peach Melba for dessert."

"All right." He threw down his napkin. "That's it. Will you marry me, Hattie Taylor?"

"No, sir, Dr. Calendar, but I thank you for the offer."

Nell scooted her chair back and laid her napkin on the table. "If you two are done carrying on, we have more serious business to discuss than Veal Oscar and Peach Melba."

"You've had a change of heart." Calendar said.

How could he see through her so easily? "If I can help find Ginny, I've got to try, but I want to do it through normal channels."

"And by normal channels, I presume you mean no visions. You're still frightened of what happened. But what is life without a good, healthy shot of fear?"

"That is easy for you to say. You've never had to be afraid of anything."

"That is most certainly not the case, but I'm not here to be the topic of conversation. Because you invited me tonight, I felt you were ready to embrace your powers and use them. If you want to go through what you call normal channels, what is it that you wish from me?"

To keep her hands from shaking, Nell anchored them on her knees and leaned toward him. "I want you to tell me what it all meant. What the things I saw meant. Why me? Why didn't I see where she is now? Why these flashes of where she has been but nothing about where to look? It was so chaotic and . . . disjointed. None of it makes any sense to me. You're the expert in the supernatural."

Calendar watched her, eyes hooded and lips drawn together. Something passed across his face, a glimmer of some kind of decision. Here it came. Any minute now, he would ask for money, and it would kill her to find out that she'd been right all along. Lord, she was a fool for going to him just because she was scared out of her wits. He didn't know anything, couldn't be trusted. Stand up. Send him home. Forget all this. Tell Luther Evans there was nothing she could do. Instead, Nell held herself upright in her chair, waiting for Calendar's response.

"When do you want to begin?" he said.

"Begin?"

"I want you to tell me everything that you saw. Everything that you felt. Every detail that you can remember. Then we'll decide how best to proceed."

"How much for your psychic insights?"

"How much?"

"How much is this help going to cost me?"

He grew very still, some battle raging inside him, although what it was, she couldn't tell. The sapphire of his eyes darkened until they seemed black, all black but for the candle flames reflected there. Like a rabbit powerless in the serpent's thrall, she forgot to think, almost forgot to breathe, watching the flames dance in the grave night of his eyes.

Then, he smiled slowly, the spell broken. The world returned. Nell shivered, swallowed, drew in air. He looked over at Hattie, who had stopped just inside the dining room door holding a tray laden with silver dishes.

"I believe this fine supper is all the payment any gentleman could require of a lady. Hattie, didn't you say something about Peach Melba, or were you only teasing me?"

"Coming right up, Dr. Calendar." She set a dish in front of Nell. "You lucky Dr. Calendar is a gentleman," she muttered out of the side of her mouth.

"Hattie, I'm going to need two servings," Nell said. The cook put a second dish in front of her, and she felt like a child told she may stay up an hour past her bedtime, but only an hour, if she is good and does not disturb the adults. "No use undertaking a quest on an empty stomach."

Throughout the meal, Bess had been remarkably quiet. Now, Nell saw her catch Calendar's eye and wink, something unexpected from a lady of her age and social station and certainly from Bess Marchand. He let out a small snort that threatened to turn into a bark of laughter. Nell looked from one of them to the other. Bess turned a smile of angelic innocence on her.

"Very wise, Miss Nell," Calendar said. "An army travels on its stomach." He dug into his own serving with relish. "Sublime, Hattie. Absolutely sublime."

—

IF ACQUIRING A MOJO SACK FROM A HOODOO DOCTOR SEEMED PECULIAR to Nell, consulting a medium about her psychic power was positively outlandish. Yet, here she was, settled face to face after supper with Calendar on Judge Marchand's sofa in the small sitting room.

"If you will not use the power within you, then you must seek out those with the greatest influence outside yourself. Who is the most powerful ally you could have in Memphis?"

"Ed Crump," Nell said without hesitation. "He may not be mayor anymore, but he still runs everything in this city. They don't call him Boss for nothing."

"Just so. Are you in his good graces?"

"I wouldn't exactly say so. He and my father were like two dogs after the same bone."

"Then you must find a way to worm yourself into his favor."

Nell chewed her lower lip. Hand in hand, Crump and King Cotton ran Memphis. As they did the city, they ruled all of Shelby County and much of the state with an iron fist, although Crump would tell you the fist was encased in a velvet glove.

He would also tell you he had the best interests of every Memphian at heart, and everything he did served those interests. Hadn't he helped clean up Beale Street so respectable business could feel free to operate there? Didn't he make sure the streets were safe at night? Didn't he see to it that Memphis had the best fire department in the country?

Nell's daddy had hated Crump and always said that if you lie down with dogs, you get fleas. Of course, Daddy had loved Ellis Marchand and was pleased as punch when Nell married him, so even he couldn't always tell who had the fleas and who didn't.

Now Nell Marchand was about to lie down with Ed Crump, if only in the figurative sense. "Anything to grease the wheels, but I'll need allies. I'll talk to my lawyer, Anton Green. He has some influence with Mr. Crump. And Oz Sherman down at the paper. The power of the press, you know."

"Have you spoken to the farmer—Luther Evans, isn't it—again?"

"Yes, Luther. I'll talk to him first thing in the morning. Then we can start." Nell picked at the fringe of her shawl. "I would . . . . Dr. Calendar, before I didn't mean . . . . Oh, good Lord, would you consider going with me to see Anton? I believe I should tell him about my visions, and I'd like to have you there in case he thinks I've lost my mind. Which I'm not entirely sure I haven't."

Calendar placed his hand over his heart. "Miss Nell, I am forever your servant. You have but to command me."

"Now you're making fun of me. Isn't that one of Karloff's lines from somewhere?"

"I assure you, I have never been more serious."

His eyes held her again, but this time, she didn't feel even the slightest inclination to flee, unless it would be toward him. No doubt about it—she had definitely lost her mind.

Chapter 22

Yes, cotton was king in Memphis, the foundation on which Memphis families like the Leytons had built their fortunes. If it was the lifeblood of the city, Front Street was the beating heart of its kingdom. From farms across Arkansas, Mississippi, Missouri, and the rest of Tennessee, the white gold poured into the Bluff City on wagons pulled by mules, on the flat beds of every description of truck, in railway cars, and on the decks of the last of the great sternwheelers plying the Mississippi. There, it was weighed and classed and sold.

In the Cotton Exchange at the corner of Union and Front, the strictly members-only realm of the princes of Memphis commerce, traders manned banks of phones and telegraph lines to disperse the precious fiber to the far corners of the globe. The Great Depression might have brought King Cotton to his knees, but no one doubted that he would rise again.

Anton Green liked to keep his law office above Cotton Row on Front Street, where he could watch the cotton factors examine and price the enormous bales stacked on the sidewalk. Now, he sat behind his desk in that office staring at Nell as though she had just declared that she wanted to dance buck naked leading a brass band down the middle of Front Street itself at noon.

"Nell, have you gone completely crazy? I didn't mind helping you when you were playing at telling fortunes, but now you believe your own fairytale? I think it's time you see a physician. These last weeks have obviously been too much for you."

"I know it's difficult to imagine, Anton, but something has happened. I don't know where it came from or why I was chosen to receive it, but I've had a message from this girl. Now, I want you to help me find her."

Anton looked past her at Joseph Calendar, who had taken up a spot beside the bookshelves to listen and lend support if Nell needed it. Anton rose to his feet and charged around his desk, bearing down on the medium, who quietly closed the history of Tennessee he'd been perusing. Anton stopped in front of him, sputtering, and directed an accusing finger back at Nell.

"Calendar, is this . . . this lunacy your doing? This kind of mumbo jumbo may be your livelihood, but how on earth can you condone this? Or are you behind it all in the first place?"

"Mr. Green, whether you are a believer or not, I think you have to remember that you are Mrs. Marchand's friend and have a long association with her family. Hear her out. She's asking you for help."

Nell came to take Anton's arm and peered up into his face. "Anton, having you with me would make what I have to do easier, but whether you're with me or not, I'm going to Ed Crump and the mayor and the police. Think I'm insane if you want to, but I believe this girl is out there. Or word of her is out there. I recognize that 16 isn't exactly a child, but neither is she a grown woman. Knowing you long as I have, I would think you'd be compassionate enough to want to stand with me."

Anton clasped both her hands so tightly that her rings dug into her fingers. "Nell–"

"After we find her, if you want me to see a doctor, I promise I will go. But for now, think what it will mean to Luther Evans and his wife to find her. Think how it may help other lost girls here in Memphis. Is it really that much to ask?"

Anton dropped her hands. "And what am I to tell Watkins Overton? That this girl came to you in a dream? He'll think I'm crazy, too."

"I'll tell the mayor how the voters will love him."

"And when we do find her," Calendar said. "I should think that would be worth a great deal to any politician, to be able to say that he's reunited a wayward girl and her family. That Memphis is the kind of big-hearted city that never forgets its own, no matter how humble."

"And I don't think it will sit very well with the mayor for the Press-Scimitar to report that his administration refused to help Luther Evans find his daughter," Nell said. "Oz Sherman is all set with the story. Ginny Evans's photograph on the front page under the banner 'Have you seen me?' and a headline that reads something like 'Callous City Officials Ignore Missing Girl's Plight.' And you know just how much Ed Meeman is going to love printing that in his paper."

Nell rested a hand on Anton's forearm. "Someone is bound to step forward after that. I asked Oz to hold off until we'd had a chance to talk things over with you, but the story runs in tomorrow's paper, with or without backing from Mr. Crump and the mayor. Even Boss Crump couldn't stop it if he wanted to."

"Blackmail. You're just like your daddy. He wasn't above a little arm-twisting if it was in the name of a good cause." Anton rubbed his face with both hands and admitted defeat. "All right. I'll go with you. It's not as though we wouldn't want to help this girl and her family. I wish to goodness you hadn't decided to involve me in this mess, though. Why on earth would you?"

"Because that's what Dutch uncles are for," Nell said. "Because you're Anton Green, sage to the great and near great. Even if they don't want to hear what I have to say, they'll listen to you."

"If it's all the same to you, don't tell them about your vision. Just say that this Evans fellow has been asking about his daughter and getting nowhere. Mayor Overton likes a story about fighting for the little man as well as anybody. So do I. And no one likes them more that Ed Crump."

"Oh, Anton, I knew you'd understand." Nell threw her arms around him and kissed him on the cheek.

"All right," he said, extracting himself from her embrace. "All right.

But promise me that you won't go telling everyone in town about these visions of yours. I might not be the only one who'd worry enough to ask you to talk to a doctor. And whatever you do, don't let E. H. Crump hear you call him Boss."

"You want me to pass up all the attention when we find Ginny Evans? Not on your life. Think how much my stock as a fortuneteller will go up. I'll be turning people away in droves."

"Now, Nell–"

She hugged him again. "You know I don't mean it. I wouldn't want to trust anyone else with that secret anyway. And if it makes you happy, I'll go talk to Dr. Roberts. He won't find anything wrong with me. Will you be satisfied then?"

"Yes. You know I worry about you since Ellis died."

"There's nothing to worry about. I promise you. Now, if you'll excuse us, I want to call on Oz and tell him to rewrite his headlines."

Nell smiled over at Calendar, and the look that passed between them deafened Anton Green with the sound of his heart shattering beyond repair.

—

OUT ON THE STREET, CALENDAR STOPPED NELL AND TOOK HER HAND. "So you've decided to go on with your work."

"Absolutely not," Nell said. She freed her hand from his grip. "I'm taking down my shingle after this is over, but I wasn't about to tell Anton that."

"You do realize that what you said is true. People will seek you out more than ever once we find Ginny."

"I'll cross that bridge when we come to it. Besides, I haven't told Oz Sherman about what I saw. He thinks I'm just trying to help the old man because he came to me for a reading and his story touched this great big old heart of mine. I may be insane, but I'm not nuts. Do you think I want to end up in Bolivar?"

"No one would ever dare think of sending Ellis Marchand's wife to the state mental hospital."

"Don't be so sure. I wouldn't be the first society matron to end up in a cell there."

"They'd have to send me as well to get away with it."

"We could ask for adjoining rooms. I bet you look as good in a straight jacket as you do in a suit."

"Thank you," Calendar said. He gave her the slightest of bows. "I'll have my tailor measure me just in case. Nothing's worse than a ill-fitting jacket, straight or otherwise."

—

"THANK YOU FOR SEEING US, MR. CRUMP," NELL SAID.

"Please sit, Miss Nell," Crump said. "Anton." He gestured to the chairs in front of his desk. "We all miss Ellis a great deal. I'm sure he would have been proud of you the day of the funeral. I've never seen anyone hold up under that kind of sorrow with such complete poise and dignity."

Nell bit her lip and nodded, unable to trust herself with a response to that.

"Now, what was it that was so urgent you felt you had to have Anton arrange a meeting with me?"

"There's a poor farmer who needs your help, Mr. Crump," Nell said. "His daughter has gone missing here in Memphis, but he hasn't been able to get anyone to look for her. Luther told me—his name is Luther Evans—he told me that even in Como, where he's from, they've heard that if something needs doing in Memphis, you come to E. H. Crump to get it done. That's what I'm here for today, to ask you to use your influence to find his girl."

Nell paused to let what she had said sink in. The ex-mayor studied her face. He looked to Anton, who nodded. Crump pressed the buzzer on his phone.

"Yes, sir?" his secretary said.

"Janice, I need you to get in here, please. And bring your notepad."

CHAPTER 23

Ed Crump strode up the long walk toward the doors of the Chickasaw Country Club, where he was about to address a luncheon of the ladies of the Memphis Beautification Committee. Memphis Mayor Watkins Overton and Police Chief Leonard Wilson scrambled out of the chief's car and hurried to keep up with him.

"I don't care how the whole thing got started," Crump said. "Something should have been done to find this girl before now." He stopped in his tracks, shook his finger in Overton's face, and uttered several of the colorful expletives for which he was famous. "This isn't Chicago or New York or some other godless hell hole ruled by gangsters and thugs. This is my city. Don't you forget that you're mayor to everyone in Memphis, Watkins. That's the promise we made to get you elected. Don't you forget it."

"I haven't forgotten, Mr. Crump," Overton said. "I've spoken to the chief about it, and he got after the officers involved. There are so many children on their own in the city, all over the country, that it's understandable if the police can't keep up with every one of them."

During this exchange, Chief Wilson nodded in time with each of the mayor's words. Crump now turned on the chief the withering glare that he had used to reduce more that one U.S. senator to compliance with the Crump agenda. "There shouldn't be so much as one child wandering the streets alone. What do you think that says about us? I want her found, do you hear? Even if it takes every man on the police force knocking on every door in the city. The people of Memphis have a right to know that their daughters are safe here. Their sons, too."

"Yessir, Mr. Crump," the chief said.

"Now, when I get back to my office, I'm going to call the Press-Scimitar and see if I can't persuade Meeman to make it clear that the city administration is behind the search for this girl. This has to look like our initiative." Crump shook his finger at the mayor again. "You make sure the chief does his part, Watkins."

"Yes, sir."

"And, Chief, you show Nell Marchand every courtesy. If she wants to sit in on an interrogation, you let her do it. If she needs anything—anything at all—I'll want it taken care of."

"Yes, Mr. Crump."

Crump waved the two men away like a farm wife shooing chickens out of the feed room. "Now, go on, the two of you. I've got to see if I can pull your fat out of the fire again. But first, I'm going to take care of these ladies who are waiting so patiently for me inside." Crump turned to his secretary, who trotted at his side. "Janice, don't forget that when we get back, I need you to get the editor of the Memphis Press-Scimitar on the line."

"Yes, sir, Mr. Crump."

Crump stopped with his hand on the handle of the door to the club. "I just hope they don't serve tomato aspic. I'd rather have a dose of castor oil." He yanked the door open and held it for Janice before he strode inside behind her.

—

AT THE BREAKFAST TABLE, FRANKLIN BRYANT SLAMMED HIS NEWSPAPER down so hard that his coffee cup levitated briefly above its saucer.

"Damn Osgood Sherman, damn the Press-Scimitar, damn Nell Marchand, and damn me for a fool."

"Franklin!" Margaret Bryant said. "I will not have you swear at the table."

"I'm sorry, my dear, but I am sick to death of reading about this missing girl. This mess with that little harlot Ginny Evans is setting this town on its ear." Franklin jumped up from his chair and started out of the dining room.

"Don't you want your breakfast?"

"I couldn't swallow it this morning. There's urgent business I've got to attend to. I'll call you later from the bank," he said and rushed out.

—

UPSTAIRS IN HIS ROOM, GAYLORD BRYANT FOLDED THE SAME ISSUE OF the newspaper quietly and laid it on his desk. He drew a creased letter from a drawer and read it. Slumping forward, he buried his face in his hands. He still couldn't understand how she could have done it.

—

AT KELLY'S, LITTLE NICK PASSED THE PAPER TO BLACKJACK, WHO SAT across from him eating a ham sandwich.

"Get a load of this," he said. "The stuffed shirt ain't going to like it."

Blackjack scanned the paper, scowled, swallowed the bite he'd been chewing, and washed it down with a swig of beer.

"No, he ain't for a fact. We'd better keep an eye out, too."

CHAPTER 24

At the enormous gilt mirror in her front hall, Nell stopped to pull on her gloves and adjust her hat. By now, Boss Crump must have shaken the police chief until his teeth rattled, and if he hadn't, Oz's stories in the paper had surely done it for him. That did not, however, mean that she shouldn't go down to headquarters herself to be sure that was enough to get the chief on the job finally. Rubbing salt into his wounds now might not be kind, but it was bound to be fun.

At headquarters, Nell and Luther followed Officer Murphy through the squad room to Chief Wilson's office, picking their way past officer after officer, all of talking to young women of every size, shape, and color imaginable.

"My goodness, it's busy out there," she said when she arrived at the chief's door.

The thing that the chief did in baring his teeth was probably intended to be taken for a smile, although made him look more like an old possum in intestinal distress and bore precious little resemblance to the one he usually plastered over his face for photographs. Nell supposed he was due some credit for having made at least a show of civility in response to her question.

"Now, you see, Mrs. Marchand, with that story in the newspaper, my men are going to be tied up talking to every Crackerjack in the city who thinks he's seen that girl. Or to some young woman who wants a bit of fame or infamy by pretending to be her." The chief gestured toward his office door. "All those girls out there talking to my men?

They are all Ginny Evanses, even the colored girls. Hell—I'm sorry ma'am. Heck, all this carrying on over that girl might drive her deeper into hiding if she doesn't want to be found."

The chief shoved both hands through his hair and drew in a deep breath through his nose. Probably didn't want her tattling to Ed Crump that he'd lost his temper with her.

"I've got two of my best men on the case, and if Ginny Evans is anywhere in Memphis, they'll find her. You can count on that. In fact, they were already hard at work on it when you stirred up the city. So, if you wouldn't mind speaking to me before you run any other public campaigns to find lost girls, I'd appreciate it."

"I understand, Chief, and I am sorry for any bother to you and the force." Nell gave him her best hostess smile. The chief straightened his tie unconsciously. "It's just that Mr. Evans and his sister-in-law had talked to your officers here at headquarters but gotten no help. Maybe there was some other way to get your attention, but at least we have it now."

A vein bulged in Wilson's forehead, but he kept his tone polite. "Your late husband and I were friends, Mrs. Marchand. You could have come directly to me. I wish to goodness you had."

"Yes, well, it sure is interesting how everyone says that now, Chief Wilson. I understand your point, but Ginny Evans has been missing for 6 months. There was no more time to be wasted."

Now, standing behind Luther's chair, she put her hands on the farmer's shoulders to drive her point home. "Luther Evans is a humble man, a poor man, and I'm afraid his pleas were simply being overlooked. Perhaps you should speak to whichever of your officers it was who gave him the run around when he asked the Memphis police for help."

"Of course, we're looking into that, Mrs. Marchand, but these are hard times for everyone," the chief said with a great show of patience that amused Nell more than it irritated her. "Desperate people from all over the Mid-South flood into Memphis looking for work or handouts or whatever they can find. Sure, a lot of them are honest folk who've simply lost their jobs or been driven off their land, but plenty of them are criminals looking to take advantage of the situation. We're stretched to the limit dealing with all of them."

"Which is exactly what I'm talking about, Chief. With your men overworked as they are, going to the paper was the perfect way to enlist all the citizens of Memphis in your search."

Veins in the chief's neck had joined the chorus on his forehead. How much longer before they all exploded was anybody's guess. If she decided to sell tickets, Nell bet people would pay money to watch.

"At any rate, Mrs. Marchand, I promise to keep you informed of whatever we discover. I'd appreciate a similar courtesy from you."

"Of course, Chief. Working together, we can do so much more. I'm sure that Osgood Sherman at the Press-Scimitar feels the same way. Besides, finding Ginny Evans will give people something to think about besides breadlines and the awful state our country is in. We can be grateful for small blessings."

The chief did not look as though he felt the least little bit fortunate.

—

THE MORNING AFTER HER VISIT TO THE POLICE STATION, NELL AND Bess were straightening up the front parlor for the garden club, whose members had decided at the last minute to meet at the Marchand house because Miss Bertha Chapman, their president and usual hostess, was in bed with a bad cold.

"You shouldn't be so cavalier about Mr. Crump, Nell," Bess said when Nell told her about interview with the chief. "You young people like to listen to all those Yankee reporters and sneer at him, I know, and call him Boss behind his back. What none of you are old enough to remember is what Memphis was like before he was mayor. There was a murder here almost every day. He fought the kind of corruption in city politics that makes what's happening today look like a church social. Mr. Crump remade city government. That's how he and the Judge got to be such good friends. If it hadn't been for them, the Klan might have taken over Memphis."

Bess reached for a figurine on the mantel and wiped it with the dust cloth. "It wouldn't surprise me at all that he took to finding that girl as though it were his idea. I know your daddy did not care for Mr. Crump, and I think that is the only foolish thing I could say about him. Deep down, Ed Crump has the best interests of Memphis at heart."

Nell closed her mouth, which had fallen open during Bess's discourse. "Why, Mother, I've never heard you say a mumbling word about politics before."

"Well, why would I, Nell? It's such an ugly business. I never could understand how the Judge found it so completely fascinating. That doesn't mean that I didn't have my eyes and ears open every time someone came to the house to confer with him. We were married for a very long time, you know."

Trying to place the figurine, a china shepherdess, back on the mantle, Bess missed. It toppled to the hearth and shattered there. She let out a squeak. "Oh, Nell. I've broken your favorite piece."

"It's all right. I'll clean it up." Nell squatted to gather the pieces into her apron. "I always hated that ugly thing anyway. The only reason I even put it out is because Miss Myrtle Dyson gave it to us for a wedding present and asks about it every single time she comes to the house."

"Oh, heavens, of course she did. What on earth are we going to tell Myrtle now?"

"I'll just say that Ellis loved it so much that I buried it with him."

CHAPTER 25

At police headquarters, Sergeant Arnold Acker hustled into his office, set the box of his wife's homemade doughnuts on his desk, and hung his black fedora on the hat rack.

"There's three more Ginny Evanses waiting for you out there, Acker," Officer Murphy said, following his nose into the sergeant's office.

"Any of them look anything like the girl in the picture?"

"One might."

"Well, that's progress anyway."

Acker untied the string on the box and handed it to Murphy. "You know they're hungry. Give them some of these, and if you haven't already, get them each a cup of coffee. I'll be out there in a minute."

Murphy lifted the lid off the box, inhaled the fresh doughnut aroma that wafted out of it, and slobbered like an old coon hound on the scent. If that boy didn't stop eating, they were going to have to bury him in a piano case.

"Yes, get a doughnut yourself, Murphy. I know that's what you came in here for, but take your nose out of there and see to those girls first. Do you hear me? By the look of you, anybody would know you're not missing any meals."

"Yes, sir." Murphy patted his belly. "If Mrs. Acker ever throws you out of the house for the dumb cluck that you are, I'll be first in line to court her."

"You think she would have anything to do with a big, ignorant

Mick like you, Murphy? Now, get on out there. I need a minute to think before I talk to them."

Jesus and his angels, why hadn't he listened to the damned old Mississippi hayseed when he'd first come in? Would have saved him all this trouble and the chief after him every waking minute asking if he'd found the girl. It was the Lord's own punishment on him for thinking it wasn't his problem if Luther Evans couldn't control his slut of a daughter. Why hadn't he considered that maybe she wasn't a slut but just a kid who wanted something better than squeezing out a batch of brats in a tarpaper shack with holes in the walls and floor?

Picking up his notebook, Acker started for the duty room. Tonight he'd ask Marta to fry up a double batch of doughnuts, and he'd drop them by the church on his way in. She'd been asking to go cook at the soup kitchen, but he'd been so worried about having her down there with all those hobos that he'd said no. Tonight, he'd tell Marta he didn't care if he ate a cold supper every night. He'd even go help her on his days off.

In the duty room, three young women sat against the wall staring back at him. This batch didn't look as beat down as the first ones had, girls and women so thin and worn-out looking that their eyes stood out in their faces and their hands were like hide stretched over bundles of string. It had taken him that first day to realize that they had come hoping for a bite of food or a cup of coffee at least. That they would have done anything, said anything so long as somebody, anybody fed them. Figuring there'd at least be eggs to eat if nothing else, some of them were even ready to go back to the farm with Evans if he'd take them.

There was no question of two of the girls watching him with crumbs on their skirts and hunger in their eyes being Ginny Evans. One of them had hair so black it shone a little blue and eyes just as dark. Italian, he'd make her for, or Mexican, maybe, and no more than 12 years old. The other one was at least 30 and pock-marked, her skin as sallow as a gourd. The one in the middle, though, she was enough like the picture of the younger Ginny to be worth a look.

Acker pointed to the middle girl. "Come in my office for a minute, please, miss."

She rose, tentative.

He put a reassuring hand on her shoulder. "It's going to be all right, now. I just want to ask you a few questions before we call Mr. Evans down here to look at you."

"May I have another doughnut, please, mister?" the dark girl said.

"Murphy, give the girl all doughnuts she wants and then take these two down to the mission and get them something better to eat. See if the father has any work they can do."

The Italian girl grabbed Acker's hand and kissed it. He pulled it sharply away but then rested it on her head for a moment. Even Murphy, hard-hearted goon that he was, looked a little teary over that.

"Nothing's going to happen to you," Murphy said. "The father'll take care of you."

In Acker's office, the girl sat across the desk from Acker, bunched in the center of the chair as though afraid to touch more of it than she had to.

"What's your name?" Acker said.

"Ginny Evans."

"And where were you born?"

"Mississippi."

"Where in Mississippi?"

"Como."

"What's your mother's name?"

"Kate. Katherine Wilkerson."

Acker tapped the end of his pencil against his paper. The mother's name hadn't been in the paper. All the other girls had gotten this far from reading the story in the Press-Scimitar, but their mother's name had tripped them up. If this girl wasn't Ginny Evans, she might know something about her at least.

"How many brothers and sisters do you have?"

"Nine. Well, maybe ten. Mama was thinking she might be going to have another one when I left."

Nothing about the baby was in the papers either. Acker picked up his phone to call Nell Marchand and Luther Evans.

—

CLAUDE BEAUMONT, PRESIDENT OF UNION PLANTERS BANK, LEFT Franklin Bryant standing in front of his desk. Beaumont folded the issue of the Press-Scimitar with Ginny Evans's photograph and slid it across the desk so that her face stared up at Franklin.

"Oh, come now, Claude," Franklin said. "What can you tell from this child's picture? It can't possibly have been the same girl. Gaylord would surely have come forward or at least talked to me about it."

"Ask him yourself, Franklin," Beaumont said. "I saw them with her, Gaylord and that nephew of yours, Benny."

"Benny has always been a wild boy. I blame his mother for spoiling him. Got Gaylord into all kinds of trouble when he went down to Greenwood to visit. I can't imagine how he made it into Harvard, but we were all relieved when he did. Thought it was just the thing to straighten him out." Franklin shifted and ran his finger around the collar of his shirt. "Still, I'd bet my eyeteeth it was all innocent. Gaylord just isn't the type to run after cheap women. I'm sure he was trying to keep Benny out of trouble."

"That's not what it looked like to me," Beaumont said. He charged around the end of the desk like a bull after a red flag. "If those boys do know anything about what happened to her, then you owe it to her family talk to the police."

Franklin took a step back. "Nonsense. I'll have a talk with the Gaylord. I'm sure he and Benny don't know anything about this missing girl anyway. No need to get the family mixed up in it. I'd appreciate your discretion in this, Claude."

Beaumont leaned his backside against his desk in front of Franklin and crossed his arms. "Franklin, we've been friends for a long time, which is why I've come to you instead of going to Chief Wilson myself. But I'm not about to let this just ride."

"I'll see to it, Claude, of course. And if there's anything gone wrong here, I'll see that they go to the police. I hope you know me well enough to trust that I will. Just look at the furor this story has stirred up. Even the slightest hint that a Bryant is involved, and they'll splash it all over the headlines. I've worked too hard to make Gaylord the kind of man I can be proud of to have him tarred with the same brush as Benny."

"All right then." Turning his back on Franklin, Beaumont picked up the paper and studied the girl's picture again. "I'll leave it in your hands. And remember that we can't afford to have that kind of scandal touch the bank. You should know that better than anyone."

"Thank you. And thank you for coming to me with this. I won't forget."

"I just hope you're right and that there's nothing to it. Mr. Crump is on the bank's board."

"You let me worry about Ed Crump."

Beaumont gave Franklin a you're-dismissed look that sent him backing toward the door.

"Better you than me. Better you than me."

—

THE INSTANT THE GIRL SHUFFLED INTO THE SERGEANT'S OFFICE, CHIN in the air and a defiant smirk on her lips, Nell knew she wasn't Ginny Evans. Nell turned to Luther, who slumped and seemed to age 10 years in a split second.

"That ain't my girl," Luther said. He raised his hand, seemed to think better of slapping the impostor, and rubbed the back of his neck instead.

"I'm sorry to bring you all the way down here, Mr. Evans," Acker said. He tossed his pencil and pad onto the desk.

"Why did you want to go saying you're my Ginny, girl? Who the hell are you?"

"I'm nobody," the girl said, the defiance gone out of her. She glanced from Luther to Nell to Acker and back again before she turned her eyes to the floor. "I heard the cops would give you dinner if you came down here. I didn't mean to hurt anybody. Besides, I was Ginny's friend. Worked at the speak with her for a while, and she had the room next to mine in the boarding house. I helped her find it."

"Yeah, and I'm your old Aunt Gertrude," Murphy said. He reached for the girl's arm and started to drag her from the room. "I'll see you get taken care of, all right."

"That's enough, Murphy," Acker said. "Sometimes people don't make sense when they're hungry. Take Mrs. Marchand and Mr. Evans to the duty room and get them a cup of coffee while I see what I can find out."

Murphy dropped the girl's arm and waited by the door. Luther shuffled out, passing the girl without looking at her again.

Nell turned to Acker. "I don't believe I care for any coffee, Sergeant. I'd like to hear what she has to say."

Acker sighed loudly but nodded. He addressed the girl. "What's your name?"

"Lois Brown." The girl thrust out her chin again.

"When's the last time you saw Ginny Evans, Miss Brown?" Nell said.

"Four months ago, I guess. I lost my job, and the old biddy who ran the boarding house put me out on the street. Said her house was for decent girls."

"Why'd she do that?" Acker said in a tone that told Nell he planned to handle the questioning, thank you.

Her chin raising a notch higher, Lois seemed to consider a lie but think better of it.

"Because she found out I was going to have a baby. That's why they threw me out at the speak, too. Said I was too fat and there was nothing fun about a girl with a big belly."

"What happened to the baby?" Nell said. She took the girl's hand, guided her to one of the chairs, and sat down beside her. "Sergeant, I think Miss Brown would like a nice, cool glass of iced tea if you have any made up. Or at least a cup of that coffee you offered us."

"Murphy!" Acker yelled out his office door. "Get us some coffee in here, please."

"St. Peter's Orphanage," Lois said, a tremor starting in her voice. She smiled a pallid smile at Nell, who squeezed her hand. "I had him there. I thought the nuns would be mean, but they were real nice. Said I could stay until the baby and I were strong enough to go home. One night, I slipped out and left him there. He's such a pretty baby, I know someone will want him."

For a long moment, no one said anything more. Acker sat down behind his desk and scribbled something. Nell simply held Lois's hand.

Hurrying in with three cups of coffee, Murphy broke the spell. Acker motioned for him to give the first to Lois. Nell thanked him and left her cup on the desk. Acker sipped from his and waited.

"Now, tell me the truth, Miss Brown," Nell said. "Did you know Ginny Evans?"

"I'm not making that up."

"Then why didn't you come to us with that information?" Acker said.

"I don't know." Lois kept her eyes on Nell. "I was scared, I guess. I thought maybe she didn't want to be found."

"The truth again. Do you know what happened to her?" Nell said.

"No, ma'am. She tried to help me for a while after I left the boarding house, but the last time I went there asking for her, that old biddy said she'd gone. Said they didn't know where." Lois turned to Acker. "Are you going to put me in jail?"

"No, Miss Brown," he said. "Just give me the address of the speakeasy where you worked, the name of the boarding house, and anything else that might help us find Ginny. Then we'll be done with you."

The girl made a soft, wet noise that became a blubber. She stuffed her fist in her mouth, which made her look very young.

"Do you have somewhere to go when you leave here?" Nell said.

Lois looked down at her hands and picked at her ragged nails. She shook her head.

"Where do you want to go?" Acker said.

"I got no place, mister. Nothin'."

"I'll ask one of the officers to take you to the mission. You can get some food and talk to the father. He'll help you."

Not looking up, Lois nodded. "I could sure use something to eat."

Nell and Acker exchanged a glance. The hard edge of official impatience had gone from his face, a shadow of concern taking over. She decided that she liked him after all.

Chapter 26

The Starlite Roof Garden at the Hotel Claridge might not have had quite the cachet of the Skyway at the Peabody, but it was plenty swank enough for Gaylord Bryant. He didn't want anything else to do with Beale Street and cheap dives, no matter how much Benny pestered him to go along. Besides, Clyde McCoy and his orchestra were down from the Drake in Chicago. Benny had promised that if anything could get all the girls in the mood, it would be McCoy's wa-wa trumpet. And if it all worked out, well, there were lots of advantages to being at a hotel with all those empty rooms.

"Get up out of that bed, Gaylord," Benny had said when he came to the house to pick him up. "I can't believe you're not ready yet. Son, half the old boys in town would be chomping at the bit to go to the Starlite tonight. I'm not about to let you mope around the house all day and all night like somebody licked all the red off your candy. We'll have a swell time, get your mind off things."

Now, Gaylord was on the dance floor holding a blonde close to the rhythms of "Sugar Blues" and hoping sincerely that his cousin had been right. The blonde wasn't exactly one of the sorority girls from Southwestern that Benny'd had in mind, but she was good-looking, and she had a dangerous kind of smile that made a fellow think that this might be his night. So far, though, things were most definitely not working out.

"Come on, baby, loosen up," he said, pulling her closer and putting his lips against her ear.

The blonde wriggled harder in response. Bryant chased her lips with his, straining to kiss her. She kicked the fire out of his shin, and he let go.

"Hey, what's the big deal?" he said.

"I came here to dance, not get mauled by some jackass, college boy or not," the blonde said. "You've got to learn to keep your hands to yourself, buster." She straightened her dress and ran a hand over her hair to rearrange the waves.

"OK, miss. Excuse me. I thought you liked me. No hard feelings?"

"I'm not going to think about you enough for hard feelings." Nose in the air, the blonde went back to the spot by the dance floor where she'd been sitting alone when he'd gone over to speak to her. Gaylord shrugged.

Back at their table, his cousin Benny grinned from ear to ear. "Your problem, old son, is that you don't know how to handle women."

"And you do?"

"Sure. First you've got to sweet talk them. Make them think they're the prettiest things you've ever seen in your life, that you're crazy for them. Then, when you've got them all buttered up, you move in. If they don't like it, you show them they're wrong. Push right on past the good-girl act."

"You forget I've seen you on the make, Benny. You're not exactly smooth."

"Oh, yeah? Just watch me."

Benny was across the dance floor in two strides, his hand closing around the blonde's upper arm before she had a chance to smile at anyone else. She rounded on him, but he changed his grip to a caress up and down her arm. Damn it if a second later he didn't have her out on the floor, all snuggled up.

"Good Lord Almighty," Gaylord said. He signaled the waiter. "Another gin, and make this one a double."

"Coming right up, sir."

His heart wasn't in it anyway.

MRS. LOTTIE REYNOLDS RAN A DECENT BOARDING HOUSE, SHE'D HAVE you know. That's why she had put that trashy Lois Brown out when it became obvious that she was going to have a baby. She couldn't have that kind of girl living here and giving her place a bad name. The police had to understand that, but here they were, the two officers making her feel as though she'd done something wrong. Making her feel cold-hearted and mean. She'd been about to offer them some tea, but now she didn't even invite them in. The porch was good enough. She stood up extra straight just to let them know she'd answer their questions but didn't give a hoot in hell what they thought.

"Now, Mrs. Reynolds, when was the last time you saw Ginny Evans?" the one called Sergeant Acker said.

The one called Murphy never said a word but just watched her, squinty-eyed, and wrote in a little notebook.

"October, it was, Mr. Acker. Or maybe November. She ran out on her bill. Just disappeared one night, and I never heard from her again. She could have come to me about it. Seemed to be such a nice girl, and she could have helped with the cleaning, something. I tell you, it hurt my feelings, her running off like that."

"So she left without telling you anything?"

"Yes, sir. Didn't even take her things. Just ran off."

"Wait. You're telling me that she didn't take her belongings when she left?"

"No, sir. There wasn't much, you know. She did have a couple of pretty new dresses and a beautiful new ivory-handled hairbrush. That surprised me, her leaving it and loving that brush much as she did. She said it was a present from her young man. Said he gave it to her so she could brush her hair a hundred strokes every night, like Joan Crawford. Ginny was a big one for the pictures. Went every time she could."

"Did you meet this boyfriend of hers, know his name?"

"No, sir. I don't let my guests bring their special friends here, especially the girls. I told you, this is a decent house. I can't have any of that kind of carrying on."

"Do you still have her things?"

Lottie pulled her sweater closer around her. She had a right to make up her rent money, didn't she? Next thing you knew, they'd be accusing her of stealing from the girl.

"I sold them. She owed me money, you know. I had to get back what I could."

"I understand. Thank you, Mrs. Reynolds. We'll be back if we have more questions."

"And you'll be welcome. I always do what I can to help the police. This is a decent house."

"Yes, ma'am. I can see that."

Lottie closed the screen door behind the two policemen and watched them walk down the porch steps to the sidewalk. She'd have offered to let them see Ginny's room, but there hadn't been no reason to because there'd been two men who had rented it since her and she'd cleared out what Ginny had left behind. She'd told them the truth about everything except the brush, and that hadn't been much of a fib. It was too pretty to sell, prettier than anything her husband had ever given her. So what if she'd kept if for herself? She wanted to see if what they said about Joan Crawford's hair was true. She put her hand up to the curl she'd tucked behind one ear, and she could swear it was softer.

Out on the street, Murphy looked back at the house, scratching his ear. He flipped a page in his notebook. "Something ain't right here, Acker," he said. "Seems funny to me that the girl would go off without all her things like that. Would have been easy enough to sneak a bundle out with her."

"That's what I was thinking. Something must of happened to her. If she'd run off with a man, she would have come back for her clothes. Unless he promised to buy her a whole new wardrobe. She wouldn't be the first girl to fall for that. We need to find this boyfriend of hers."

"Any idea where to start looking?"

Acker pushed his fedora forward and scratched the back of head. "That speak on Beale Street." He flipped open his notebook, too. "Kelly's. You ever been there?"

"What, me go to a place that sells whiskey? Don't you know that's against the law?"

"What came over me?" Acker said, grinning. He slapped Murphy on the back.

Murphy grinned back at him.

"Come on," Acker said. "It's three doors down from the One Minute. Maybe they'll have a nice cup of coffee for us."

—

ALL NIGHT THE NIGHT BEFORE, IT HAD RAINED HARD IN MEMPHIS, BUT by 10 o'clock the next morning, the clouds had moved on, and a soft breeze swept across the river. A gorgeous late-spring day. A black Packard stopped on the bank just below the bridge that spanned the Mississippi between the city and Arkansas. Two men got out of the back. They reached inside, pulled out a girl, and began to drag her onto the bridge.

She slumped against them, her legs rubbery. The left side of her face was one enormous bruise, that eye had swelled shut, and her lip was split and still bleeding a little. It took both of the men to walk her along to about the middle of the bridge, lift her over the rail, and hold her there.

The girl looked up at the sky and thought what a sweet, soft blue it was. The moon hadn't quite set and was still just visible, a tiny, perfect, pale sliver. It was about the prettiest thing she'd ever seen. The breeze was cool against her face.

Far below her, the rain had stirred the Mississippi into a chocolate torrent that swept branches, a dead cow, and other odds and ends past her feet. It looked dingy and cold. She shivered.

One of the men counted to three. On three, they let go of her arms. Then she was falling toward the river. She grabbed at the rail but missed it. She tried to hold her breath, but when her body hit the surface with a slap, both of her legs snapped at the knee and all the air whooshed out of her lungs. As the dark water closed over her head and the tips of her grasping fingers, Lois Brown thought of her little baby boy, safe with the sisters, and hoped the new mother he would have some day would never tell him anything about her.

—

THE NEXT DAY, THERE WAS A SMALL ITEM ON THE THIRD PAGE OF THE paper deploring the number of men and women, driven to desperation by the privations of the Depression, who chose to fling themselves from the heights of the Harahan Bridge into the raging torrent of the mighty Mississippi. The article mentioned Lois Brown by name as the latest such unfortunate whose lifeless form had been found battered against a pylon and fished from the heartless embrace of the river. The reporter asked if there were nothing more the city could do to relieve the suffering of those forced to depend on the charity of others and to take their own lives when there was no charity to be found.

Joseph Calendar read the article. Lois Brown, the false Ginny Evans. He wondered if someone had helped Lois into the Mississippi. Perhaps Ginny had not simply run away after all. Perhaps they would never find her because she had met a fate like her friend's. He also wondered if Nell had read the story and understood what it might mean. From now on, he could not allow her to question anyone on her own. Perhaps even that precaution might not be enough to keep her safe.

CHAPTER 27

Before he squatted to line up his shot on the third green of the Memphis Country Club, Franklin Bryant pulled out his flask and offered it to Ed Crump.

"For the life of me, I can't figure out how you allowed yourself to be dragged into the circus around this girl, this . . . what's her name?"

"Ginny Evans," Crump said. He narrowed his eyes at Franklin and pointed with his club for him to putt. "Go on, boy. You're holding up the whole parade."

"That's right. This Ginny Evans. What does anybody know about her anyway, E. H.? Can you be sure there even is a Ginny Evans? This could be a publicity stunt Nell Marchand cooked up to promote that damn fool fortunetelling of hers."

Franklin positioned himself over the ball. "Why, even if the girl exists, she's probably run off with some man. Maybe she's a whore and doesn't want her mama to find out. She could be dead. Hell, for all we know, she could have jumped off the Harahan Bridge. People are already beginning to mutter about the fact that she hasn't turned up yet."

"You got something against this girl?"

"Of course not." Putt sunk, Franklin signaled for his caddy to retrieve the ball. "But how's it going to look for you when you can't find her? Bad. That's how it's going to look. And you know people are going to blame you."

"Nice shot," Crump said. He picked his marker up off the green and replaced it with a ball. The gentlest tap sent it rolling to the hole where, before it dropped home, it circled like a desperate ant swimming to avoid being sucked down a drain. "But not as nice as that one. Now, how do you propose that I withdraw gracefully, Franklin? I've pledged myself and the whole city of Memphis to find her."

Franklin removed his cap and swiped at his forehead with the handkerchief he pulled from his back pocket. "You could say that the city has spent enough of its scarce resources looking for the girl. That we've done everything we can but that she's nowhere to be found."

"Hurts me to think of her out there alone. What if she were mine?"

"Come on, now, E.H. You're letting your soft heart cloud your judgment. You and I both know the kind of girl this Ginny Evans is. Wherever she is, I guarantee you that she's alone. You've got no business wasting any more of your time or anyone else's on her."

The caddies shouldered their bags and headed toward the next tee. Crump reached for Franklin's flask, took another pull, and wiped his mouth with the back of his hand.

"Well, if I do call off Chief Wilson, at least it will keep that old boy from getting the ulcer that he has been working on. Ever since this whole business started, he has been just about as nervous as a long-tailed cat in a room full of rocking chairs."

—

FOR ALL THE SENSATION THE HEADLINES ABOUT GINNY HAD CAUSED, when the newspaper reporters stopped writing them, it didn't take long for the people of Memphis to shuttle her to the back of their minds. Had she been found, she might have lived on in their thoughts, but because there was no sign of her, other, more pressing concerns took her place. There was still the milkman to pay and shoes to be bought for children somehow and recipes to be stretched with as much cabbage and water as they could.

Nell wouldn't have believed it, but even stalwart, dependable

Oz Sherman had thrown up his hands. Ginny Evans, he said, was yesterday's news, and he had other fish to fry.

"I was so sure we'd find her," Nell said. She plucked a can of green peas off a shelf in the Piggly Wiggly and showed it to Hattie, who screwed up her face like she'd smelled a skunk. Nell returned the can to the shelf.

"Don't you go getting all down at the mouth about it, Nell," Hattie said. She studied a can of yams, grimaced again, and put it back on the shelf. "Maybe that girl doesn't want to be found. Just because her daddy wants her home doesn't mean she wants to go. Nobody thought about that, did they?"

"I guess not." Nell studied the yams Hattie had put down. "We've been going along thinking she'd disappeared and there's something mysterious about it."

"There are lots of reasons a girl might not want to go home. Maybe her daddy took the strap to her. Maybe she didn't want to work herself to death on a farm. Nobody knows what she wants but her."

"Maybe so, Hattie, but there was something I sensed, you know, when Luther Evans first came to see me. The things I saw as Ginny. She felt lost. Maybe it wasn't home she was looking for, but I got the feeling she wanted to find some place, some thing. That she was looking for something."

Hattie dropped a jar of pickled beets into her basket. Nell shuddered. Bess and Hattie could have her share of beets.

"You thought about trying to ask her?" Hattie said.

"Ask her? You mean going into some kind of trance again? No." Nell drew out the last word.

"I'm just saying, you talk mighty big about wanting to find that girl, but you're not doing anything about it. Not the way you could."

An elderly woman in a dress that had been stylish at the turn of the century appeared at the end of the aisle. Nell shushed Hattie and waited for the old lady to pass before she answered in a voice just above a whisper.

"Hattie, please don't start that again. I don't even know if anything I saw was real. Maybe I'm just crazy. Have you thought about that?"

"No. Your grandmamma wasn't crazy, was she?"

"A lot of people thought so, and Mared Blayney didn't go around telling everybody that she saw things, either. If she had visions, she kept them to herself."

"Maybe she shouldn't have. Might have helped you. Maybe you're afraid of what you'll see."

"There's no maybe about it, Hattie. Of course, I'm afraid. And what if I don't wake up? What if I go to wherever it is I'm going in the trance, but I can't get back?"

"I don't know, honey. Only way it find out is if you try. Maybe you ought to talk to Dr. Calendar about it."

Just then, Bess fluttered up with a jar of marmalade and a tin of salmon that she displayed proudly to Nell and Hattie before she added them into the basket. "My mother used to order oranges for us at Christmas, and she made marmalade as a special treat for New Year's breakfast. And salmon! Goodness, I don't think I've tasted tinned salmon since the Judge passed on."

Bess poked through the basket's contents and sighed contentedly. When she looked up at Nell, her smile vanished. "What's troubling you, my dear?" Bess said.

"Hattie thinks I ought to use my powers—just saying that makes me want to laugh—to find Ginny Evans," Nell whispered, having spied a young matron and her little boy at the end of the aisle.

"But you still don't want to," Bess said in a normal voice, oblivious to the fact that Nell might want her to keep her voice down.

Nell pulled Bess and Hattie to a corner from which she could keep an eye on the other Piggly Wiggly patrons and pretended to consult with them over a box of oatmeal. "I want to find her, of course, Mother, but it's not as though I have any idea how to do it or if I can, even. I haven't had any inkling of anything about her since that first day with her father."

"You have nothing to lose by trying, my dear."

"That's just it, Miss Bess. What if none of it is real?"

"I suppose you can't know any of those things, Nell, but it doesn't seem possible that the Lord would give you this ability without also letting you learn how to use it."

"What if I don't find Ginny Evans?"

"Then she and her family will be no worse off than they were when all this started. But if you do find her, Nell, think what that would mean to all of them. A family reunited, a girl rescued from who knows what kind of distress. Wouldn't it mean something to you to be able to do that?"

"You know something, Mother? I think I'm more afraid of finding out that I do have some kind of psychic power than of finding out that I don't. If I do have it, what on earth am I to do with it?"

"As the saying goes, my dear, we'll cross that bridge when we come to it."

"I wish I'd never started this."

"Too late for that," Hattie said. She took the oatmeal from Nell's hand, put it in the basket, and started toward the registers.

—

"YOU HAVEN'T GOT ANYTHING FOR US, SERGEANT?" NELL SAID. SHE, Joseph Calendar, and Luther Evans sat across from Acker, who looked like a boy whose daddy just had to shoot his dog.

"The chief has pulled everyone off the case. I'm sorry."

"Well, since it don't seem like we're going to find Ginny, I can't stay in Memphis no longer, Sergeant," Luther said. "Been gone too long already."

"We might still turn up someone who really knows something about her," Acker said.

"How do you expect to do that if you're not really looking anymore?" Nell said.

Acker looked even more miserable but said nothing.

Luther creased the crown of his hat where it sat in his lap.

"Anyway, I got to get back, see about getting the rest of my fields planted. No crop this year, and come fall, I won't have a farm no more. I got all them other children to worry about. And Kate. Maybe she'll fret herself less if I'm back home." He rubbed hard at his eyes with a knuckle.

"We'll get word to you if we find her, Mr. Evans."

"Thank you, Sergeant."

"You got enough money for the train back home?"

"I rode up from Como on my old mare Sal. Going back the same way. Got to get her back home before she decides she forgets how to pull a plow. She's going to miss the life of Riley she's been living, eating her head off down to the livery stable."

Acker laughed. "I bet she will that. I could use a vacation like that myself, nothing to do and somebody feeding me regular."

"Thank you, Sergeant Acker." Luther stood and stretched his hand across the desk. "You been right decent. I appreciate what you tried to do for Ginny."

"Good luck, Luther." Acker shook his hand.

"Why don't you go on downstairs, Luther, and ask Jenkins to bring the car around for us?" Nell said. "We have one little thing to talk to the sergeant about, and then we'll be down."

Battered hat settled on his head, Luther walked away through the duty room with a slump to his shoulders but a nod for anyone who greeted him on his way out.

Acker tossed his pencil on his desk. "Dammit. Dammit to hell." Avoiding Nell's eyes, he sat in his chair and reached for the next report from the stack in front of him.

"I could go to Mr. Crump, tell him we need just a little more time," she said.

"Where do you think the order to stop came from, Miss Nell?" he said, his mouth a hard line of disgust. "But you didn't hear that from me."

"That's worse than I thought."

"I suppose further inquiries—even quiet, unofficial ones—are not possible," Calendar said.

"I don't like giving up, but there's nothing I can do. At least not officially. Not if I want to keep my job."

"Of course." Calendar handed the man one of his ornate visiting cards.

"But I will keep an ear to the ground." Acker pocketed the card. "Something might still turn up."

"That's very kind, Sergeant Acker," Nell said.

Nell went to the window and looked down at Luther, who stood on the curb with his hands in his pockets, staring down into the gutter. Calendar came up behind her.

"I was so sure we would find her, Joseph."

He rested his hand on her shoulder.

From a window in his office, Chief Wilson watched Nell and Calendar emerge on the street below a few moments later. Nell took Luther's arm and ducked into the car with him while Calendar held the door for them. Wilson smiled.

CHAPTER 28

Sometimes things don't work out so bad. Benny might be just a kid, but he was a looker. And he was no snob. He was just as happy taking her to the Galindo or to Kelly's or even out to the Silver Slipper in Mason if they were feeling wild. And he was always on time. Mildred Epps liked that in a man. It showed respect. His pockets might not be quite a deep as Ellis Marchand's had been, but, then, he wasn't nearly as much trouble as Ellis. And he was tall. She liked them really tall, too. She might make younger men a specialty from now on.

"You look gorgeous, Mildred," Benny said when she opened the door. "Just like a million bucks."

"You don't look so bad yourself, sugar."

Mildred put her hands on Benny's chest and leaned against him, her face upturned for a kiss. Benny obliged quite nicely. She pushed him away when she was done.

"Any more of that, and we'll miss our reservations at the club," she said.

"That wouldn't be so bad, would it?" Benny tried to kiss her again, but Mildred slipped out of his arms.

"Are you kidding? I'm starved. Positively starved. All day long, I've been thinking about that steak at Galindo. I can taste the béarnaise already."

Benny pulled her back, nibbled at her ear. "You could cook something here, and we wouldn't have to go out."

"Not a chance, buster." Mildred shoved him away, hard. "You want someone to cook for you, you go home to your mama. Mildred Epps is nobody's kitchen help."

Benny held his hands up in surrender. "Oh, now, darlin', I'm sorry. I just thought if we stayed in, we'd have more time to cuddle. I've been lonesome."

"Did the big strong man miss his little Mildred? Aw, that's so sweet." She leaned against his chest again but pulled back before he could kiss her. "Keep that thought about cuddling. Buy me a nice, thick, juicy steak, and you'll get all the cuddling you can stand. But first, you've got to feed me."

"All right. Come on. I suppose you're going to want to go to the Skyway to dance, too."

"You got it. I'm getting tired of the Starlite. And Paul Whiteman's broadcasting from the Peabody tonight. You think I'm about to miss that? Besides, you want all your friends to see you've got a new girl, don't you? They'll all be eating their hearts out with envy."

And they did. Every time Mildred and Benny hit the dance floor, someone was cutting in. It was starting to make Benny a little hot under the collar.

"I thought you were here with me, Mildred."

"I'm sorry, college boy. Can I help it if there isn't another woman in this room half as good-looking? Think of what I'm doing for your reputation."

The big lug was going to pout. Je-sus. Couldn't a girl have any fun? It was going to take the works to keep him in a good mood. Mildred pulled her chair right up against Benny's and slid her arm through his. She rested her head on his shoulder, gave him her best doe-eyed gaze, and ran her fingers along his lapel.

"Look, Benny, we can sit out the rest of them out if you want. I'm here with you, and I promise I won't dance with anybody else the rest of the night. Why should I, anyway, if I'm with the handsomest fellow in the room?"

Benny smiled in spite of himself. What a pushover.

"There, that's my lamby pie. I knew you couldn't stay mad at your little Mildred. Let's just listen to the music and have a good time. Don't you just love Paul Whiteman?"

Some geezer and the prune-puss who must be his wife stopped at their table, and from the looks on their faces, her lamby pie was in for trouble. From the look on his, he knew it, too.

"Benjamin, what on earth are you doing in Memphis?" the woman said. "You're supposed to be at school."

"You'd better explain yourself, son," the man said.

They both stared at Mildred until she wanted to ask what was eating them.

"I'm waiting for an explanation, Benjamin," the old coot said.

Benny rose from his seat, hauling Mildred up by the elbow as he did. "Aunt Margaret, Uncle Frank, this is my friend Mildred Epps. Mildred, these are my aunt and uncle, Mr. and Mrs. Franklin Bryant."

Time for the society girl manners. "Mr. and Mrs. Bryant," Mildred said, "Benjamin talks about you all the time. I hope you won't be angry with him. You see, today is my birthday, and he came to Memphis especially to take me out to celebrate." She faced him, hands on her hips. "Benjamin Bryant, I can't believe you came to town and didn't tell your aunt and uncle. Shame on you. You need to apologize to both of them right this minute."

"I'm sorry, Aunt Margaret, Uncle Franklin. I should have let you know."

All regret and contrition, Mildred put her hand on Prune-puss's arm. "I apologize, too, Mrs. Bryant. I had no idea you and Mr. Bryant didn't know Benjamin was here. I'm so glad that there's someone taking care of him when he's in Memphis. He just goes on and on about you both, of course. I'm so happy to meet you finally."

She gave the aunt and uncle her brightest smile. "I hope you'll forgive me for luring him away from Cambridge. Really, I told him he shouldn't come, that it's important for him to stay in school, but he just would not listen. He didn't want me to be alone on my birthday.

Isn't that sweet?"

"Well," Mrs. Bryant said, starting to soften up.

"And what about your studies, Benjamin?" Franklin Bryant said. "Your father has told me that you're already on academic probation. One more violation, and they'll kick you out. All the Bryant men have graduated from Harvard. I'd hate to have to call your mother and father and speak to them about this. You don't want to disappoint them, do you?"

"No, sir."

So, the old man was going to be the tough nut about Benny. Better turn it on. "Oh, Mr. Bryant, I'm sure it's all going to be all right. Benjamin is so intelligent. He just has to apply himself a little more. If we all encourage him, I'm sure he'll do splendidly, won't you, Benjamin?" Mildred rested her hand on Benny's shoulder and squeezed it.

He looked at his aunt and uncle like a sullen six-year-old. "Sure, I guess so."

"Now, won't you join us at our table? We'll be so cozy, the four of us, and I've been positively dying to get to know you. Here's our chance."

"I suppose it couldn't hurt anything," Franklin said. "Margaret?"

"I suppose it's all right," Prune-puss said.

Good. Eating out of her hand already. Maybe she could play this for all it was worth. End up being Mrs. Benjamin Bryant. Or the old man wasn't so bad once you got a good look at him. Get him away from that hatchet-faced old heifer, and he might be worth a few laughs. And he was here to take her out whenever she wanted, not way up north in some snotty school. Why not? It might be fun. The old boy would never know what hit him.

"Where are your people from, Miss Epps?" the old woman said.

A shack just across the river, if you really want to know. "St. Louis. I came to Memphis to go to school, but when Papa and Mama were killed . . . well, I had to make my way. It just seemed better to stay here than go back and be reminded of them constantly."

"Why, bless your heart," Mrs. Bryant said. "Haven't you any other family?"

"I was an only child. Papa and Mama, too. But Papa always taught me to be self-reliant, and so I manage as best I can."

"You never told me any of that, Mildred," Benny said.

Now, the big, brave smile. "It's not a happy story. I didn't want to worry you with my troubles."

"You poor child," the old man said.

This was going to be fun.

CHAPTER 29

They rang the doorbell, and Joseph Calendar himself answered. The wave of relief that swept over Nell at the sight of him took her breath away. He offered his hand, and she took it, grateful for its warmth and strength.

"I'm afraid we're a bit late," she said, desperate to break the tension that clamped her shoulders together and left her hands like ice. "I wasn't sure what to wear for my debut as a seer."

"You could wear a tow sack and look like a queen," Calendar said. He eyed the burgundy silk she had chosen. "But this is much more suitable. Are you ready?"

"No." She attempted a brave smile.

He returned her smile and linked her arm through his to escort her to the Spirit Room, which they had decided was the best place for Nell to reach out to Ginny again, set up as it was for just such undertakings as this. She was at the table by the window with Calendar, Bess and Hattie sat on the gold sofa, and Simon waited by the door in case anything were needed.

Teeth sticking to her parched lips, Nell reached for the water that Simon had set beside her. Her hands shook so that she had to use both to pick up the glass.

"There is no need to be anxious, Miss Nell," Calendar said. "I'll be right here with you."

"You know you might as well tell a child not to scratch a chigger bite."

His chuckle was like a pair of warm arms enfolding her. "Ready?"

Nell nodded.

"Do you remember what card you touched when you had the vision of Ginny in the night club?" Calendar said.

"Luther had just turned it over. I remember thinking it was a particularly fascinating card, and I was trying to remember what Mathers said about it in his book. I picked the card up to talk to Luther about what it might mean when the flash came."

"Close your eyes. Put yourself back in the room with them. See if you can take yourself to the exact moment when you're about to pick up the card. Are you there?"

"Yes." The room was warm, but Nell shivered. She was both herself now, sitting in Joseph Calendar's Spirit Room, and a past Nell, reaching for Luther's card.

"Do you see the card?"

"I don't know. It's not . . . Lord, there it is. The World. What does it mean?"

"We can worry about the meaning later. You never finished the reading, so I don't know that it matters in that context. What we want to do is to see if you can touch it and trigger another vision. Put your hand out and pick it up."

"I can't reach it somehow." Nell wiggled her fingers and squeezed her eyes tighter. "The table is getting wider so it's always just beyond my grasp."

As though he had moved to stand just behind her, Calendar's voice came soft and low in her ear, soothing. "I believe that's you not wanting to see what the card is trying to tell you. Relax for a moment, clear your mind, and tell yourself that you're calm and open and ready to accept its meaning. That you're eager to know what's waiting for you."

She opened her eyes again to find him still seated across from her, his expression neutral but for the intensity of his gaze. The strength that emanated from him washed over her, and she felt the last bit of fear that had possessed her slip away. Eyes closed once more, she sat back and rested her hands quietly on the table. She felt her fingers grip the edge of the card. She flipped it into her hand.

"I've got it. Joseph, it's glowing. I–"

Nell gasped.

She lay on a thin, bare mattress on a narrow cot that was hard against her back. High above her on the wall, a tiny window showed the night sky with a few stars visible. Her hands rested on her stomach, and the fabric of the plain white shift she was dressed in was rough under her fingertips. Outside her door, she heard women laughing and talking. Every now and then, one screamed. She tried to sit up, and . . . .

She was back in the Spirit Room. She breathed out in a great hiss.

"Don't open your eyes," Calendar said. "Quickly, what did you see?"

"Not much. A small room. A simple bed. Ginny was alone. But she's alive, Joseph. She's alive. I was there now, not in the past. It was different this time, warmer. I wasn't simply looking out of her eyes and feeling what she had felt. Her lungs breathing in and out were mine. Her heart beating was mine." Nell laughed, caught up in the wonder and hope of what she had seen and felt. "She's alive, and that means we can find her."

"But you don't know where you were?"

"No, it was too quick." She strained after the last tendrils of the memory that were just out of her reach. "A flophouse, maybe. I don't know."

"Try to go back. Reach for the card again."

Steadying herself as best she could, Nell sent her mind in search of the card. Nothing. Not the deck, not the table, not the salon. Only blackness.

"It's gone." She slumped and covered her face with her hands.

"That's all right, Nell. We can try again when you're ready, but for now, at least you saw something. It was real."

Nell opened her eyes. She had never been happier to see anything in her life than she was to see his face. His wonderful, wonderful face.

"And I came back, Joseph. I don't think I can try again tonight, but I can do this again."

"That's my girl." Calendar grasped her hands. "You're like ice, Nell. How do you feel?"

"That's funny. I don't feel cold at all. Not like the first two times. I feel warm, safe even, and sleepy. Lord, I could sleep for a week."

"Then let's get you home and put you to bed." Calendar rubbed Nell's hands between his. He draped her shawl around her shoulders and helped her to her feet. "Miss Bess, will you allow me to escort you and Miss Nell back home? I don't want to leave her so soon after her trance. She's perfectly safe, I'm sure, but nonetheless, I'd like to be nearby tonight. May I impose on your hospitality?"

"Of course, Dr. Calendar. Hattie can fix up the blue bedroom for you. That's between Nell's and mine."

"Perfect. But if there's a chair in her room that I could sit in for a while and watch her until she's asleep, I'd like to do that. Miss Nell, is it all right with you?"

Hardly able to keep her eyes open, Nell struggled to follow his exchange with Bess. She felt peculiar, heard them as through they were speaking somewhere on the other side of the room. She dragged out an answer.

"Of course. Anything would be all right as long as I can go to sleep. And I have the strangest desire for a big glass of buttermilk."

"Perhaps it was the effort of summoning and controlling what you saw that has fatigued you. Do you usually take buttermilk before you retire?"

"Lord, no. I can't stand it. That's why it's so strange. All I can think of is some cold buttermilk and a piece of cornbread."

"I'll keep you company for a while at least, Dr. Calendar," Bess said. "After all the excitement this evening, I don't believe I could sleep a wink."

—

"THAT WAS CLOSE," BENNY SAID BACK IN MILDRED'S APARTMENT, sliding his arm round her to pull her close. "You know, sugar, you're really something else. You had Uncle Franklin wrapped around your little finger in no time. And my aunt? She's so tickled I'm with someone who has been gently reared, as she put it, that she's beside herself. She said you're a lovely, lovely girl."

"You saying I'm not?" Pouting her mouth, Mildred pretended to push him away.

"You know that's not what I mean. It's just that, well, I've never seen anything like the act you put on tonight."

"You'd better be glad I can think on my feet, lamby pie. You were about to be in big, big trouble with your old man, and we can't have that, can we? We've got to keep them thinking everything's on the up and up so they let you keep seeing me."

"They couldn't stop me." Benny nuzzled her neck.

Mildred pushed him away for real this time and went to her bar to fix herself a drink. She did not offer Benny one. "Sure they could," she said, sipping her gin. "Old Uncle Franklin could call your daddy up, and he could take away your bank account. Then where would you be? You know I'm crazy about you, but I like nice things, too. A girl's got to look after herself. I'd hate to have to choose."

"Don't talk like that, Mildred." Benny crossed to the bar and took her manfully by the shoulders. "I don't know what I'd do if I lost you."

"Then you'd better get yourself back up to Harvard U and stick your nose as deep in those books as you can. Study hard, and I'll keep the home fires burning for you."

"There's no one else in the world like you."

"Now, come on, and let's see what kind of performance we can cook up before you have to go home for your dear auntie to tuck you in."

She didn't have to ask Benny twice.

—

MARGARET BRYANT WAS BRAIDING HER HAIR FOR THE NIGHT WHEN Franklin came in with the two glasses of water he brought up every night and set one on each of the bedside tables, being careful not to spill a drop.

"You know, Franklin, I have the funniest feeling that I've seen Miss Epps before, but I can't quite place her," she said. "I don't believe I know any Eppses. Do you think we could have met her and her people when we were in St. Louis for your bank meeting? I must remember to ask her what her father's work was. Thank goodness Benjamin has chosen such a nice girl for a change."

"You know, my dear, I felt the same thing. I don't know where we would have known her, though. I can't think of an Epps among our acquaintances. Where did she say her family was from?"

Margaret turned from the mirror to look at her husband, who had sat down on the bed and removed his right shoe. "Were you listening to me at all just now, Franklin? She said she was from St. Louis. That she doesn't have any family left there. The poor thing is an orphan."

"I'll pack Benjamin back off to Boston tomorrow morning." Franklin dropped his shoe and began to untie the left one. His mind had obviously wandered off again.

Margaret shook her head at herself in the mirror. When that man's mind drifted, it was like talking to a brick wall. "Franklin!"

He started. "Yes, Margaret?"

"Perhaps we should invite Miss Epps to Sunday dinner with us. It sounds as though she's all alone here. I hate to think of that. Such a lovely, sweet girl."

"Yes, quite charming. Perhaps I'll look in on her, tell her she should think of us as her Memphis family. An impressionable young thing like that needs someone to guide her. And who knows but that Benjamin might decide to make the arrangement permanent one day. He seems quite smitten. Even if we don't know anything about her people, he could do worse. And Lord knows he has. We should encourage him to keep seeing her."

He dropped his left shoe and stood to remove his trousers, which he draped over the rack at the foot of the bed. "Yes, I'm going to pay her a call. I believe she said she's staying at the Parkview Apartments. Her people must have left her a little money if she's able to afford a place there."

"Oh, I think that's a wonderful idea, Franklin. And ask her for this Sunday, will you?"

"Yes, my dear. I'm sure she'll appreciate the kindness."

Margaret turned back to the mirror. "Good. Now help me with the clasp on my necklace will you? I can never quite manage to unfasten it myself, and I've been waiting for you to come up."

And so he did, but it was another neck altogether than Franklin thought of—a slim, smooth young neck instead of the rather older, somewhat creased one under his hands.

CHAPTER 30

Nestled on the back seat of the Duesenberg, Nell fell asleep almost as soon as they pulled away from Calendar's house. Her head sank onto his shoulder, and he shifted to support her neck. The urge to kiss the top of her head was so powerful that he focused on Bess Marchand's face with all the will that he had.

Bess smiled coquettishly at him. "Doesn't Nell look like an angel when she's sleeping, Dr. Calendar?"

"Yes, she does."

"Tonight must have been absolutely exhausting. She's a strong girl, but these last few weeks have been more than anyone should have to deal with. It means so much to both of us to have you guide her, someone who understands her gift. It must be terrifying."

"We're all afraid of the things we don't understand, Miss Bess. As she learns to use her abilities, they'll be less frightening. I hope one day, she'll be able to summon her visions at will and read and understand them as easily as you or I would study a written text. For the true adept, controlling the gift becomes second nature."

"Will she have a spirit guide like Imhotep, do you think?"

"Each gift is unique. She may be able to summon spirits when she wishes, or her powers may be such that she doesn't require intermediaries. Only time will tell."

Once home, Nell roused herself long enough to get upstairs and get into bed. The moment her head hit the pillow, she was asleep again. Bess had no sooner sunk into her chair than her head dropped to the side, and she began to snore softly. Calendar smiled at the two women and settled himself.

Joseph Calendar had never stayed in one place more than 5 years. Often, he moved on before 2, but Memphis drew him, held him. Perhaps it felt too much like home, was too close to it. The culture, the cadence of the voices, the very smell of the air said home.

It was a power that he resisted, a danger that he understood. The call of his old life, desperate and impoverished as it had been, was strong. He would never be that boy again, but the comfort of being someone more than the façade that was Joseph Calendar the medium appealed to him. To be able to relax and simply be someone real would be a blessing. But this life in Memphis that he'd grown to relish so could bind him, pull him down like a frog in quicksand. He knew he should go.

But now there was Nell Marchand, and he could not leave her. She was beautiful, yes, but he had known many beautiful women before. Indeed, some far more lovely than she. Intelligent, brave, good humored, compassionate, generous, witty, selfish, capricious, greedy, fearful—he had known them all in abundance in various female forms. Even talent and sensitivity to the spirit world, he had known before.

The pain of what had happened to that other beautiful creature, what had been done to her, was something he never wanted to endure again. But at the first touch of Nell Marchand's hand, he had been lost. Enthralled. Her slave. Her protector. Her guide. Whatever she wanted him to be—or did not want—he was doomed to obey, had always been doomed to obey. Fleeing would be futile. She would draw him back.

Watching her in repose, her fingers curled at her face like a child's, her red-gold curls a halo across her pillow, he felt at peace at last with knowing that he must love her twice in this lifetime. Perhaps Memphis was as good a place as any to stop, rest, be after all. He let his head drift back against the chair, closed his eyes, and slept a dreamless sleep.

CHAPTER 31

What kind of loony knocked on a girl's door at 10 o'clock in the morning? It was practically the middle of the night, for crying out loud. Mildred threw on her dressing gown and answered the door to find Franklin Bryant there, hat in hand.

Well, well, well. That hadn't taken long. "Mr. Bryant. Why, goodness, I'm surprised to see you. Is something wrong?"

"No, my dear, we'd simply like to invite you to share our dinner with us this Sunday. Mrs. Bryant insists that you think of us as your family here in Memphis. If you arrive a little after 1 o'clock, that should give you time to get home from church and freshen up if you like. I know Margaret—Mrs. Bryant—finds she has so much visiting to do on her way out of the sanctuary that it's often almost 1 by the time we get home ourselves. Of course, we'll be expecting you, so you won't have to worry about not finding us at home."

Sure, she'd hustle straight over from church. "Oh, how kind and thoughtful of you both. I'd adore having Sunday dinner with you. I am so on my own here. I confess that it's a little lonely sometimes."

"I'm afraid I've disturbed you, though. I do apologize." He made as if to go.

Mildred put her hand on his arm to stop him. "Not at all. Today is my day off, and I was out later than I should have been last evening, as you know. I was indulging myself with a lazy day. You've caught me in my pajamas." She pulled her robe closed at her throat and looked up at Bryant through her lashes, just enough of a smile on her lips. "But please come in. If you'll give me a moment, I'll put on something a little more suitable and fix you a cup of coffee."

"I really should get back to my office. I just wanted to deliver Mrs. Bryant's invitation."

Sure. That's what telephones are for, buddy. "All right, but I'm about to fix a pot for myself. I'm no use to anyone, including myself, until I've had my coffee in the morning. If you'd like some, I'd be glad of the company."

Franklin Bryant hesitated, turned again to go, thought better of it, and came in. "Well, perhaps just one cup. It will give us a chance to get better acquainted. I like to know Benjamin's friends."

Gotcha! "Wonderful. Just make yourself at home. I'll be right out. How do you like your coffee?"

"Black."

"Oh, I don't see how you can do that." Time to turn it on. Mildred gave a dramatic shiver that allowed her dressing gown to open just a little bit at the neck. The old boy's eyes went straight there. Let it open just a little more, and his eyes all but bugged out of his head. This was going to be almost too easy.

"I take mine with cream and lots and lots of sugar. I've got a terrible sweet tooth, you see, and I simply can't swallow it any other way. My dear mother, Lord rest her, always teased me about my extravagant nature, but what's life about if you can't taste a bit of sugar every now and then? Don't you agree? Now, excuse me, Mr. Bryant."

—

NELL WAS ON HER WAY TO LAY THE CASE FOR FINDING GINNY AT E.H. Crump's feet again. He would have to listen to her now. Anton might think she was bearding the lion in his den, but it was worth another try. So, Nell had left Anton fretting in his office and enlisted Calendar to accompany her. As many society matrons as the medium counted among his clientele, the politician was bound to have heard of him.

"I'll do the talking," Nell said, climbing out of the car when Calendar held the door for her. "When he hears what I've got to say, he'll have to believe me. If he doesn't, you can tell him you were there."

"I'm not sure he'll put any more faith in my veracity, Nell."

"Well, he's the one who said I should come to him if I ever needed anything, wasn't he? Let's see if he's as good as his word."

—

WHEN NELL AND CALENDAR APPEARED AT HIS OFFICE DOOR, CRUMP came around his desk to greet her, both hands outstretched.

"Mrs. Marchand, what a pleasure. It does me good to look at your pretty face. Now, what brings you to my office today? What can I do for you?"

"I want you to help us find Ginny Evans," Nell said.

Crump's face fell, taking his broad smile with it. His lips twitched to one side, then the other. He shot Calendar a poisonous glance, settled deliberately into his chair, and interlaced his fingers.

"Ginny Evans? Why, Mrs. Marchand, we've been way down that road already. The entire city turned itself upside down looking for her. For all we know, she ran off with someone. Or she's dead. Of course, we all hope that's not the case, but I don't see how there's anything else any of us can do. It's time to put that sad business behind us."

"Ginny Evans is not dead, Mr. Crump, and I believe she's close by."

"And why do you believe that, Mrs. Marchand?"

Nell hesitated and gripped the arms of her chair. "I sense it, Mr. Crump. I know in my heart that she's alive and that we just can't give up now when we're so close."

"I see. Ah, yes, of course. You're a fortuneteller, aren't you? I'd heard something about that from my wife and her friends. You're practicing as some kind of psychic medium."

The glower of which Nell was now the beneficiary was decidedly darker than the glare Crump had visited on Calendar.

Crump was calling her a liar, and part of her couldn't blame him. She took a deep breath and went on. "Yes, sir."

"And did the spirit of Ginny Evans come to you in a trance?"

"As a matter of fact, she did."

Crump now looked at her the way a patient parent looks at a slow child who asks where the moon goes in the morning. He leaned back in his chair. "Mrs. Marchand, I knew your father-in-law and your husband. They were great friends of mine. Your daddy and I might not always have seen eye to eye, but I had nothing but respect for your family. I cannot, however, see how we can commit any more of the resources of this city looking for a lost girl because you claim you saw her in some kind of dream. There are too many other people who deserve our help and concern. We've done everything we can."

"You think I'm a fool."

"I can attest to the fact that Mrs. Marchand is remarkably gifted, Mr. Crump," Calendar said. "I'm sure you don't mean to make light of her abilities."

"I know exactly what Mr. Crump means," she said, leaning toward him. "You think I'm some kind of ninny who imagines things and has nothing better to do that chase after phantoms. Or you think I'm crazy. Well, I'm here to tell you that I'm neither, Mr. Crump. I saw Ginny Evans just as clearly as I see you sitting before me now. Believe me, it's not easy to say that because I know what you think, but she is in trouble. Someone has to help her before it's too late."

"And you know where she is."

"Well, no, but I'm sure it's just a matter of time before we do."

Tapping his fingertips together, Crump studied Nell. Just as she thought he might be about to relent, his lips drew back in a reptilian smile that left the rest of his face unmoved. Nell shivered. He rose from his chair and offered her his hand to dismiss her.

"I'm sorry. If you insist on looking for this girl in spite of everything, then I'm afraid there's nothing I can do for you. People will finally have proof that you are just as crazy as a loon. Especially if word of your vision leaks out somehow. None of us want that, now do we? I think you should stick to reading palms at ladies' teas."

Oh, Lord, how she wanted to slap him for that. Haul off and send those stupid spectacles flying across the room and wipe that superior smirk off his face. People might very well believe she was crazy, unless she found Ginny. Might even when she did, but she would just have to risk that. Ladies' teas, her left hind toenail. Somehow, she managed to keep her voice even and rose without touching his hand.

"When I find Ginny Evans, Mr. Crump, I'll remind you of what you said to me today."

"If you do find her, Mrs. Marchand, then that's exactly what you should do. I'm always glad to see an old friend."

Old friend, ha! He made it clear just how little friendship she could count on.

"Meanwhile, I hope you'll excuse me." Crump opened his office door. "I'm expecting a call from Cordell Hull any minute now and am not about to keep the new secretary of state of the United States waiting. Thank you for coming by. Good to see you, Anton."

He held out his hand to Calendar, who shook it.

"Mr. Crump," Calendar said. He grasped Nell's elbow and pushed her out of the office, down the hall, and onto the street. Once there, Nell exploded.

"That arrogant old jackass!"

"Going against him could be dangerous."

"You mean he's going to send his thugs to throw me around if I don't stop?" Nell stood, feet planted and hands on her hips. "You don't really believe that, do you, Joseph?"

Calendar took on the grave look of a doctor telling a patient that she has only a few months to live. "It wouldn't be the first time he's dropped a hint about wishing he were rid of someone the same way Henry II wished to be rid of Thomas Becket. If you will remember your English history, that didn't end well for the Reverend Becket. Crump would never let on that he had anything to do with it, not even to himself. No one would be able to trace it back to him, but your house might burn down mysteriously. Some of his cronies might pay you an unfriendly visit. Or Miss Bess or Hattie. I'd hate to see any of you get a beating . . . or something worse."

"Good Lord, Joseph." Nell grabbed at his arm. "He wouldn't dare."

"I just want you to understand that this is serious business. Remember what happened to Lois Brown."

Nell suddenly felt like Horatius with the Etruscans storming the bridge. She suppressed a shiver. "Ginny Evans is out there somewhere waiting. I've got to find her."

"We'll have to be very quiet about Crump."

"Crump is the one picking a fight. Not me. I'm perfectly happy to let him go on governing all of Tennessee, or the rest of the dadgum world if he wants it. He should show me the same courtesy and let me look for Ginny." She stopped Calendar before he could protest. "All right. I'll be quiet, and he shouldn't have anything to complain about. It's not as though I were pointing my finger at him and accusing him of abandoning her."

"That's probably how he sees it."

"Well, there's nothing I can do about that." Nell tapped her chin with an index finger. "If there's any way I can use the law to help me, Anton will know. We can still count on him. Now that I've seen where she is, maybe I can describe it well enough for someone to recognize it."

"I don't think the Good Lord himself could compel the Memphis Police Department to help you at this point. They're in Boss Crump's pocket."

"I'm not talking about the Memphis police. What about all the little towns around Memphis? Couldn't Anton call and say you're Ginny's attorney and that you've got to find her?"

"I imagine at least some of those sheriffs read the Memphis papers."

"It's worth a try. Maybe there's some kind of federal statute or something that he can invoke. Or I'll call myself, say I'm his secretary or something."

"Mr. Green isn't going to like it."

"He doesn't have to like it. He just has to do as I ask."

Chapter 32

When E. H. Crump closed the door on something, it stayed closed.

The society ladies who had been her regular clients stopped coming to Nell's salon for consultations. At the First Methodist Church, the usher seated her on the back pew off to the side instead of the fourth in the middle where the Marchands always sat. Not even her regular girl at Lowenstein's would take her calls. They way things were going, they might have to take in laundry again, something Nell didn't want for any of them.

"I don't understand it, Miss Bess." Nell dug through Bess's sewing basket and passed her the black thread she had asked for. "You'd think I was trying to pass off blue john as whole milk for orphans."

"Going against Ed Crump wasn't the wisest thing to do in Memphis," Bess said. "He's let it be known that he's unhappy with you."

"But I'm not going against him." Nell couldn't help the fretful tone that crept into her voice.

Bess put her sewing aside. "My dear, why don't I take us for an ice cream? We can talk about how to entice people to see you again. Go back to the way things were, and I'm sure the girls in the bridge club will be glad to come back. Why in time, you'll be just as busy as you ever were. Everything will go back to normal."

"Thank you, Mother." Nell tried but could not manage a smile. Even her mother-in-law was taking Crump's side.

Bess hugged her. "Of course, my dear. And afterward, let's go see Dr. Calendar, shall we? With him standing by you, his friends must certainly be willing to consult with you. And they may have other, more discreet methods of inquiry that you haven't tried yet. There's more than one way to skin a cat, you know."

Maybe Bess Marchand wasn't afraid of the game after all.

—

THE BUZZER AT MILDRED'S DOOR WAS INSISTENT. WHY DIDN'T THAT idiot maid get it? She was going to fire the lazy, no-account girl in the morning and demand they send a replacement. It shouldn't be so hard to find good help, especially with a Depression on. Seven o'clock. Dammit, Franklin was early, and she wasn't ready yet. She'd told him to pick her up at 8. Punctuality was one thing, but being overeager was decidedly unattractive. She might have to punish him by forbidding him to see her for a day or two. It wouldn't hurt him to feel a little desperate. She pasted on her most-welcoming smile and opened the door.

Benny? What in the hell was he doing here?

"Surprised?" He thrust an elaborate bouquet at her.

"What are you doing in Memphis?"

He stopped half way to the smooch he was about to plant on her. "Aren't you glad to see me, Mildred?"

"Well, of course, I am, but we talked about this. You should have told me you were coming. You're supposed to be up at Harvard studying hard to make your mama proud."

"Why? Are you expecting someone else? If you're seeing another man, I swear, I'll break his neck."

She dragged him through the door, took the flowers, and let him kiss her before she wagged a finger at him. "Benny, I've told you that I don't like jealous men. I'm going to supper with some friends, that's all."

"Call them up and tell them something better came up."

"You know I'm not going to do that." Mildred took the flowers into the kitchen, grabbed a vase off the top of the icebox, and filled it with water. She gave the flowers a little shake so they fell just so and put the vase on the kitchen table. "I do have a life when you're not here, and I've never been the kind of girl who throws her friends over for a man. Besides, you wouldn't want me to do something like that to you, would you?"

"I guess not, but I don't like it."

"Then don't show up at my door unannounced. I'm happy you're in Memphis, of course, but these are old friends of mine. I'm not about to disappoint them." Mildred dragged Benny to the door, opened it, and motioned for him to step out. "Toddle along to your aunt's house. I bet you can keep her company. Call me tomorrow. We can make plans together."

"You're sure you're not stepping out with another man?"

"Cross my heart and hope to die."

"All right. But tomorrow, it's just you and me, Mildred. Understand?"

"Yes, darling. Tomorrow, I'm all yours. Now, run along."

"Give us a kiss first." He ran his hand up and down her arm.

"All right. Just one, though. And don't muss my hair." Mildred allowed Benny to peck her on the lips before she shoved him into the hallway, closed the door behind the big idiot, and leaned against it. That was probably the closest call she'd ever had. It would be just her luck to come face to face with Benny while she was out with his uncle. Maybe it was time to let the boy down easy. Tell him she knew it could never work out and that it was time for them to go their separate ways. She'd find some way to make him believe it was his idea. She always did.

Mildred tossed Benny's flowers into the trash, emptied the vase, and returned it to its perch. Keeping everything straight sure did get complicated though.

—

BY THE TIME FRANKLIN ARRIVED AT 8, MILDRED HAD HER PLAN IN place. No sense taking a chance of running into Benny.

"Franklin, darling, I'm afraid I have a bit of a headache. Would you mind terribly if we go somewhere quiet tonight? I don't think I'm up to the crowds at the Galindo or the Skyway. Let's find some quiet, intimate place where nobody knows us. Won't that be romantic?"

"Of course, Mildred. If you don't feel up to going out, though, I can have supper sent to us. The chef at the Galindo is a friend of mine."

She leaned wearily against his shoulder. "Would you be disappointed if we do stay in? We can build a fire in the fireplace and pretend that we're newlyweds on our honeymoon at some romantic lodge in the French Alps. That would be fun, wouldn't it? I've given the maid the night off, so it will be just the two of us, all alone."

"That sounds wonderful. I'll arrange for our supper."

"You are the most thoughtful man in the world. Let me take your jacket. Shall I pour you a drink?"

Two lobsters, fresh asparagus, two Caesar salads, and a berry-drenched pavlova later, Mildred snuggled against Franklin in front of the fire. "Isn't this nice, Franklin? It really is as though we were married. Sometimes, I wish we could be."

"Mildred–"

She stopped him with a kiss. When the old buzzard started snorting like a winded mule, she pulled back and looked dreamily up at him. "It's all right, darling. I know you'll never leave your wife. I would never ask you to. You're too honorable. It's one of the many reasons I love you." She leaned her head on his shoulder. "This is enough for me. Really it is. If I can just have you all to myself every now and then, well, I can't ask for any greater happiness than that."

"You're a remarkable girl, Mildred. I don't believe I've ever known anyone as selfless as you. I'm a lucky man."

"Yes, you are. And don't you forget it. Now, would you like a little more champagne? You know I'm not going to drink the rest of this bottle by myself, and it would be a crime to waste it."

"Later. Right now, I have something else on my mind."

In the most masculine way he knew how, Franklin Bryant crushed Mildred to him. She yielded as only she knew how. The champagne was on ice and could wait. Besides, there would be plenty more where that bottle came from. Franklin would keep her in all the champagne and caviar she could swallow and would wrap her in fine furs and festoon her with jewels. And best of all, he would thank her for the opportunity to do it. They always thanked Mildred.

CHAPTER 33

Nell's team, as she had begun to think of them, gathered in the Spirit Room to discuss strategy. Only Hattie was missing, having taken herself off to confer with Aunt Mary.

"We should wait a few more days, let Mr. Crump believe he has quashed our efforts for good," Calendar said, taking a glass of sherry after Simon had served Nell and Miss Bess.

"Let's start with the last places we know she was," Nell said. "Luther said the police talked to the speakeasy owner and the woman at the boarding house but that they didn't know anything. I want to go to them myself. Maybe they'll be more forthcoming with me. Not everyone is comfortable talking to the police, especially not a speakeasy owner."

"You're not going to any of those places alone," Calendar said. "I'm coming with you. I am quite practiced in uncovering what people haven't said."

"I'm sure that proves useful in all kinds of situations." Nell grinned at him, a little ashamed of herself for being so relieved that he insisted on accompanying her.

ROY MERTZ WAS BEHIND THE BAR OF HIS SPEAKEASY HIMSELF, POLISHING glasses and counting his stock.

"What can I do for you folks?" he said.

"We've come about Ginny Evans," Nell said, puzzled that she didn't recognize the place from her first visions. She checked the address in her hand again, crumpled it, and did her best to sound assured. "We know she worked here."

"Y'all are just about to wear me out asking about that girl," Mertz said, dropping his rag and leaning both hands on top of the bar. "I told the po-leece I don't know nothing about what happened to Ginny after she left here."

"We're so sorry to disturb you like this." Nell smiled brilliantly, careful to season it with apology and regret. "If you could just answer a question or two, there might be something that could help us find her."

Mertz wiped the bar in front of them. "All right. Have a seat. Can I get you folks a drink? I've got iced tea if the lady would prefer it."

"Tea sounds wonderful, Mr. . . ," Nell held out her hand to Mertz, and he took it.

"Mertz. My name's Roy Mertz, ma'am."

"I'm Nell Marchand, and this is Dr. Joseph Calendar."

"Nell Marchand?" He squinted at her and dug his teeth briefly into his lower lip. "You the lady that started this whole thing about looking for Ginny?"

"The very same," Nell said.

"I'll have those teas for you lickety-split." Mertz took two tumblers from under the bar and went to fill them with ice.

"What do you think?" Nell said out of the side of her mouth to Calendar.

"He knows more than he's telling. He cared about Ginny, was possibly in love with her."

"How on earth can you tell that much from half a minute of conversation?"

"I don't usually reveal my trade secrets, but since you're a fellow adept, I'll make an exception."

Nell wrinkled her nose at him.

He smiled. “Watch the eyes. When people are interested or reacting emotionally, their pupils enlarge. The courtesans of Venice used drops of belladonna to dilate their pupils. Unconsciously, their clients read that as sexual excitement and responded, believing themselves more virile.”

“The things you know amaze me, Joseph.” Nell nudged him with her shoulder. “Did you experience this first hand?”

“I have never resorted to a courtesan, although I have counted many among my friends. The practice was prevalent in Renaissance Venice.”

Mertz returned with the two glasses of tea brimming with chipped ice and topped with sprigs of mint. “My old granny loved mint in her tea,” he said, placing a glass in front of Nell first. “Mint and lots of sugar. That’s how I always make it for myself, too. I hope you like it.”

Nell took a tentative sip. “It’s heaven, Mr. Mertz. Thank you.” She waited for Mertz to settle himself on a stool behind the bar.

“Now,” she said, “please tell us everything you know about Ginny Evans.”

“Like what? There’s not that much to tell, Mrs. Marchand.”

“How long did she work here?”

“A month or two. She was a good waitress while she worked for me, and then she was gone. That’s all there is to it.”

“That doesn’t seem very long if she did a good job, as you say.”

“She came here looking for work as a singer. She was pretty good, but I didn’t tell her that.” He glanced down at the bar, shook his head, and looked back at Nell. “I told her she sounded like somebody squeezing a cat.”

“Why, Mr. Mertz?” Nell said.

“Because that’s what they all want. They been to the pictures. They got these big ideas that singing is their ticket out. They don’t want to be maids like their mamas or farmers’ wives. They don’t want dirt under their nails from anything.”

Mertz reached behind him, took down a bottle of whiskey, poured himself a drink, and threw it back. "There's a hundred, a thousand who end up in cheap dives working for peanuts. Excuse me for saying this, ma'am, but a lot of them end up working as whores. Ginny was a nice girl. I didn't want to see any of that happening to her. I gave her a job as a waitress so I could keep an eye on her. Poor kid." He tossed back another shot of whiskey. "She looked so fresh and clean, coming in here that first day."

"That was very generous."

Mertz shrugged. "Nobody ever called me generous, Mrs. Marchand. I just took a shine to Ginny. She was something special. A lot of girls, they're always out for something, but Ginny wasn't like that. She was a sweet girl. A real sweet girl."

"Still, she didn't stay here long," Calendar said.

"No. One of the other girls working here put a lot of ideas in her head. Made her change her looks. Bleached her hair, plucked her eyebrows. Told Ginny she was a dead ringer for Jean Harlow. Now, I like Jean Harlow as much as the next red-blooded American man, but she's got nothing on Ginny. That girl was beautiful."

"This was Lois Brown you're talking about?" Nell said.

"Yeah. How'd you know about Lois?

"She tried to pass herself off as Ginny, though how she expected to get away with it, I can't imagine. That's how the police found this place, Mr. Mertz. Didn't they tell you? Lois said she and Ginny worked here together, that Ginny was her friend."

"Well, I'll be damned. Oh, excuse me, Mrs. Marchand." Mertz returned the whiskey bottle to the shelf behind him. "It's just that I never figured Lois for doing anybody any favors. Remember what I said about girls who was out for all they could get? Lois was one of them. Hard as nails, she was, but too dim to pull off any of her schemes. Went after some society boy, thought she'd get her hooks into him. Got herself knocked up—excuse my language again, ma'am, and I'm sorry for bringing up something like this in front of a lady—and when she told him, he disappeared faster than a deadbeat on rent day. This may not be the Peabody, but I try to run a respectable place. I feel sorry for that kid, having Lois as its mother."

"She gave the baby up, Mr. Mertz," Nell said. "Left it at the orphanage."

Mertz picked up another bar rag and began absently wiping out more glasses. "Well, I'm telling you, the baby's better off. Lois wouldn't know what maternal instinct was if it hit her over the head."

"Lois is dead," Calendar said.

Mertz dropped the rag and leaned against the bar. "Dead? Well, damn me. What happened to her?"

"They fished her out of the river. The report in the paper said that she jumped off the bridge and drowned. A suicide."

Something flickered across Mertz's face. Nell glanced at Calendar to see if he had caught it, too. He had not taken his eyes from Mertz.

"Does that surprise you?" Calendar said.

"Jesus, I never took her for that kind of girl. Tougher than that. Hard as nails, like I said."

"Do you think perhaps someone killed her?"

A chill swept over Nell, and she rubbed her arms to fight it off.

Mertz shrugged, wouldn't meet Calendar's eye. "Oh, I don't know. Maybe she tried one angle too many, and I can guarantee you that she tried them all. Must have tried one on the wrong guy." He stopped, apparently lost in thought.

Nell and Calendar waited.

"Anyway, like I was saying," Mertz went on, reaching for another glass to shine. "Lois takes Ginny and turns her into this platinum blonde. But inside, Ginny's the same sweet girl from the Mississippi sticks. I can see, though, that she's eating her heart out, wanting to be a singer. She just won't let go of it. So, finally I decide if that's what she really wants, then, I'm going to help her. This fellow I know hangs out over at Kelly's over on Beale tells me they're looking for a girl singer to front the coon band that plays there. I tell Ginny, and next thing I know, she's got the job."

"Did you go hear her sing there, Mr. Mertz?" Calendar said.

For what seemed like forever, the barman paused in polishing the glass in his hand before he put it down carefully. "Just once. I couldn't take it after that."

"Why not?" Nell said.

"Because she was the class in that joint, but nobody was listening to her. It was going to wear her down, I could see it. She already had this look in her eyes, you know, that people get when they find out that what they dreamed about maybe ain't all that great. I tried to talk her into coming back to my place, but it was no dice. I never went back."

"And you never spoke with her again?" Calendar said.

"No. If she was going to turn into a tramp, I didn't want to have to watch. You want to know what happened to her, go talk to the boys at Kelly's."

"Did you tell the police any of this?" Calendar said.

"Are you kidding? And get Blackjack Kelly on my back? I figure Ginny is dead or in some whorehouse. Either way, it's better nobody finds her."

"But her family would want to know, Mr. Mertz," Nell said. "Didn't you think about them?"

"No. What do you want to break their hearts for? She was never going back to that farm anyway. They're better off forgetting."

Nell pushed her glass away from her. "I see. That is for them to decide, don't you think, Mr. Mertz? Thank you for the tea and for your time."

Mertz took Nell's glass and dumped it into the bucket of swill at his feet. He wiped out the glass with the cloth and set it back under the bar. Nell and Calendar rose to go. They were halfway to the door when Mertz spoke again. He didn't look up, his eyes on the next glass.

"If you do find Ginny Evans, Mrs. Marchand, tell her she can still come back whenever she wants. It don't matter where's she's been or what she's done. Tell her Roy Mertz always has a place for her."

—

FROM THE CORNER OF THE BUILDING ACROSS THE STREET FROM MERTZ'S place, Little Nick watched the Duesenberg pull away. He dug his quarter from his pocket, and strolled in the direction of Kelly's, flipping the coin as he went.

CHAPTER 34

Jenkins was driving back to the Marchand house. At first, Nell and Calendar rode in silence, digesting what they had heard.

"Did you see Mertz's face when you told him about Lois Brown?" Nell said finally breaking it. "Do you think he knows something about what happened to her?"

"I'm sure he knows it wasn't suicide," Calendar said.

"Do you think he knows it had something to do with Ginny?"

"Possibly. The news shocked him, but he wasn't about to tell us that. He has an idea who killed Lois, and he's afraid."

"If that's love, Joseph, I never want any part of it."

"I think Mertz honestly tried to help the girl, but he didn't know how. He probably loved her as best he could in his own way. His story reminds me of Beauty and the Beast, only this time, Beauty didn't stay around long enough to transform the Beast."

"Why, you're a romantic, Joseph."

"Guilty as charged."

They fell silent again, but Nell peered at Calendar out of the corner of her eye. "Have you ever been in love, Joseph?"

"I have tried to afford myself that luxury as little as possible."

"Love is a luxury?"

Pensive, almost melancholy, Calendar regarded her. Nell clenched her fists in her lap to keep from reaching out to touch his face.

"For some, it is," he said. "For me. I've always felt that my mind should be clear, my heart unencumbered. Would it be presumptuous of me to ask if you loved your husband, Nell?"

Nell stared out the window of the Duesenberg, watching but not seeing the streetscapes they passed. She thought about herself and Ellis and wondered how to answer Calendar's question. A sudden, shocking urge to weep swept over her—she hadn't cried over Ellis Marchand in years—but was gone again before she could blink or reach for her handkerchief. She sighed deeply and spoke, not looking away from the window.

"From the time I was a little girl, I worshipped Ellis Marchand. He was 10 years older, you know, and the first time I remember seeing him, he came to a dinner party at the house with his parents. I think he must have been at Yale by then. I was dazzled in the way little girls are with their first crushes. I thought he was the most dashing man who ever lived.

"I was always afraid that he would marry someone else before I was old enough, so every night, I started my prayers by asking God to make him wait for me. When he finally did notice me, I was studying at Southwestern. He asked if he could take me to the movies. I thought I had died and gone to heaven."

She faced Calendar, and the fierce hurt in her eyes shot through his heart so hard that he almost gasped aloud. If he could have, he would have kissed that and every other grief she'd ever known away. Instead, he listened as Nell went on.

"My grandmother tried hard to get me not to marry him. She said Ellis wasn't everything I thought he was, but I wouldn't hear it. Hattie tried to tell me, too. I was determined to have him, though, and we were happy for a little bit. A very little. By the time I understood that they were right, I hated him."

"I'm sorry, Nell. Why didn't you leave him?"

Her wry smile sent another pang, worse than the first, clear through him.

"Because by then, I had no one else. My mama and daddy died in the influenza epidemic when I was a child. Mared Blayney reared me. But she was gone then, too, and I was alone, except for Hattie, of course.

"Anyway, there were still benefits to being Mrs. Ellis Marchand. I had a comfortable life. Half the women in Memphis envied me. The ones who knew better gave me their sympathy, whether I wanted it or not. It was just easier to go on as we had been, playing the part of the happy couple when it was important, and, when it wasn't, being at least civil to each other."

"And then, he died."

"Yes, and then he died. Suddenly, there was no money. He'd lost it all. I had to find a way to support myself and Miss Bess and Hattie and Jenkins. You know all that." Now, Nell's smile was ironic. "I thought telling fortunes would be fun. If I'd had any idea on earth what would happen, I would never in this world have done it."

Calendar took Nell's hand and squeezed it. "You're very brave, Nell, whether you realize it or not. And you're not alone. Whatever you may think, you're not alone. You have many friends. I am honored that I am one of them. And one day, I'm sure you will find the right man to love, someone who will be capable of loving you as much as you do him. That is what I wish for you."

"Thank you, Joseph," Nell said. She squeezed his hand in return, pulled hers gently from his, and turned to look out the window again. He wanted to reach for her again but didn't let himself. "I don't have time for love either. You're right about unencumbered hearts. They're the best kind to have. I can't imagine ever marrying again. I think I'll stick with being wed to my gift, as you call it. I don't want to have to put up with anything else again."

And that struck straight at his heart, too.

CHAPTER 35

It was day of the annual benefit for the Crippled Children's Hospital, and the Peabody ballroom was awash in Memphis society.

Months before Ellis died, Nell had agreed to chair the luncheon. She might no longer be society's darling or able to lead the way with an eye-popping donation, but she could still organize and encourage others to reach deep into their pockets, even in these hard times. In fact, she pointed out, the hospital had taken on more patients than ever before, and the children needed them.

Bess and her bridge and garden clubs pitched in to arrange the seating. Hattie advised her on the menu. The hotel had done them proud, placing centerpieces of pink roses and tiny white crutches at each table. With the program about to start. Nell and Bess were at the door directing the late arrivals to their tables. The black cloud Boss Crump had put over Nell had lifted somewhat, and most of the crowd greeted her as though most of her transgressions had been forgotten.

"I don't believe my eyes," Nell said, gazing out over the gathering. "Miss Bess, pinch me. I'm either having a nightmare, or I have gone completely crazy."

"What is it, my dear?" Bess said.

"Look over there. Isn't that Franklin Bryant with Mildred Epps?"

"Good heavens, you're right. What on earth can he be thinking?"

"I don't know, but I'm going over there to find out."

Nell marched up to Franklin's table and stuck her face in Mildred's. "What do you think you're doing here?"

Mildred simply smiled.

"Mrs. Marchand, do you know my friend, Miss Mildred Epps?" Franklin stood to introduce them. "Miss Epps, Mrs. Marchand."

"Oh, I've had the displeasure, all right," Nell said. "What I want to know though, Franklin, is if you know her."

"I'm not sure I understand what you mean, Miss Nell. Miss Epps is a friend of the family. Margaret didn't feel up to coming to the benefit today. It seemed a shame to let her ticket go to waste. Miss Epps was kind enough to come in her place and keep me company."

Nell turned on him. "My goodness, wasn't that generous of her? This is Ellis's mistress, Franklin. You know, the mysterious blonde who phoned the police when he dropped dead because she happened to be right there under him when he did. I know why Ellis got mixed up with her, but you . . . . I would have thought you had more sense that to let this gold-digging little tramp get her claws into you."

Franklin puffed himself up like a Mississippi bullfrog. "I don't believe I like your tone, Mrs. Marchand."

Nell moved around to his side of the table and stood before him, hands on her hips. "This is Mildred Epps of the West Memphis Guttersnipe Eppses, Franklin. Bar hostess and professional party girl. I don't know what kind of baloney she's been handing you, but she was Ellis Marchand's mistress and who knows who else's before him. She makes a habit of hornswoggling rich old jackasses like you. Ask her."

Mildred rose and hooked her arm through the old idiot's. She never took her eyes off Nell. "Franklin, I've told you there are things in my past that I'm not proud of. When Mama and Papa died, I was left all alone. I found my way as best I could, and, yes, sometimes I accepted gifts from gentlemen."

"Is it true what she says about Ellis Marchand? Did he keep you?"

Gazing up at Franklin, Mildred was all wronged innocence and remorse. "Yes, I knew him." She let her eyes drop demurely. "He was very kind to me when I needed a friend."

Nell snorted. "And you were very, very kind to him in return, weren't you, Mildred? Listen, Franklin. You remember the story in the papers about Ellis dying quietly at home, loving wife and mother by his side? Well, it was a lie intended to spare Miss Bess's feelings. He was really in a room here at the Peabody in bed with our little Mildred here. She's a cold-blooded, scheming, shameless hussy. I bet she even went through Ellis's pockets before she called the police to tell them he was dead."

By turns, Franklin went fish-belly white and beet red. He grabbed Mildred by the shoulders. Nell was just waiting to enjoy the spectacle of him shaking the life out of her. The other guests at the table had all gone silent after the first mention of the word "mistress." That silence rippled through the room in widening circles until it seemed everyone was caught up in enthralled anticipation.

"Is this true?" Franklin said.

Mildred looked up at him again, wide-eyed. She placed her hands over his wrists tentatively, her lower lip trembling ever so slightly. "She makes it sound so ugly, Franklin. So cheap. But it wasn't that way at all. Yes, Ellis Marchand was my special friend, but she's wrong about our relationship. Ellis truly cared for me, and I for him. We never meant to hurt anybody. Can't you forgive me for a young girl's foolish mistake? It has nothing to do with what we have now, with how I feel about you."

"Young?" Nell said. "Have mercy, Franklin Bryant, I can't believe you're standing there listening to all this hogwash. She'll lie as soon as look at you. Are you going to throw your wife and family away for this?"

Franklin let his arms drop to his sides. Mildred watched him. He wore the expression of someone a mule had just kicked square in the forehead. Nell half expected him to fall over backward. She had to admit that Mildred was good, very good. If she hadn't known better, she would have believed the harlot's story herself. Men were idiots.

"Why don't you ask to see the official police report?" Nell said. "It will tell you exactly where Ellis died and who was with him."

"I don't need to do that," Franklin said.

"If you're that big a fool, then I pity you."

Nell stomped off to find Bess. The murmurs that had started as she marched away gradually swelled into a buzz and had become a soft roar by the time she reached her.

"What on earth happened, Nell?" Bess said, breathless.

"Well, I told him, but I don't think he believes me. She'll suck him dry and then toss the husk aside when she's ready for the next one. I don't understand it, Miss Bess. Why would someone like Franklin Bryant let himself be taken in by a man-eater like Mildred Epps? Can't he see her for what she is? Can't anyone?"

Bess pulled a chair out for Nell and settled her in it before she took the one next to it herself. She paused, no doubt rummaging for the most genteel way to phrase her answer. "Men are wonderful at looking the other way until they've persuaded themselves of what it is that they want to believe, Nell. He's not the first old fool who has wanted to think that a pretty young thing could find him desirable. It lets him feel young again too, at least for as long as the affair lasts."

Nell gasped. "Don't tell me the Judge ever–"

"No! No, good heavens, of course not. I never had to worry about that with my Daniel."

"But Franklin's throwing away everything. I like Margaret Bryant, and I can't stand seeing her humiliated like this."

"I don't know. I suspect that Margaret will take him back when the time comes. Society wives are also good at looking the other way as long as they can keep their homes intact."

"Don't I know it."

"Oh, my dear, I'm sorry. I didn't mean that you–"

"It's all right, Mother. That's exactly what I did. I let Ellis run around and make a fool of me all over town just so I could go on being a Marchand. I'm surprised Franklin didn't remind me that I was the pot calling the tea kettle black. I bet Margaret has more backbone than I did."

"I'm sorry my son made you so unhappy, my dear Nell. I'm not sure how the Judge and I went wrong, but we shouldn't have allowed it. I shouldn't have, anyway. At least while the Judge was alive, Ellis did keep up a pretense of being a proper husband and son."

Mildred appeared suddenly behind them. "Your son wasn't as bad as you make him out to be, Mrs. Marchand. Maybe he was a little weak, but a lot of people are that way."

"Where's Franklin?" Nell screeched her chair back and jumped to her feel. "Did he finally come to his senses and leave you to streetwalk home?"

"He's fetching my coat, the dear lamb." Smirking, Mildred stood her ground. "You gave him quite a turn back there, but I think I smoothed it over. You shouldn't worry. I'll give him back to old Prune-puss when I'm done with him, and he'll be none the worse for wear. She may even thank me for teaching the old boy a few new things. But not just yet. I'm getting to like him."

"You are unbelievable," Nell said.

"You know, you ought to give me a chance," Mildred said. "You might find out that I'm not so bad. We could still be friends. I bet we could find a way to help each other if we just put our minds to it."

Nell grunted, which was more ladylike than uttering the vulgar retort that sprang to her lips.

Mildred shook her head. "Suit yourself, but if you ever need help finding something you're looking for, I might be just the girl who can do it."

Franklin came up behind Mildred, a mink coat draped over his arm. "I think we should go, Mildred."

Mildred reached back her hands. He slipped the coat up her arms and around her shoulders. "I'm ready, Franklin. I just wanted to thank the Mrs. Marchands for a lovely afternoon. I don't know when I've enjoyed myself more. Remember, if I can ever return the favor, let me know."

Franklin managed nothing more than a nod to Nell and Bess before he trotted off after Mildred.

"What an odd young woman," Bess said. "She seems to have no shame whatsoever."

Nell looked after Mildred and Franklin as they made their way through the crowd. "She's something, all right."

"And she seems so insistent on ingratiating herself with you."

"I know. I wonder what her game is? If I were someone's mistress, the wronged wife is the last person in the world I would want to chum around with."

Bess wriggled in distress and whispered to Nell behind her hand. "Do you think we ought to tell Margaret what her husband is up to?"

"Lord, no, Mother," Nell said, patting her. "I think there are plenty of people here who will be willing to do just that. Some of them are probably at the pay phones right now. Besides, everyone was always so eager to tell me about Ellis's latest exploits, and it was awful. Let Franklin Bryant work that out himself. I wish Joseph had been here to read Mildred Epps, though. I can't tell if she knows something or if she's just trying to get my goat."

Chapter 36

"Why did you never tell me you knew Ellis Marchand?" Franklin said in the car on the way back to Mildred's apartment.

The old boy didn't sound jealous exactly, but something was up. Maybe Nell Marchand had messed everything up for her after all. Mildred decided to go on with the lamb-returning-to-the-fold act. Appeal to his forgiving Christian nature.

"That's all in the past, so there's no reason I should have, Franklin. I've told you, I'm with you now. But I was about to ask you the same thing. What was he, one of your golf buddies?"

Something must be sticking in the old goat's throat the way he kept clearing it before he answered. Maybe he was jealous. Let's face it. Ellis Marchand had been a hundred times better looking. And younger. It might take something extra special to get back in Franklin's graces.

"A client. A friend, too, of course, but I've handled the Marchand finances for years, first with the Judge and then with Ellis, who was, I'm afraid, not as wise in the way he safeguarded his money."

"You don't say. You were Ellis's banker, then."

"I was."

Mildred scooted away from Franklin and stared out at the sky where it winked in and out of view between the taller downtown buildings as they passed.

"You're upset about what happened today, aren't you?" He reached for her hand.

She didn't answer.

"Mildred?"

She pulled herself out of her reverie and sneered. "What? Oh, those two holier-than-thous? Are you kidding? As long as you believe and trust me, I couldn't care less what they think about me. Or what anyone else thinks, for that matter."

"I'm sorry our afternoon was spoiled."

"Not at all, Franklin." Mildred let him take her hand but didn't snuggle back into her accustomed spot right up against him as he drove. "It was quite an interesting outing. I just have a headache, that's all. Would you mind terribly not coming up with me? I'm going to take an aspirin and go straight to bed."

"If that's what you wish, darling, I wouldn't think of imposing myself on you. I'll escort you to your door, of course."

"Thank you. You're always so understanding."

At the door, Franklin tried to pull her into a big kiss, but she pushed against his chin and turned her face away. "Please, Franklin."

"Are you sure you're all right, Mildred? You really mustn't let what happened today distress you. We've put that behind us now."

"I'm just feeling a little unwell, and I want to be alone."

"All right, then. I'll call in the morning to see how you're doing."

Mildred closed the door and went to her window to look down at the street. Below, she watched Franklin emerge and glance up at her window before he climbed into his blue DeSoto sedan and drove away. Long after he had disappeared from view, she stood like that, watching the street below, resting her forehead against the pane and remembering.

If Ellis was going to leave a juicy, gorgeous hunk of steak sitting on his plate like that, she sure wasn't going to let it go to waste. Mildred reached her fork across and speared it. She grinned before she cut off a big bite and popped it into her mouth. He didn't even notice.

"Hey, how come you're all down in the mouth tonight, sugar?" Mildred said around the meat. "You haven't smiled at me all night, and you're about to hurt my feelings. Ellis?"

Nothing. He really was off somewhere else in his head. She poked him with the back of the hand that held her fork before she sliced off another chunk of meat. "Yoo-hoo! Remember me?"

He started and looked at her as though he didn't know who she was.

"Got some bad news today, Mildred."

"I'm sorry, sugar. Bad bad? One of your dogs lose at the track?"

"I wish it were something that simple. No, I talked to my banker today. It seems I'm flat, dead broke."

Mildred laughed and nudged him with her elbow. "Broke? You can't be. You told me yourself that you've got more money than Rockefeller."

"I thought I did."

Mildred put down her knife and fork and swallowed the bite she'd been chewing. "Wait a minute. You're not kidding, are you?"

"Wish I were."

"What happened to all of it?"

"It seems that my trusty banker had a run-in with some of his shadier clients. He mishandled their investments, found out more than once when they came to withdraw big hunks of it that he didn't have enough to cover their withdrawals. He's been taking the Marchand family trust to pay them off. The old skunk let me down. I can't believe it, especially after what I've done for him lately."

All of a sudden, that steak tasted like sawdust going down. "But he can't get away with that! You've got to get that money back. Go to the police or the mayor or somebody."

"I'm afraid I can't do that, Mildred. You see, I was a partner in handling these particular investments. If I blow the whistle now, as the popular expression goes, he'll expose me, too."

"So what? A little scandal can't hurt you. I thought you were used to it."

"That kind of scandal is nothing compared to what could happen, honey. If he exposes me, then the whole operation with our hoodlum friends comes crashing down as well. That would make them very unhappy, which could be particularly unhealthy for him and for me. I'm in a great big old mess, you see, and I don't think there's any way out."

Mildred put her knife and fork down and thought. "So, what are you going to do?"

"I'm not sure I've got any choice. I think I'm going to have to go to the police and hope that fessing up keeps me out of jail, gets me some protection. I don't think I'm going to enjoy being ruined, though."

An Ellis Marchand with no money was quite a different critter from the one with oodles and truckloads of it. Ordinarily, this would be the signal for her to stand up, say, "Thanks, it's been swell," and walk out.

But what do you know, she didn't feel like walking. Instead, she felt bad for Ellis, felt something that must be pity although it was hard to know for sure because it was an emotion she'd never experienced before. And then, Lord God Jesus Christ, she realized she felt something else that was much, much worse. She realized that she loved the damn fool.

"Aw, don't worry, sugar. There's always a way out. We just have to find it." She kissed him and patted his arm.

He blinked at her, astounded. "I thought this would be your cue to leave."

"Yeah, me, too. Funny, huh? But I guess I'm staying."

"Thank you, Mildred."

"Come on. Let's go up to the room. I'll make you forget about all your troubles."

When he took her to supper at the Peabody, Ellis always got them a room. It was their special treat. Tonight, she noticed that the room was much smaller and more ordinary than their usual suite, but what the hell. She really didn't care, as long as she was with him.

When she'd done everything she could to make him forget the mess he was in, Mildred slipped out of bed and into the bathroom. There was nothing like a long, hot soak after a roll with a man. She turned on the taps full force and pulled back her hair to keep it from frizzing in the steam. When the water was the way she liked it—just short of boiling, Ellis said—she eased in up to her chin and rested her head against the back of the tub.

She heard the door to the room open, and she called out to Ellis, "If that's room service, I want mine in here."

She had left the bathroom door open a crack to let some of the steam out, but now it was yanked shut. Ellis screamed, "I'm sorry." Then there was a loud pop. The door to the room slammed. She jumped out, threw a towel over herself, and snatched the bathroom door open. Ellis was face down on the bed with a pillow over his head. There was a hole like a burn in the pillow. It seemed like feathers had scattered all over the room.

"Oh, no."

She sat next to him, her throat closed up so tight that she couldn't breathe. She knew what she was going to find. She didn't want to see it, but she pulled the pillow off and looked anyway. Blood oozed out of a hole at the base of his skull.

God. She should get out of here. Run.

As carefully as a mother draws a blanket up over a sleeping baby, Mildred put the pillow back in place. Wiggling as close to him as she could, she laid down next to Ellis and slipped her arms around him. For the first and only time in her life, she cried for someone else.

After she called the police, Mildred got dressed, pulled a chair over beside the bed, and sat down to wait. When they showed up, Chief Wilson himself was with them. She should have expected that. After all, Ellis was a Memphis big shot. The chief looked at the body and signaled the cops with him to wait in the hall.

"Look, Mildred," he said. "We don't want what really happened here to get out, do we? I mean, there'd be an investigation and a trial and all kinds of trouble for everybody, most of all you. Now, I don't think for a minute that you did this."

"But I—"

The chief held up his hand to cut her off. "Once people start poking around, they're going to want to know what you were doing here with Ellis Marchand, and somebody is probably going to decide that having you take the fall is better than asking too many questions of the wrong kind of people. You get what I'm saying?"

She nodded dumbly.

"Now, I'm going to put in my report that Mr. Marchand had a heart

attack under some very personal circumstances. That will be so embarrassing for the family that I think they'll want to drop the whole thing without asking for any further investigations."

"But I need to know who did this. Who killed him."

The chief took her chin in his hand and turned her face so she had to look at him. "No, you don't. Not if you've got any idea of what's good for you. All right?"

She had to force the words out. "All right."

"Good girl." He opened the door and motioned for the two men leaning against the wall outside to come back in. He went to the closet, took down Mildred's coat, and held it out for her to put on. "Now, I'll drive you back to the Parkview while the boys get Mr. Marchand down to the morgue. The doc there will fix him up, and nobody will be the wiser. It'll be our little secret."

Except that now Mildred Epps had a pretty good idea who had killed Ellis Marchand . . . or had him killed. She might be able to get even with them after all. At last, she closed the curtains, poured herself three fingers of gin, and went to run a hot bath.

CHAPTER 37

Nell went straight from the Peabody to Calendar's house. Simon led her to the study, where Joseph listened until she wound down.

"I never saw such a thing before in all my life, Joseph. She was in the middle of my luncheon hanging on Franklin Bryant's arm and laughing at everybody. And then she keeps goading me, hinting that she knows something that's important to me, but I have to cozy up to her to find out what it is."

"Perhaps you should consider making this woman your ally, at least until you discover what it is she claims to know," Calendar said.

"I'm not sure I could do it." Although she had already washed them three times since her confrontation with Mildred and Franklin, Nell wiped her hands on her skirt. "Talk about clutching a viper to my bosom."

"It needn't be for long. If you're careful enough, she won't have a chance to strike."

"Why don't you cozy up to her?"

"I'd rather nuzzle a 'possum, but if that's what you really want, I could try." He wrinkled his mouth as though he'd just taken a bite of lemon.

Nell weighed his offer and found she didn't like the idea at all either. "No, forget it. She's all snuggled up with Franklin Bryant right now anyway. Not that I think she's too particular about having more than one mule in her barn as long as she thinks she's not going to get caught."

"Then, I'm afraid it's up to you, Nell.

"I could offer to read for her." She flopped down in the chair by Calendar. "She did come to see me at the salon, but I turned her away. You think it might work?"

"Well, it can't hurt to try."

"All right." Nell shuddered. "It'll be just like wading barefoot in the hog pen, but I'll call her and ask for a truce. Would you be there, though? I don't like having to be in the same room with Mildred Epps, let alone facing her by myself. She makes it awfully hard not to lose my temper."

"I'll be at your side or in the shadows. Wherever you prefer."

"Stand behind me. I'm more interested in what you see than in what I see."

"I'm not the one with the gift."

"You're the one who really sees."

"As you wish."

SOMEWHAT LESS INSOUCIANT THAN USUAL, MILDRED POSITIONED herself across the table from Nell. Before she opened her mouth, the woman did manage a simper for Calendar where he stood in the shadows just behind and to the side of Nell.

"You surprised me, calling up the way you did, Mrs. Marchand," Mildred said. "Especially after you threw me out of your fancy society party."

Nell smiled brightly and tried to keep from clenching her jaw when she spoke. "I thought about what you said. I decided I was being ungenerous and unchristian and that we ought to try being friends. After all, Ellis Marchand isn't worth fighting over, is he? Especially now that he's dead. Please sit down, Miss Epps."

Something flashed across the woman's face, but it was gone before Nell could decipher it. "You're a lot cooler customer than I gave you credit for, Mrs. Marchand. This is going to be fun. I've never had my fortune told before."

"Let's begin. Think of the question you'd like answered." Nell waited for another wisecrack that didn't come.

Thinking, Mildred glanced up and to the right. "I got my question." She leaned her forearms on the table, eying Nell expectantly.

Passing her the cards, Nell told her to lay them out in a five-card spread. Mildred turned over the first one. Death. She blanched. Nell repressed a smile and reached for it.

"That card doesn't necessarily mean you or anyone you know will die," Nell said. "It means change or transformation. Because this card represents the present in this reading, it may mean you are changing or something about your life is. It could be the dying of the old order, whatever that is. We'll know more as we go on. Turn over the next card, please."

It was The Fool.

"That looks like—what do they call it?—a court jester," Mildred said.

"It's the Fool. It can mean innocence or hopefulness. That card represents the past and its influence on you in terms of your question."

That there had ever been anything innocent about Mildred, Nell doubted. The next card was the Magus.

"This is getting downright interesting," Nell said. "Three major arcana so far."

"Arcana? What the hell does that mean?"

"They're not part of any of the suits, and they have special significance. This can mean that very powerful forces are at work in your life. This card, the Magus, is in the position of the future. It may mean that you have to envision what you want for yourself if you're to achieve it."

"Honey, I've never exactly had any trouble doing that."

"No, I don't imagine you have. Next card, please."

The Priestess.

"This is the Priestess. She tells us to look inward so we can open our eyes to the true meaning of the things around us. Because she's in the position of the reason behind your question here, I think she's telling you that what you seek is right in front of you. For some reason, you don't want to see it, or you don't know what to do about it."

Mildred reached for the next card. The Hanged Man.

"That one doesn't look so good either. This whole thing is starting to give me the creeps."

"The Hanged Man," Nell said. "Remarkable, really. All major arcana. What I'm seeing is that everything points to change, to the search for fulfillment and the change necessary to find it. You feel something is missing in your life. You're not sure what it is, but you're looking for it. The Hanged Man can mean a spiritual quest, so perhaps you're looking for meaning beyond the material."

"All I've ever looked for is the right man to keep me in diamonds for the rest of my life."

The utter gall of Mildred's saying such a thing to her of all people was almost too much. Pretending to study The Hanged Man, she brought the card close to her face. Deep breaths, Nell. Remember that you want to know if she's hiding something. Card back on the table.

"That may be what you think on a conscious level, Miss Epps, but perhaps your heart is telling you something else."

"I don't have a heart, Mrs. Marchand. Can't afford one. Hearts are for saps and suckers. It's what's over the heart that most men are after." Mildred positioned herself in the chair to make her breasts even more prominent so there could be no question what she was talking about. "I got those and a brain. They've done a pretty good job for me so far."

"I can only tell you what I see. It's for you to decide how to apply it to what you seek."

Staring at Nell, Mildred tapped the table with her index finger until Nell thought she would scream. She finally seemed to decide something and leaned across the table toward Nell.

"That part about not seeing what's right in front of you? Well,

I think you're right, Mrs. Marchand. I've been trying to tell you all along. Did you get a good look at Ellis before you buried him?"

"What?" Nell blinked.

"Did you look close enough to see the bullet hole in his head? Or did they cover it up so good that you couldn't tell? I hear they can do that, you know."

"What on earth are you talking about? Ellis had a heart attack. You should know. You were there." Nell felt her breath coming faster.

There was nothing of the brazen, conniving Mildred that Nell expected in the air of the woman now. She seemed deflated somehow and much, much older. When she spoke, her voice was ragged. "You're right. I was there, and I'm telling you, somebody shot him. They shut me in the bathroom, but I heard it. I saw the hole in the back of his skull. The bullet had to come out the front of his head somewhere. You had to have seen it."

"What complete and utter bullshit," Nell said when she managed to find her voice. Even after all the lies Ellis had told her during their marriage, this was the first time she had ever said "bullshit" out loud. Behind her, she heard Calendar shift his stance.

Mildred jerked back as though Nell had finally delivered the slap she'd been expecting from the moment they met. "You don't believe me? Why don't you ask his buddy Franklin Bryant? Or the chief? But you'd better find a real sneaky way to do it because they went to a lot of trouble to keep anybody from finding out."

"Why would anyone shoot Ellis?"

"He was about to blow the whistle on some deal that went bad."

"Why are you doing this?"

"Because they took Ellis away from me." Mildred's face crumpled, but her voice took on its former snap. "Because he didn't deserve a bullet in the head."

"And you've suddenly gotten religion and decided to tell someone what happened. Why wait until now? Why tell me?"

Remorse, an emotion no one could have imagined was part of her repertoire, was written clearly on Mildred's face. "They told me I'd better keep my mouth shut if I knew what was good for me, so I did. But lately the idea of someone getting away with murdering him has been choking me. I thought maybe you could do something about it. Maybe instead of looking so hard for this girl nobody gives a damn about, you ought to be finding out who killed your husband."

Whatever anger Nell thought she had felt before, it was nothing compared to the cold, hard, implacable fury that consumed her now. "Get out," she said, her voice shaking.

Mildred stared back at her, shame giving way to disbelief and blossoming into outrage. She rose, flung her mink around her, and stalked out.

Calendar rested a gentle hand on Nell's shoulder. "You don't think she may have been telling the truth?"

"Of course not. That whole performance was to get back at me for embarrassing her at the luncheon."

"Are you sure?" Calendar took the chair across from Nell that Mildred had occupied. "I didn't get that feeling from her."

"Well, isn't that something? Exactly what did you get and where did you feel it?"

"I'm serious, Nell. That woman is afraid. And why would she accuse Franklin Bryant?"

"The only thing she's afraid of is ending up back in the gutter. After the luncheon, Franklin probably put her out on the curb. She wants to get back at him. Besides, if someone did shoot Ellis, it was probably someone's husband, and he deserved it."

"Why not tell you the truth, then? And why would the police say it was a heart attack?"

Nell chewed her lip. "They were covering up something. Someone important called in a favor." She shivered. "I don't want to talk about Ellis or that Epps woman any more. Just having her in here made me feel as though I need a bath."

Before Calendar could say anything more about the bizarre idea that Ellis had been murdered, Nell pointed to Mildred's cards. "That was a fascinating spread, though."

Calendar picked them up and examined them, laying them out again one at a time. "You could say that the cards support what she was telling you, but I think there's more to this reading."

"Like what?"

"Mildred may have been the querent, but think about it. This was about you, too, Nell. Sometimes the adept unconsciously dwells on a question as the cards are being dealt, and that is the question that the reading answers. Every card could certainly apply to you and what's happened over the last few weeks. You're the innocent struggling your way to understanding, exploring a gift that many would envy."

Nell laughed. "So, I'm the Fool. That certainly fits."

"You are the Fool, the innocent striving toward knowledge. Contemplate this spread and everything that you told Mildred Epps and consider how that interpretation could apply to you. Then let's see where it leads. It was a remarkable reading, by the way. Insightful. Yes, I'd say that you are definitely getting the hang of it."

Like a plain girl unexpectedly told she's a beauty, Nell blushed.

"Well, of course, I'm looking for something. I want to find Ginny Evans. If the answer is right in front of me, I can't for the life of me see it, though."

"Not yet, perhaps. That's the literal interpretation of the meaning. What could the cards mean on a broader level?"

"That the answer to all my problems is right in front of me if only I reach out and grab it. But what's the answer?"

"Your abilities, I believe. Learn to trust your gift and your instincts and you can never go wrong. And keep your mind open to all possibilities."

That was one interpretation, anyway.

CHAPTER 38

A dream can shrink to a room no bigger than a chicken coop, to a narrow bed and only a tiny patch of sky high up to remind you that there's a world outside. A dream can shrivel to meals eaten among women who babble and hoot and claw their faces until someone ties mitts over their hands to make them stop. Food that makes you long for something as simple and good as potatoes for supper again. A dream can be all that you have left to hold on to when the world hides you away and you know that everyone has forgotten that you ever lived. A dream can be all that keeps you sane.

Ginny Evans still dreamed, but each day made it a little harder to remember. The music and the sound of her own voice drowned by the noise of the men and women who came to the speak to forget. Sometimes now, she couldn't remember the words to any of the songs she used to sing.

Every night, she lay on that bare mattress and looked out at the stars. The same stars she'd seen from her bed back home in Como with her little sisters breathing softly beside her in the night. The same stars that had made her dream in the first place. How cramped and crowded that bed had felt with Ruth and Lizzie pressed against her. But this bed was cold and hard. She would give anything to be back on that ticking mattress in the shack on her daddy's little place, looking up at the stars out that window.

"Lord, if you will just get me away from here and let me get home, I promise I will never leave again. I will be good and do what Mama and Daddy say. I will look after my brothers and sisters and work hard. I will never think of singing anything but what's in the Cokesbury hymnal at church. I promise. Please, let me go home."

Ginny curled around herself against the cold and closed her eyes. She tried to conjure her mother's face. "Sing something sweet to me, Mama. You know I can't get to sleep unless you sing."

And as clear as though she were right there in the room, Ginny heard her mama's voice start up "The Solid Rock" all soft and low.

"On Christ the solid rock I stand," Ginny whispered in time with her mother's voice.

If the attendants heard her singing, they reported it to the doctor the next day. She didn't want the doctor to give her any more shots. They made her sick and gave her the weak trembles all over before she passed out. She was afraid the guards would do things to her before she woke up. Sometimes she was afraid they already had.

"All other ground is sinking sand. All other ground is sinking sand." Her mother's voice faded slowly until she couldn't hear it any more.

"I'm sorry I ran away, Mama. I won't never do it again."

"I know, Ginny," her mother said. "You get on home, and we'll keep you safe. Remember, we always love you."

"I love you, too, Mama."

Then she was asleep. The new dream began of walking the rows, dirt under her feet and the sun on her back and buttermilk and cornbread for supper.

SEEMED LIKE SOMETHING HAD TO BE HOLDING NELL BACK FROM finding that girl. Hattie was beginning to think that maybe somebody had put a curse on her. Somebody who didn't want that girl found, who meant her evil. Nell hadn't been sick or had the night chills or complained that the back of her hands were itching, but that didn't mean there wasn't a confusion spell out there on her.

Aunt Mary would know what it was, and she would know how to put the good magic against the bad. Hattie went down to Beale Street to see the hoodoo doctor again. They needed to get that girl home and get back to tending to their own business.

"We've got to have something to go with the mojo sack, Aunt Mary," Hattie said. "Have you got a finding spell?"

"I heard Nell Marchand is the only one still looking for that fool Mississippi gal," Aunt Mary said. "Going up against Mr. E. H. Crump and everybody else what's ready to forget her. Makes me proud."

"I'm afraid she's got something besides Boss Crump against her."

"Well, if she does, I'm going to make her a charm to fight that, too." A finger resting against her lips, Aunt Mary turned to the powders and herbs in the jars behind her on the shelf. She lifted three down and put them on the counter.

"We need something from that Mississippi girl. Something she touched or wore."

"All we have is this picture."

"That will have to do, then."

Aunt Mary studied the photograph. "Fine girl, mighty fine. Shame she went and worried her mama like that."

Aunt Mary took down another jar and extracted a root that looked like a hand. At her table, she put it on an old, chipped plate with a faded pattern of blue flowers in the center. From each jar, she extracted a pinch of the contents and sprinkled it over the root hand. All the while, she hummed "Amazing Grace."

When she had seasoned the root to suit her, she covered it with both her hands. Then she recited the 23rd Psalm once more. Hattie joined in.

"Now, you take this root and tell Nell Marchand to hold it and the girl's picture and say the psalm again. She got to do it every night right before she goes to sleep so the right dream going to come to tell her where to find the girl. Then she got to empty her mind and lie right down and be still so she don't think about something else that the hand thinks it has to find. And tell her to take the mojo sack I give her and sleep with it under her pillow or around her neck, too, to make the dream stronger. Leave the girl's picture beside the bed with the hand resting on top of it, and the dreams be real strong."

—

NELL DID AS AUNT MARY SAID. FOR GOOD MEASURE, SHE ALSO DID A reading for herself before bed. But it was no use. Not only did she not dream of where to find Ginny, she didn't dream of anything at all.

"It's the strangest thing," Nell told Calendar. She had gone to his house again to consult him about her difficulties. "I've always had lots of dreams, but ever since I saw Ginny in that little room in my vision, I haven't had a single one. No inkling of other visions either. My power, if I had it, is gone."

"Something else is at work here," he said. "I have no doubt that you did see Ginny Evans and that she is still alive. Perhaps there is some reason that part of you doesn't want to find her. If you were conscious of it, then we could counteract it."

"But that's ridiculous. There's nothing I want more than to find her. It's all I think of all day long."

"With your waking mind, yes. On some level, you know the clue to finding Ginny, but your conscious mind doesn't want to recognize it. Perhaps it poses some dilemma of choice that you're simply not ready to face."

"Why not?"

"Only you know the answer to that, Nell."

"You're talking in circles, Joseph." She pressed her fingers to her temples. "I know, but I don't want to know, so I can't know. We're no better off than we were in the beginning. I wish I'd never heard of fortunetelling or Luther Evans or his daughter. This isn't my idea of a gift. What use is it?"

"And now you're thinking in circles. I know it's difficult to be patient when you felt that you were so close that you could almost touch Ginny and now she seems to be drifting farther and farther away. All you can do is keep up your daily practice, go on with your readings, and know that the vision will come back to you in its own time."

"This is worse than trying to keep track of everyone's cards in bridge. Bess writes them down. Maybe that will help. I'm going to make a list of what we do know so far."

Nell took out a pad and wrote down "Ginny Evans" at the top. Beneath that she wrote "Como, Mississippi," "Roy's Place," "Kelly's Nightclub" in one column and "Luther Evans," "Sadie Rainey," "Lois Brown," and "Roy Mertz" in another. In a third column, she noted "Ginny at Kelly's" and "Ginny in cell with bed." She sat tapping the pad with the eraser end of her pencil.

"See any connections you haven't noticed before?" Calendar said.

"No, dadgummit. We've been over all this too many times."

"Let's try a new perspective. Take your deck and draw a random card for each entry in each column. Line the cards up alongside their entries and see if they say anything to you."

Nell counted out the cards and sat looking at them. "Still nothing."

"Squint your eyes as much as you can without completely closing them and look at the cards out of the corner of your eye. It's a ruse the Viennese medium taught me for overcoming resistance. Trick the brain into working for what it sees, and the unexpected or sought-after may come up."

Nell squinted and turned her head until she was practically looking out of the back of it. She held the cards with her eyes closed. She held them with her eyes open. She shuffled the deck and tried new alignment after new alignment. Nothing.

"We might as well try Pin the Tail on the Donkey for all the good this is doing. If we don't stop now, I really am going to go crazy."

"Then let it go for a while," Calendar said. "Let your mind work on it. When you're ready, the answer will come."

CHAPTER 39

Nell was just coming into the front hall with an armload of late tulips for the dining room table when she heard a crash in the front parlor and a shriek. She ran in to find Bess standing by the overturned case, staring at General Oates's leg, which had rolled out of its resting place and come to a halt beside her.

"I don't know how I could be so clumsy," Bess said. She waved her hands, bent to pick up the leg, didn't, and clutched her hands to her bosom. "I stumbled over my own feet and fell against the case and knocked it over. I shall never forgive myself if the General's leg is damaged."

"Oh, I'm sure it's not hurt, Mother. It has survived worse than this. Please go ask Hattie to bring the broom and dust pan before anybody steps on all this glass. I'll take care of the leg."

Nell bent to lift the General's leg. As her hand closed on it, everything went black.

The girl wheeled the General behind the main building so he could see the patients turning over the rows in the vegetable gardens. He enjoyed watching everyone else being productive and industrious, as he liked to put it, even if he couldn't take part in any of the farm and dairy work himself, not with that leg of his that was never made to bend.

"Fine work, men," the General hollered out. "Keep it up. We want to be well-provisioned before the damned Mexicans attack."

A couple of the patients snapped to attention and saluted, but most of them paid no attention, lost in their work weeding and turning the soil.

Fall was here, and they were getting it ready to plant the spinach and kale that would provide greens for the hospital kitchens throughout the mild Tennessee winter.

Daddy and Mama and them would probably be doing the same thing down on their place, except they'd be planting collards instead of spinach. Wouldn't be long before it was cold enough to kill hogs. There would be bacon and pork chops and all kinds of good eating. Daddy would hang the hams in the smokehouse, and when the greens were ready to eat, Mama would cook a big mess of them down with streak-o-lean that made the best pot liquor in the world.

She shivered and pulled the gown closer around her. It was about time to take the General in for lunch anyway. Wrestling his wheelchair a little forward and then pulling it back to turn it, Ginny Evans looked straight at Nell as she wheeled him past her toward the red-brick Victorian building.

Still clutching the General's leg, Nell came to in the front parlor. "Mother!"

Bess rushed in bearing the broom and dustpan. "What is it, dear?"

"I think I know where Ginny Evans is."

"That's marvelous, dear! Shall I call Dr. Calendar?"

"I guess you'd better. Find somewhere for this."

Nell handed Bess the leg, took the broom, and began to sweep up the broken glass. When Calendar arrived, she was pressing a piece of stale bread against the floor to pick up the last tiny shards. She led him into the kitchen and put the kettle on.

Sipping tea and trying to collect herself, she faced him across the kitchen table. He encircled his cup with his hands but made no move to drink.

"Oh, Joseph, you don't think Ginny could possibly be at Bolivar, do you? I've only driven by it, but it sure felt like the asylum. I was there watching Ginny and General Oates, but it was such a crazy vision with her and the General together in it when he died before I was even born."

"There's one way to find out."

"Jenkins!"

The driver appeared at the kitchen door, brushing dirt from his knees from where Hattie had him weeding the vegetable patch. "Yes, ma'am?"

"We're going to need the Duesenberg."

"Yes, ma'am. Right away."

—

WESTERN STATE MENTAL HOSPITAL IN BOLIVAR, TENNESSEE, DATED from the late 1880s and was one of the last to be built according to the Kirkbride plan, with the central administration building flanked by tiered wards to ensure that natural light and fresh air reached each lunatic. Dr. Thomas Kirkbride, who developed the system, believed placing patients in a more natural environment away from cities both stimulated and calmed their minds. In their day, the buildings had been state-of-the-art and a far cry from the prisons and madhouses that had entombed the mentally ill before the doctor's reforms.

To Nell, who knew nothing of this history, the four-story red-brick building with its main central and smaller side steeples loomed cold and forbidding in the late morning light. Jenkins stopped the car by the entrance along the chalk drive that swept the length of the façade.

As Nell and Calendar hurried in, the stone-faced nurse at the front desk observed them. "May I help you?" she said, her tone implying that assistance was the last thing they could expect from her.

"Oh, I hope you can help us, please," Nell said. "Someone we've been looking for may be in the hospital."

"And you figured you'd stop off here to see," the nurse said.

"We've searched everywhere else."

"What's the name?"

"Ginny Evans."

The woman glanced up sharply, but Nell wasn't sure if it was because the name was familiar to her or because all her looks were sharp. "No one here by that name."

"Are you sure?" Nell said. "Don't you have some kind of list you can check?"

"Don't have to look. I know every woman in this hospital, ma'am. There is no one named Ginny Evans here."

"But–"

Nell started around the desk, but Calendar put a restraining hand on her arm. His smile sad, he drew Ginny's photograph out of his pocket and put it on the counter in front of the nurse. "We don't want to be any trouble, ma'am, but Ginny worked for us, and my wife has been so worried about her."

"Yes," Nell said, catching on to her part of the act. "We've searched and searched for her, and when we finally had an inkling that she might be here, well, we rushed right over." She took out her handkerchief and rubbed her eyes.

Calendar leaned forward and dropped his voice so only the nurse and Nell could hear him, his tone was regretful, mesmerizing. "You see, I'm afraid my brother seduced her, abandoned her when someone younger and prettier presented herself, and then brought her here to hide his shame. As you can see from this old photograph—the only one her family had, I'm afraid—she was a simple farm girl who came to work with us to help support her family in these dark and difficult times. I believe she sent every penny she ever made home to feed her little sisters and brothers, keeping almost nothing for herself. I can't bear to think that such an innocent young girl languishes here because of my brother's . . . depravity."

The nurse's eyes softened. Nell could almost believe that she'd once been a young girl done wrong by some cavalier cad. The woman picked up the photograph and held it closer to the light to study it.

"This could be Mary Lou Baker. Her family had her committed here a few months back." The nurse flicked the edge of the photograph, dredging up a memory. "Yes, it was the talk of the hospital for a couple of weeks. I was on duty that night. The doctor who brought her said it was an urgent case. That she had tried to kill herself and threatened to drown her baby in the bathtub and that she had made up a wild story about being someone else to hide her guilt over having an illegitimate child in the first place."

"That doctor was probably my brother," Calendar said, his demeanor now tragic. "He is totally without scruple, I'm afraid."

"We have to see her," Nell said. "Please, nurse."

"I'm sorry, ma'am, but I can't do that."

"Why not? It has to be our Ginny you've got."

"Only family and people the patient's doctor has approved are allowed visits."

"Is there someone else we could speak to, please?" Nell dabbed at her eyes again. "Her doctor or the hospital director, perhaps? We'd appreciate it if you could put in a good word for us."

Calendar took the photograph from the nurse gently and put it back in his pocket. "We understand, of course. You have your rules, and they're meant to protect everyone concerned. It's just that we'd about given up hope. This is our last chance."

The nurse studied Calendar's face and wavered, captivated. "I reckon it won't hurt if I call the doctor on duty. He won't let you see her, but maybe he can tell you how to get permission."

"That would be very kind." Calendar reached across the desk to touch the nurse's arm and smiled. A blush crept up the woman's neck.

"Oh, yes," Nell said, summoning her broadest, most-sincere smile. "We're so grateful for anything you can do."

"All right then. I'll be right back."

She disappeared around a corner, returning with an impossibly young man in a doctor's lab coat behind her. He stopped in front of Nell and Calendar and peered at them over the top of his glasses. His face was anything but welcoming.

"Am I to understand that you want to interview one of our patients to find out if she's your missing parlor maid?"

Calendar squeezed Nell's hand to keep her from speaking. "Yes, doctor. I don't know how much the nurse told you about this poor girl's plight, but we believe that my brother wronged her and then abandoned her here to escape any blame."

"I wish I could oblige you folks, but without specific instructions from the doctor who brought her here, I'm afraid I can't let anyone see her."

Nell bit the insides of her cheeks in frustration. Why was it that people always said that they were afraid they couldn't do something when what they really meant was that they were just plain not going to do it?

"Of course, we understand," Calendar said. He kept his voice even. "Could we perhaps see the paperwork on this patient? If we know the doctor's name, we can petition him ourselves to implore his permission."

"I can't show you her commitment papers. They're confidential." The doctor looked over his glasses at them again. "But I don't see any harm in giving you the name of the referring physician. We'll need a letter from him stating that you have his permission to talk with his patient, Mary Lou Baker." He scribbled a name on a slip of paper he took from his pocket and handed it to Calendar.

"Thank you, doctor."

Back in the car speeding toward Memphis, Nell checked the name and address the young man had given them. "I don't know every doctor in Memphis, of course," she said, "but have never heard of this man. Alistair March."

"I imagine there's no such person. Or if he does exist, his practice is in such a place or of such a sort that there would be no reason for you to know of him. We'll check as soon as we're back."

"And if there's no Dr. March, we'll go straight to Ed Crump with the fraud and get Ginny Evans out of there. He'll help us spring her if I have to drag him to Bolivar by the scruff of the neck."

CHAPTER 40

Driving back to Memphis, Jenkins burned up the road. A quick check of the phone book revealed no Dr. March, and Jenkins had Nell and Calendar at Crump's building in no time. Before his protesting secretary could stop them, they pushed past her into the former mayor's office.

"It's all right, Janice," he said, waving her away. "Mrs. Marchand, it's a surprise to see you here. I don't believe there's an appointment with you on my calendar."

"No, sir, but you're my only hope," Nell said. "Will you listen to me for just one minute, please?"

Crump sighed, put down the papers he'd been reviewing, and pushed his spectacles up the bridge of his nose. "Sit down, then."

Nell ignored the chair he offered her. "I've found Ginny Evans."

"Not again, Mrs. Marchand." Crump looked at Calendar as though to say, "Can't you do anything with her?" He pushed his glasses even farther up. "I told you I didn't want to hear anything more about that business."

"Mr. Crump, I don't mean that I've had a vision of where Ginny Evans is." Nell leaned her hands on the desk to bring herself as close to him as possible. "I've found her. We've been there. I've not seen her in the flesh, but I know she is there. The nurse and one of the doctors recognized her photo. I need your help to rescue her. You must come right away."

"What on earth are you talking about?"

"She's in Bolivar."

"Bolivar," Crump said, puzzled. He leaned toward Nell. "At the state hospital?"

"Yes, sir. But she doesn't belong there. Someone must have put her there to hide her away, maybe to cover up a secret that someone will do almost anything to keep her from revealing. The doctor on duty told me that once they've had an order from the court or a recommendation from a doctor with the approval of the family, patients are committed until the court or the family petition to have them released. You've got to help me get her out."

"You've been to see this doctor who put her there?" Crump watched her now, almost persuaded. "You've tried the proper channels to have her released?"

"He doesn't exist. There's no doctor in Memphis named Alistair March."

"Mrs. Marchand and I checked," Calendar said. "The papers list a false name and address. Whoever did this somehow forged a medical license and the court documents."

"Mr. Crump, please. We have got to go now." Nell moved to crouch beside his chair, bringing her eyes level with his. "If whoever hid Ginny there discovers we've found her, they might move her or do something worse. She's guilty of nothing more than dreaming of a different life and of having trusted the wrong people. Surely she doesn't deserve to rot away for that."

Crump seized Nell by the hand, strode across the room, and grabbed his hat off the hat rack. "Come on, Miss Nell. Time's a wasting. We'll take my car." He charged out of his office, Nell in tow. Startled, his secretary leapt to her feet. On the way toward the outer door, he shouted orders over his shoulder. "Janice, call the state hospital in Bolivar. Speak to the director and tell him that Congressman Crump is on his way there to see a patient named Ginny Evans."

"They're calling her Mary Lou Baker." Nell scrambled behind him.

"Right. Mary Lou Baker. Tell him that if he doesn't produce her when I arrive so that I can talk with her right that minute, I will have his job and the hides of anyone who tries to interfere with me."

"Yessir," Janice said.

"I want my driver and my trooper escort out front by the time we get downstairs. And call Dr. Roberts and tell him to drop whatever he's doing and get ready for me to pick him up in front of his clinic in twenty minutes. He's going with us." Crump turned to point at Janice. "Make that 10 minutes."

"Yessir."

Calendar caught up with them at the door. A breathless laugh of triumph bubbling to her lips, Nell grabbed his hand and dragged him out behind her.

—

GINNY JUMPED WHEN THE HEAD MATRON TORE OPEN THE DOOR TO her cell and planted herself beside the cot.

"Come on, girl," the matron said. "No less than the mighty E. H. Crump himself is here to see you. Get yourself up and brush your hair. I'm taking you to the director's office."

"Mr. Crump?" Ginny sat up on the bunk and blinked. "I don't understand."

"You don't have to understand, girl. Just get yourself together and let's get a move on. Mr. Crump don't like to be kept waiting."

—

HAVING A ROOM FULL OF PEOPLE ON HAND WHILE DR. ROBERTS examined Ginny was not how Nell would have done it, but Crump insisted that he would not let her out of his sight. She stood close to the girl, hoping that having another woman in the room would put her more at ease. When the doctor had asked Ginny a raft of questions including what her name was, what year it was, and who was president and examined her head to toes as thoroughly as was decent, he removed the stethoscope from his ears and turned to the hospital director.

"What do you think, Doc?" Crump said.

"Far as I can tell, there's nothing wrong with this girl that a bath, a few good meals, and a little regular sleep won't cure," Roberts said, leveling his remarks at the director, who suddenly found the floor of his office intensely fascinating.

"Then she's not insane," Nell said.

"No, ma'am. I see no evidence of that. No more than is normal for a 16-year-old."

Crump approached Ginny. "Do you have any clothes besides this gown, Miss Evans?"

Ginny clutched at the neck of the gown and tried to pull the hem down. "No, sir. They took everything away when they brought me here. I didn't have anything but the clothes I was wearing anyway."

"Who brought you here, Ginny?" Nell said. She stood in front of the girl and smiled kindly.

"I don't know, ma'am," the girl said. She began to shake, and her eyes filled with tears. Nell squeezed her hand, dug a handkerchief out of her back, and gave it to Ginny.

"There's time for questions later," Dr. Roberts said. "Right now, let's just get this young lady back where she can get proper care."

"Of course," Nell said. She glanced at Calendar, who nodded.

"Well, Miss Evans, we are going to get you all fixed up," Crump said. He stepped in front of Nell and put his arm around the girl's shoulders. "Don't you worry about that. We'll get you a whole new wardrobe when we get you back to Memphis. Mrs. Marchand will take you shopping anywhere you want to go, won't you, Miss Nell?"

"Ginny, as soon as we get you to my house, we'll find a nice dress you can wear until I take you to Lowenstein's."

Pulling the girl gently to her feet, Crump shrugged out of his overcoat and draped it around her shoulders. "Meanwhile, this will keep you warm for the ride home."

Ginny blinked first at Crump, then at Nell, and then at Dr. Roberts. "Y'all are taking me out of here?" Her voice cracked.

"Yes, Miss Evans," Crump said. "We're taking you back to Memphis. I will call your mother and father myself when we get back and arrange for them to catch the train from Como. They'll be in Memphis in no time, and you can see them as soon as you want."

"And Ruth and Lizzie, too?"

"Who are Ruth and Lizzie?"

"They're my little sisters."

"We'll bring your whole family up if you like," Crump said. "How many brothers and sisters do you have?"

"Ten."

Crump threw his head back and laughed. "Then I'll reserve a special car for your family, and they'll all come. Would you like that?"

Ginny nodded. A tear spilled down her cheek. "We don't have a telephone. You've got to call Mr. Drucker at the general store, and he'll send his boy to fetch my daddy."

"There now, Miss Ginny," Crump said. He buttoned the coat around her. "I'll call Mr. Drucker just as soon as we get back to Memphis. You'll be back with your mama and daddy in no time. Are you ready to go home?"

Ginny collapsed against Crump and buried her face against his chest, sobbing. He patted her and looked over her at Nell, who came to take her by the arm.

"It's all right now, Ginny," Nell said. "We've got you. You're safe, and everything is going to be all right."

CHAPTER 41

Dr. Roberts wanted to put Ginny in Baptist Hospital downtown to observe her, but Nell was adamant that the girl had had enough of such places, even if Baptist was no Bolivar. If Ginny was well enough, she said, she was taking her home with her, and there were no two ways about it.

Once they were at the Marchand house and the flurry over their arrival died down, Nell saw to it that Ginny had a glass of buttermilk and some cornbread—which was all she wanted—a bath, and a clean nightgown. Nell tucked her in herself in the guestroom. Before she could close the blinds and turn off the lights, Ginny was asleep.

Nell's daddy might be rolling over in his grave knowing that Ed Crump was sitting at her kitchen table, but the congressman said he wanted to stay until they had her settled.

"Y'all can fix your own plates," Hattie said, setting out fried chicken, dressed eggs, half a pound cake, and a jar of bread and butter pickles. "I'll start some coffee."

Crump stuffed an egg in his mouth and reached for a chicken leg. Dr. Roberts put a wafer-thin slice of cake on his plate.

"Now, give the girl a day or two, Mr. Crump, before you subject her to any kind of interrogation," the doctor said. "You saw how she reacted to Miss Nell's question. She's undernourished, and the Lord alone knows what kind of mental anguish she suffered. She's very fragile. Let her rest and recover herself."

"What are you talking about, Roberts?" Crump said. "Nobody is going to interrogate the girl, as you put it. But we will have a lot of questions for her when she's ready. We want to find out how she ended up there. There's not one person in Memphis who isn't going to want to know her story."

"All I'm telling you is that you should proceed slowly."

"Don't worry, doc. We'll take good care of the girl. I'll see to it myself."

Behind Boss Crump's back, Nell smiled at Calendar and shook her head.

—

JOSEPH CALENDAR DROPPED THE MORNING PAPER ON THE DINING room table in front of Nell. She and Bess were just finishing their breakfast. When Nell peeked in on her, Ginny had still been asleep. They were going to let her stay in bed all day if she needed to.

"Hattie," Nell called to the kitchen. "Dr. Calendar is joining us for breakfast. Bring him a cup of coffee, please."

Nell picked up the paper and flipped it open. On the front page was an enormous photograph of a smiling Ed Crump with his arm around a startled-looking Ginny Evans, still wearing his coat. The headline read, "Crump Rescues Missing Girl," with the subhead, "Where has Ginny been?" Nell handed the paper to Bess, who scanned the story.

"Mr. Crump doesn't miss a trick, does he?" Calendar said. "He's taking all the credit for finding Ginny when it's your photograph that should be on the front page. If it weren't for you, she'd still be in the asylum."

Hattie bustled in with a steaming cup of coffee and plate with two hot biscuits dripping butter that she set before Calendar. The near-worship on his face when he thanked her made Nell smile.

"Let him have the limelight," Nell said. "All I care about is that Ginny is back and safe."

"Can we be sure she's safe? We still don't know who sent her to

Bolivar."

"Why exactly did you think Oz and his photographer met us here last night? No one would dare touch her now that she's E. H. Crump's protégée. Whoever shut her up in Bolivar could just as easily have killed her if he'd wanted her dead. Besides, the paper doesn't say where she is."

"Even a cornered rabbit will fight, Nell. What about asking Crump to put a trooper at the front gate?"

"That would be just like waving a flag saying she's here."

"Then sooner we find out who put her there, the better."

"Ginny hasn't said anything yet. She doesn't want to tell us what happened. I don't think we should force her to say anything until she's ready."

Having skimmed the Crump-Ginny story for herself, Bess tut-tutted, folded the paper, and placed it back on the table in front of Nell.

"That poor child is frightened half to death," Bess said. "And my goodness, who wouldn't be after what has happened to her? Perhaps when her father arrives, he can get her to talk."

—

NELL HAD JUST ASKED HATTIE IF THERE WERE ANY MORE BISCUITS when there was a pounding at the front door that startled Bess so that she almost dropped her coffee cup. She gaped at Nell and Calendar. They could hear Jenkins cross the foyer to open the door. Whoever was there cut him off before he could ask who was calling.

"Where is she?" the voice said. "Where's Ginny? They told me at Mr. Crump's office that she's here. I've got to see her."

Nell, Calendar, and Bess exchanged looks and rose as one to see who was causing all the ruckus. In the front hall, they found Gaylord Bryant, eyes frantic and hair in disarray. When he saw her, he grabbed Nell and shook her.

"Miss Nell. Miss Bess. Please, you've got to tell me where Ginny is.

I've been half out of my mind ever since I saw her picture in the paper this morning. I've got to talk to her."

"What do you want with Ginny Evans, Gaylord?" Nell said. "How do you know her?"

"She's my girl, Miss Nell. Hasn't she told you? Ginny is my girl."

CHAPTER 42

The shouting downstairs roused Ginny from her sleep. She bolted up, her heart pounding and her breath coming in gasps. She must have dreamed it all. She was still in the hospital. She had dreamed the rescue and the ride back to Memphis and the reporters and the wonderful, soft bed. They were coming to strap her down and give her another of those horrible injections. She was about to scream when she realized that the bed was, indeed, soft and covered with fine sheets. The fabric against her skin was silk, not rough cotton. Sun streamed through the double windows of her room, where someone had opened them to let it in.

She was in Mrs. Marchand's house. But what if they had found out and were coming for her? Scrubbing the sleep from her eyes, she pulled on her robe and ran out on the landing to see who was carrying on so. She looked down, and there he was, standing with Miss Nell and Miss Bess and she didn't know who else.

Gaylord. In spite of everything, he was there. He looked up, saw her, and broke into a grin. It was all there in his eyes. Everything that had happened to her, every last minute of terror and despair was forgotten. Gaylord was here.

She flung herself down the steps and into his arms. He kissed her eyes, her hair, her lips, crying and saying her name over and over again. He held her so tightly that she almost couldn't breathe, but she didn't care. She clung to him. His arms around her were enough, everything. He had come for her, wanted her after all.

"I was afraid I'd never see you again," Ginny said into his shoulder.

"Darling, I thought you didn't love me anymore. At Kelly's, they told me that you'd gone away, that you'd played me for a fool. When I read your letter . . . well, I felt like a dead man. Then, when I saw the paper this morning, when I read what had happened to you, what they'd done to you. Oh, Ginny, can you ever forgive me for believing what they said, for letting them put you in that place? No matter what anyone said, what you said, I should have looked for you."

"What letter? I never wrote you any letter, Gaylord."

"You didn't write saying you never wanted to see me again, that I made you sick, that you'd rather be dead than ever have me touch you again?"

She nestled as close to him as she could get. "Oh, sweetheart, of course not. I don't know what letter you're talking about, but even if I had thought anything like that, I would never have written it. I don't know who that letter came from, but it wasn't me."

"Ginny, I'm so sorry. I should have known." He kissed her wildly again.

"It doesn't matter now. We're going to forget all about it. You're here now, and you'll never let go of me again, will you? Promise you'll never let go."

He brushed his fingers across her cheeks to wipe away her tears. "Never, sweet girl." He took her face between his hands and tilted it up to his. Gently, tenderly now, he kissed her, and the rest of the world dropped away.

—

LITTLE NICK LOOKED UP FROM PARING HIS NAILS WHEN FRANKLIN Bryant burst through the door of Kelly's and waved the newspaper in his face.

"I thought we agreed that you would take care of this," Franklin said.

"Hey, is it our fault we couldn't find her either? How was I supposed to know your pal left her out at the nut house?"

"Where's Kelly?"

"Keep your shirt on. He's back in his office."

"Well, get him. Now!"

As Little Nick weighed the pleasure of shivving the old bastard on the spot against the trouble of explaining it to Blackjack afterward, Franklin's life hung in the balance. He decided to err on the side of discretion and went to find Blackjack instead.

"The stuffed shirt is out front making a big stink because they found Ginny," he said, leaning against the door to the boss's office.

"What does he want us to do about it? It's his mess, which he should have cleaned up in the first place. Jeez, I'd turn him over to the cops myself if I didn't think it would make too much trouble for us." Blackjack sighed and followed Little Nick back into the bar.

"Have you seen this?" Franklin said, this time shoving the paper in Blackjack's face.

Blackjack knocked the paper aside. "Of course, I've seen it. I ain't blind, and I can read."

"What to you propose that we do about it?"

"Are you crazy or something? I don't *propose* to do nothing. So they found her. So what? We got nothing to worry about long as you're smart enough to keep your mouth shut and stay out of it. She's got no way of knowing that we were mixed up in this with you. And you said she saw you only that one other time, right? So, how's she going to figure out who you are? I say lay low, wait until they send her back to her old man's farm, and you'll be clean as a whistle and free as a bird."

Franklin threw his homburg to the floor, dragged both hands through his hair, and looked as though he might swallow his lower lip. "And if she does find out, what then? I want her done away with." He hooked his finger at Nick. "Send your goon here and make sure he doesn't make any more mistakes."

"Hey, you old–"

Blackjack silenced Little Nick with a glance. "Well, then you're going to have to take care of her Bryant. We're not touching her. Not with Crump and the papers and everybody in Memphis breathing down our necks. That would be bad for business. Very bad. She's too hot."

"This is a fine mess you've gotten me into."

"That I've gotten you into? You should have taught your kid to keep it in his pants or save it for the whores down on Gayoso."

Franklin grabbed his hat up off the floor and stomped out. Blackjack and Little Nick watched him go.

"Maybe you should keep an eye on our banker friend."

"Sure thing, Blackjack." Little Nick grinned.

Flipping his quarter, Little Nick strolled out onto Beale and leaned against the wall. He watched the stuffed shirt hop into his crate and drive away. He reached into his pocket and felt the edge of his shiv, just to be sure it was nice and sharp. He could almost feel it slide up between the old gink's ribs now. Just give him one excuse. Just one.

CHAPTER 43

Nell gathered everyone in the kitchen. While Hattie fixed a fresh batch of biscuits, Nell, Calendar, and Bess sat around the table with Gaylord and Ginny.

"Ginny, if you're ready, I think it's time for you to tell us what happened," Nell said, handing Ginny a cup of tea.

Ginny looked at Gaylord, who squeezed her hand and nodded for her to go on. The girl shivered, but when she spoke, her voice was clear and strong. "Two men came to the club one night to watch the show. An old man I'd seen there before talking to Mr. Kelly and a younger one I didn't know. After the first set, Mr. Kelly told me they'd asked me to come to their table. I didn't usually do that, but he said it was all right. They looked nice, and they were so well dressed that I didn't think there would be any trouble. The older man didn't say anything. He just looked at me as though I smelled bad."

She took a deep breath before she went on.

"The younger man said he was a friend of yours, Gaylord, and that you'd asked them to take me out to supper after the club closed because you couldn't be there that night. He said you didn't want me to be alone, so he'd come to look out for me as a favor to you. He knew so much about you that I thought he must be your friend."

Ginny's eyes filled with tears. Hattie put a glass of water in front of her. Gaylord reached over and blotted her eyes with his handkerchief.

"It's all right, sweetheart," he said. "We need to hear what happened."

"Take your time," Nell said. "Just let it come out any way that you can."

Ginny nodded and sipped the water.

"We stopped in front of the Peabody. The older man got out of the back seat and looked at me through the window. I thought he was going to open the door for me the way you always do, Gaylord. But he nodded at the younger man, who pulled away. We left him standing at the curb, watching us drive off.

"That scared me a little, so I asked where we were going. The man who was driving said not to worry, that we were going to a special place out in the country that was really hard to get into but where he'd gotten us a reservation. Then we were at the hospital. He took me inside. I heard him tell the director that he was a doctor and that I was his patient, that he wanted me committed because I had just tried to kill myself in front of my whole family and a house full of people. I guess he said that to explain why I was all dressed up for going out and why he was wearing a tuxedo. He showed them some papers. I kept telling them who I was and that nothing he said was true, but they wouldn't believe me. They wouldn't even listen."

She gulped, took Gaylord's handkerchief from him, and pressed it against her eyes.

"Perhaps you're not quite ready to talk about this," Nell said.

"No, I need to," Ginny said. She scoured her eyes with the handkerchief and clutched it in both hands. "I asked that man why he was doing this. He told me that you had asked him to take me there." Her voice began to tremble, but she took another deep breath and went on. "He said you told him I was nothing but a dirty little whore and you didn't want me bothering you anymore. He said you were afraid I'd go to your family, tell them all about us, and demand money from them. He said you didn't want your mother soiled by being in the same room with me."

"How could you think that, Ginny?" Gaylord said. "After all the times I told you how much I loved you, how could you believe him?"

"What else could I think, Gaylord? I always knew your family wouldn't like me, that they'd think I wasn't good enough for you. And here was this man who looked so rich and important and acted like he knew you saying that I was too cheap for you. After he said all those things—I don't know—I felt like daddy's old mule had kicked me in the stomach. Like I was dying. Like it didn't matter what happened to me."

"Bless your heart," Bess said, blurting out the words and then covering her mouth with her hand as through embarrassed at having interrupted.

Ginny managed a weak smile. "That man said all those things, and then he just turned and walked way. He left me there without looking back even once."

"When I find that bastard, I'm going to kill him," Gaylord said.

"Ginny, would you recognize these men if you saw them again?" Calendar said.

"I think so, Dr. Calendar. The one who drove me to the hospital and left me there? Him, I could never forget. He had the meanest eyes I've ever seen. The other one? Yes, I think I'll know him if I see him again."

"If they are Memphis society, we may have some difficulty," Calendar said. "It's not as though their photos will be on file down at the police station."

"The society pages," Nell said. She glanced at the kitchen clock. "The Evans's train will be in soon, and I want to meet it. First thing in the morning, though, we'll take her down to the Press-Scimitar and get Oz Sherman to help her go through the society pages. And she can describe the two men to the police. Maybe they can draw likenesses that will help us recognize them."

CHAPTER 44

Over the years, there had been plenty of big parties in the Marchand house, but Nell didn't think it had ever quite felt as overflowing as it did with Ginny's family there. Luther, Kate, and all ten of her siblings down to the new baby, whom they were simply calling Baby until they could think of a name for him, had arrived on the train that afternoon.

When she saw her mother and father, Ginny hesitated.

"Girl, you got less sense that just about anybody I ever saw in my life," Luther said. "You know how much you worried your mama?"

"Yessir, Daddy. I know. I'm sorry."

Luther held out his arms to her. "Now come here and let me 'n' your mama hug your neck."

After that, it was all kissing and crying and carrying on about how everybody had known all along that it would all turn out all right.

Gaylord refused to leave Ginny even for an minute, so Nell sent Jenkins to his house with a note for his mother asking her to send some of Gaylord's clothes and telling her that Nell would explain later.

Thank goodness the house could accommodate them all without too much crowding. Bess insisted on giving up her room to Kate, Luther, and the baby and said she would be just as comfortable sleeping on the daybed in her sewing room as she would be in a suite at Buckingham Palace. Ginny remained in the guest room, it having been decided that she'd had enough crowding in Bolivar. Dividing up the two other Evans girls and six boys was easy.

Hattie, who loved a party more than anyone else Nell knew, was in her element. She made beds, fluffed pillows, and asked each of the children what their favorite things to eat were. When each said fried chicken because that was always what they ate at home for a special treat, Hattie decided that she would serve a big mess of it at every meal just so they would have something familiar.

Bess and Nell went through their closets and pulled out dresses for the girls and Kate. Half the boys were in Ellis's room. Nell had found that, despite what she said to the vagrant George Baxter in her kitchen, she'd had neither the time nor the inclination to make herself go through her dead husband's things to give to charity, and a good thing it was, too, Bess said, because now the older Evans boys would look as though they had just stepped out of the fashion pages. Bess went through the closet there picking out suits, shirts, and trousers to make over for them.

Bess was bent over a pair of trousers, shortening them just a hair for Luther, Jr., who was 14 and already almost as tall as Ellis had been, when a knock came at the door of the sewing room. Ginny stopped there with her sister Ruth, who looked as though she'd been caught stealing a watermelon.

"I'm sorry to bother you, Miss Bess, but Ruth snagged the pocket of this nice new dress you gave her on the doorknob and tore it," Ginny said. "She's awful upset, but I told her you could fix it in no time."

"Why, of course, I can." Bess motioned for the girls to come in.

"Come on in. Now dry your tears, Ruth, slip that dress over you head, and give it to me. I won't take a minute to fix that pocket, and it will be as good as new. You and Ginny come in and keep me company while I work on it."

Ruth did as she was told and sat on the daybed to look at the copy of "The Saturday Evening Post" that Bess had open beside her. When her sister didn't join her, Bess looked up. Ginny stood in the doorway, whiter than a cotton boll and trembling. Bess leapt to her feet and went to the girl, who stared past her to the sewing table, where Bess's favorite photograph of Ellis sat.

"What is it, my dear? Are you ill? Tell me what's wrong."

Ginny choked back a wail and bolted from the room, Bess hot on her trail. She stopped Ginny in the hallway and folded her in her arms. The girl clung to Bess, sobbing and whimpering as though the worst thing in the world she could ever have imagined had just come to pass.

"Ginny. Ginny. What is it, darling? Tell me, please."

The sound of Ginny's weeping brought Nell running from the kitchen, Hattie close behind. Gaylord bounded down the steps, taking them three or four at a time. He eased Ginny out of Bess's arms and into his own. "Ginny!"

"Mother, what on earth happened?" Nell said.

"I have no idea, Nell. One minute we were talking about repairing a tear in Ruth's dress, and the next, Ginny was standing there as though she'd watched the dead rise from their graves. I haven't been able to get her to stop crying long enough to tell me."

"Ginny?" Nell said. "What has upset you so, sweetheart?"

Ginny lifted her face from Gaylord's shoulder and gulped hard three times before she could summon enough of her voice to speak. "In there. The man who took me to Bolivar."

Nell turned to Bess, who looked as mystified as she felt. "What are you talking about, honey?" Nell said. "What man? Where?"

"On the table," Ginny said. "There's a picture of him on the table in Miss Bess's room."

Nell went into the sewing room and come out with the photograph of Ellis, the only one on the table. What could the girl be talking about? "Surely you don't mean this man, do you, Ginny?" She held the photo out for her to study. The girl hid her hands behind her as though to keep them from being burned and backed away.

"Yes, Miss Nell. That's him. That's the man who took me to the hospital and left me there. That's the man who told me Gaylord never wanted to see me again. That's him."

Lord help us, Ellis. What did you do?

"But that's impossible, my dear," Bess said, going to Ginny and pointing to the photo in Nell's hands. "This is a photograph of my son Ellis just after he graduated from the university. This couldn't possibly be the man you're talking about."

"It is, I tell you. It is. I would know those eyes anywhere. He's younger in the picture, but it's the same man."

Inconsolable, Ginny collapsed into sobs again. Gaylord rocked her, whispering to her and smoothing her hair. Bess stumbled toward the stairs to crumple onto them as her legs gave way. Nell clutched the photograph to her chest to keep herself from flinging it across the room and tried to think of something to say. Not a single word would come. She took a deep, shaky breath.

"Get Dr. Calendar, please, Hattie," Nell said when she could find her voice again. "Call him and tell him we need him right now."

Hattie ran for the phone.

"Gaylord, take Ginny into the sitting room. There's a decanter of whiskey on the desk. Pour her two fingers of it, and be sure that she drinks every drop. Bess, get a basin and a cloth and help her wash her face. I'll be along in a minute to wait with you until Joseph comes."

The group dispersed to do as they'd been told. Nell held Ellis's photo at arm's length and studied it, trying to see what Ginny had seen in his eyes.

—

CLAUDE BEAUMONT, PRESIDENT OF UNION PLANTERS BANK, FOLDED the newspaper that he had just plucked from the pile in front of him and set it beside his chair. He really must do a better job of keeping up with the news. He gazed thoughtfully out the window. Several moments later, he was still lost in thought. Mamie's voice drifted into his consciousness.

"Claude?"

"Yes, my dear?"

"Are you ill, Claude? I've been calling your name over and over, but you haven't responded. I was beginning to worry that you'd had some kind of fit."

"I'm sorry, my dear. I was thinking."

Mamie reached into her knitting bag for a new ball of yarn. "About Ginny Evans, no doubt. It's remarkable that she's been found, isn't it?"

"Yes, remarkable, Mamie. I was thinking about her as a matter of fact. Will you excuse me, my dear? I must go back to the office for a while."

"But I was just about to ask the cook to start supper."

"Don't wait supper for me. I can fix a sandwich when I get home."

"You're absolutely sure that you're feeling all right?

"Yes, dear. I'm well. Just preoccupied. I'm sorry to worry you, but I really must go."

"Well, all right, Claude."

Deciding on the crimson yarn, Mamie cast the first loops onto her needles. Maybe she would give the cook the night off and have a sandwich herself. There was still some pimento cheese left from the bridge club. Claude could fend for himself.

—

NELL CLOSED THE DOOR TO THE SITTING ROOM AND TOOK HER PLACE beside Calendar on the sofa facing Ginny and Gaylord. Calendar held the photograph of Ellis Marchand out to Ginny, who shrank back from it as far as she could.

"I know this is difficult, Ginny, but I want you to take this picture and study it carefully," Calendar said.

The girl held the image in front of her. After a few moments, Calendar took it from her and set it on the table so that it faced the group. Ginny wiped her hands on her skirt.

"Try to empty your mind of everything except this man's face," he said. "Now, forget it. Close your eyes. Think back to the night you were taken to Bolivar. You are in the car on your way out into the country. There's a man on the seat beside you. I want you to concentrate on his face. When you can see him clearly, I want you to open your eyes again."

Ginny opened her eyes.

"Are you sure that the man in the photograph is the same man who took you to the hospital and left you there?"

"Yes, sir. It's him. He's younger in this picture, but it's him. You won't tell him I'm here, will you?" The girl cowered against Gaylord, who put a protective arm around her shoulders.

"Ellis Marchand is dead, Ginny," Nell said. "He can't hurt you or anyone else ever again."

"He was your husband?" Ginny said, her eyes wide with disbelief. Or was it revulsion?

"I was married to him, yes."

"I'm sorry Mrs. Marchand."

"So am I, Ginny."

"What happened to him?"

"It doesn't matter now. He's gone, and he can't find you."

Ginny leaned her head against Gaylord's shoulder. Her whole body relaxed, and she smiled.

Gaylord kissed her hand and held it between both of his. "What can we do now, Mrs. Marchand? With Mr. Marchand dead, how will we find out why he took Ginny to that place?"

"There's still the older man, Gaylord. He's the key to the whole mystery, and we'll find him. I promise you."

CHAPTER 45

At the Press-Scimitar offices the next morning, Osgood Sherman placed the book of bound newspapers on the table in front of Ginny Evans.

"I figured we'd start with the last year first and work backward if we have to," he said.

"Thank you, Oz," Nell said. "We're looking only at the society pages, so I hope this will go fairly quickly. But, there's no need to hurry, Ginny. Take all the time you need."

Dragging the book over, Gaylord opened it. He put his arm around Ginny's shoulders and turned the pages for her when she was ready. Nell and Calendar waited and hoped.

After half an hour, they had been through three years' worth of papers. Gaylord pulled another volume in front of her and had just begun to flip to the society section when Ginny grew very still.

"Go back," she said, her voice the barest whisper.

"Where, darling?" Gaylord said. "Did you see something?"

Ginny paged back to the financial news and stopped at the photo of Ed Crump with a panel of bankers. She put out a shaking finger and let it come to rest on the image of the man seated at Crump's right.

Gaylord went as pale as a new moon. "That man? That's the man you met with Ellis Marchand?"

Ginny nodded. "Do you know him?"

Gaylord didn't answer. He put his head in his hands.

"Gaylord?" Ginny touched his shoulder.

He sat up, his face a mask of despair. "That is Franklin Bryant. My father."

"Oh, sweet Lord," Ginny said. "What are we doing to do?"

Nell and Calendar peered over their shoulders. Nell gasped, the world spun for a moment, and she grabbed at Calendar's arm. Puzzled, he turned to her.

"Lord have mercy," she said. Her heart flipped in her chest. "Mildred was right."

"Tomorrow, we're going to get married, Ginny," Gaylord said. "We're going to get married, and I'm going to find us somewhere to live. I'm never going back to his house again except to tell him exactly what I think of him. I'll give him the chance to admit what he did to you. If he doesn't, then I'm going to give Mr. Sherman an interview and expose him myself."

"That will ruin him, you know," Nell said quietly, praying that Gaylord would do exactly that.

"I know, and I don't care. He almost destroyed Ginny and me. I don't think he deserves any consideration. I would kill him, but he's not worth that. Making sure he pays for what he did is second best."

"What about your mother?" Nell said.

"I'm sorry about what it will do to her. He's already hurt her so much, but I can't help that. If Mama wants to come live with us, she can, but after that, I will never see my father or speak to him again, even if it means we have to leave Memphis."

His newshound's nose twitching, Oz appeared at the table. "Any luck?"

"Gaylord and Ginny aren't ready to talk about it yet," Nell said. She rested a hand on each of their shoulders.

"Oh, come on, now." Oz pulled out a notebook. "Haven't I been on your side all through this thing?"

"You'll get your story, Mr. Sherman," Gaylord said. "One way or another. But we need a little time."

"OK, son. But when you're ready, remember your old buddy Oz."

"Thank you for understanding, Oz," Nell said. "Let's get Ginny home, get that wedding planned, and decide what we need to do next."

—

BACK AT THE MARCHAND HOUSE IN THE JUDGE'S STUDY, NELL POURED healthy glugs of whiskey for herself and Calendar. She kicked off her shoes and sat beside him.

"I don't think I've ever had a drink before noon before," she said. She clinked her glass against his and tossed her drink back. "I may have another."

"That was rather a startling way to discover that your husband was most likely murdered." Calendar swirled his drink, sipped it, and studied her face. "Are you all right, Nell?"

She leaned her head against the back of the chair. "I don't know. I suppose there's no way to know for sure if someone really shot Ellis without digging him up and taking a good long look at his skull." She shuddered. "What would that accomplish anyway, other than more pain for poor Bess? After what he did to Ginny, I believe he got the justice he deserved. And when the truth comes out about what happened to her, Franklin will be destroyed, too."

"I wonder if that will be enough of retribution to suit fierce little Mildred."

Nell reached for the decanter and started to pour herself another drink. Thinking better of it, she returned the decanter to the Judge's desk. "You know what? I don't give one hoot in hell if it does. Besides, we've got a wedding to put on tomorrow."

—

THE NEXT MORNING, THE WEDDING PARTY GATHERED IN THE FRONT hall of the Marchand mansion. Nell, Bess, all the Evanses, Hattie, Jenkins, and Joseph Calendar. Gaylord and Reverend Hezekiah Sharpe stood at the foot of the stairs, waiting. Ginny appeared on the landing, breathtaking in the gown Bess had worn when she married Daniel Ellis Overton Marchand III. Bess sniffled.

Gaylord gazed up at Ginny as though he could not believe she was real. She floated down the stairs and into his arms like a ship coming to safe harbor after a typhoon. By Reverend Sharpe's final benediction, a lot more sniffles joined Bess's.

Afterward, they all went into the dining room, where Hattie had laid out a wedding lunch.

"Happy, darling?" Gaylord said.

"You don't know how happy," Ginny said. "I just wish your mother could have been here, though."

"So do I. I didn't want to run the risk of my father finding out and trying to interfere. Once I've told her everything, she'll understand." He kissed Ginny, who blushed and looked around the table at everyone who was watching. "I'm sorry I can't take you on a proper honeymoon, but I promise one day I'll take you all over Europe. I'll take you anywhere you want to go."

"I'm going to like being Mrs. Gaylord Bryant."

"I'll have to get a job, but we'll manage somehow. I'm going to take good care of you from now on."

—

AFTER THE LUNCH, GAYLORD TOLD GINNY THAT NOW THAT THEY WERE safely married, he didn't want to put off confronting his father another minute. Nell stood on her front steps with the boy, waiting for Jenkins to bring the car around.

"I wish you would let me go with you, Gaylord," she said. "I've got a few things to say to your father myself."

"No, Miss Nell. Thank you. This has to be between my father and me. If I don't go face him, I won't ever be able to call myself a man. But don't worry. Much as I might want to kill him, I won't. I promised

Ginny that I wouldn't lay a hand on him, no matter what he says or does."

"Ginny is right. It's not worth it. Say what you need to say and come back home." She hugged the boy. "We'll be here, waiting."

"You sure are good to let us stay with you, Miss Nell."

"As long as you want, Gaylord. You know you and Ginny are welcome."

Jenkins stopped the Duesenberg at the front walk. Gaylord climbed in. Before the car pulled away, he gave Nell a gallant smile.

Nell thought to herself what a good thing it was that he took after his mother's side of the family.

CHAPTER 46

Pounding on his parents' front door, Gaylord reminded himself that he had promised not to hit his father when he saw him.

Franklin opened the door himself and looked fit to be tied when he discovered his son standing on the stoop. "What business did you have taking yourself off to Nell Marchand's house? You have worried your mother half to death. And let me tell you, I'm none too pleased with you myself."

"I don't give a damn what you think."

Franklin rocked back on his heels as though he had been slapped across the face. "Watch your mouth, boy. Have you completely lost your mind?"

"Gaylord!" his mother said, coming into the hallway in time to hear their exchange.

"Mama, you need to leave me alone with him, please. Wait for me in the parlor. I want to talk to you after we're done." He turned to his father. "In your study, now."

"Do you presume to give me orders in my own house, Gaylord Bryant? I've a good mind to take my strap to you even if you are almost 20 years old."

"Try it, and I'll kill you."

"Gaylord, please!" his mother said. She rushed to grab him by the arm.

He pried her fingers off gently. She stepped back, looking from him to her husband. Gaylord pushed past his father and stood waiting at the door of the old man's office.

"Go along to the parlor, Margaret," Franklin said. "I'll get this straightened out."

She shot an anxious look at the two before she disappeared into the parlor. Gaylord stood aside to let his father pass into the study, drawing back as though the old man were a leper and to touch him would mean certain infection.

"Explain yourself, boy." Arms crossed, Franklin positioned himself in front of his desk.

"You're the one who has the explaining to do. I know what you did to Ginny. I know you sent her to rot away among a bunch of lunatics in Bolivar. I know you tried to destroy her."

"You don't know what you're talking about." Franklin screwed up his face like a man who has just stepped in dog's leavings. "That trashy girl came to me asking for money, wanted me to buy her off, and I did." All righteous innocence, he drew himself up and glowered down his nose at his son.

"Don't lie anymore. Ginny identified you and Ellis Marchand. She told us exactly what happened, that you had him take her to Bolivar and leave her there. You can't get out of it this time. Not even Ed Crump will want to have anything to do with you."

The old man sat down hard in the chair beside his desk, every iota of arrogance vanished. "I did it to protect you, son. I thought that girl was out for your money. She wasn't the kind of people I wanted allied with the Bryant name." He buried his face in his hands.

Gaylord clinched his fists at his sides. It was becoming harder and harder not to punch him. "And what kind of people should I ally myself with? Liars? Philanderers? They're your kind. Ginny's father is a farmer, a poor dirt farmer, yes, but an honest man, which is more than anyone will ever be able to say about you again." Gaylord went to stand over his father where he huddled in the chair. "How could you send her to that place?"

"I'm sorry, son. Ellis Marchand said he was going to give her money to go away. He said he was going to tell her that you were through with her in such a way that she'd never want to come near you again, but I never dreamed . . . . " Franklin stood, tried to put a conciliatory hand on his son's shoulder. Gaylord slapped it away and took a step back. His father slumped.

"I am at fault, of course, Gaylord. When Marchand offered to help with the problem, I was relieved and grateful. I thought I didn't care what he did as long as he got Ginny Evans away from you. That was wrong. I should have made sure that the girl wasn't hurt, but I swear to you, I had no idea what he was going to abandon her in that place. I hope you're still enough my son to know that I am not that depraved."

"I will never believe anything you say ever again." Gaylord backed toward the door. "If you ever put your hands on me or Ginny or come near us again, I'll kill you."

"Come home, son. We can work through this, you, your mother, and I. Won't you give me another chance?"

"Ginny and I married this morning, Pop. Pop. It makes me sick to say that word. Do you think I would ever bring her here to the same house with the bastard who sent her away?"

"Son, please." The old man held out both hands, pleading.

Gaylord started toward him. He cowered, expecting a blow.

"No. There's only one thing that might make up for what you did," Gaylord said.

"I'll do anything you say."

"Then go to the telephone and call Osgood Sherman at the Press-Scimitar. Here's the number. Tell him you have the solution to the mystery of Ginny Evans and that you're ready to tell him everything. You will make a full confession to him. You will tell him that it was you who took Ginny to Bolivar. You will not say a word about Ellis Marchand's part in this. You will say that it was all your doing, that you abandoned her there."

A condemned man on his way to the noose could not have moved more slowly than Franklin Bryant did crossing to the telephone. He sat behind the desk, raised the receiver to his ear, and asked the operator for the Press-Scimitar.

"Mr. Sherman, please," he said. There was a pause. "Mr. Sherman, this is Franklin Bryant. I need to speak to you about something important. Would it be convenient for me to come to your office this afternoon? Yes, that's fine. Thank you." He hung up the receiver and turned desolate eyes on his son. "There now. I will do what you ask."

Gaylord felt a little of the rage go out of him, just a little. "Someone needs to tell Mama now. She has to know before the story comes out in the paper tomorrow. Will you do it, or do I have to?"

"We'll go together, Gaylord. But before we speak to your mother, please understand that what I did, I did out of love and concern for you and for her."

The old fraud was determined to keep up the charade to the end, wasn't he? "Don't talk to me about love. I know all about you and Mildred Epps. Everybody knows. I've been waiting for you to wake up and realize what you were doing. I thought you'd come back to Mama in time. But it's too late now. It will be up to her to decide what she wants once she knows what you have done."

"You're not going to leave me anything, are you, Gaylord? Can you really hate me that much?"

The old man had no idea just how much. "You did this to yourself. As you've always been so fond of telling me, you've made your bed. Now you've got to lie in it."

"All right, son. Let's get it over with."

—

AFTERWARD, GAYLORD WOULD REMEMBER MOST HOW CALM HIS mother had been. In her shoes, he would have clubbed Franklin bloody, ripped his tongue from his lying mouth and fed it to the dogs, and cut off his rancid old pecker and given that to the dogs, too. But his mother heard her husband out before she responded. She believed in being a lady always.

Margaret Bryant opened the door of her husband's study before she turned back to him, her expression composed and her hands clasped in front of her.

"You will go upstairs right this minute, Franklin, and pack a bag. Then you will leave this house. Don't imagine that you will ever set foot within these walls again. From this moment on, the house and everything else you own are mine. I'll phone Anton Green and ask him to draw up the papers. You will sign them without question and without hesitation. Once that is done, you will never attempt to speak to me again. If you do, if you dare to oppose me in any way, I will leave you without so much as the clothes on your back. Do you understand me?"

"Yes, Margaret," Franklin said, he voice barely audible.

She addressed her son. "Gaylord, you and your bride are welcome to come and live with me. This is a big house, and I wouldn't know what to do with myself without you here. If in the future you decide to have anything to do your father again, it cannot be here, of course. Otherwise, this will always be your home. Ginny and all of her family will be welcome here."

"Thank you, Mama."

She turned back to her husband. "Go on, Franklin, and close the door behind you. Ask Fanny to tell me when you are gone. As long as I live, I never want to rest the weight of my eyesight on you again."

"I'm sorry, Margaret."

She crossed to the window and looked out until she heard the parlor door close behind him. After another minute, she went to Gaylord, smiling as though no one more troubling than a tedious guest had been sent on his way.

"Take the car, dear. Bring Ginny home. She can have her pick of rooms in the house, including mine. I will never sleep in that bed again."

"I'm sorry, Mama. I wish I hadn't had to put you through this."

"Go on, Gaylord." She kissed him on the cheek. "I've got to call Anton, and I don't want you to have to listen to what I say to him."

CHAPTER 47

Blackjack Kelly was as much of a patriot as anyone, but there were days that he cursed the Kaiser, Archduke Ferdinand, and even Woodrow Wilson, for whom he usually had nothing but praise. The German bullet that had lodged in his left shoulder at the Second Battle of the Marne was giving him fits.

"It's going to rain today." He pressed his fingers over the scar through his shirt.

"Shoulder bothering you again?" Little Nick said.

"Yeah, it's killing me." Blackjack rotated his arm, trying to work a little of the stiffness and ache out. "Sometimes I wish I had let the docs take my arm off like they wanted, but it's too hard holding a machine gun with one hand."

Little Nick cackled the same way he did whenever Jack Benny started to maul his violin. "You're a riot, Blackjack. A regular riot. If we ever get out of the booze business, you oughta get a job on the radio."

"Yeah, well, we got away easy on this Franklin Bryant deal. Now Prohibition is on its way out, I'm thinking it's time we both retire and look for something else to do, kid."

"You don't mind that so much, do you, Blackjack? You said we'd go legit one day anyway. Have a real restaurant."

"This is going to push us along. I hope you like wearing a white jacket and carrying a napkin over your arm. You'll have to clean up your language, too. I can't have no tough-talking waiters if we're going to have a genteel clientele in the joint."

"I thought I got to be the maitre d'." Little Nick pronounced it "mater dee." He looked at himself in the mirror behind the bar and ran a hand through his hair. "I want to wear the monkey suit and stand up front. One of those double-breasted jobs like they got at the Congress Hotel in Chicago."

"That'll be my job. I can't carry a tray with this bum wing of mine."

"I thought you was going be the owner. The class. Sit at the bar and stroll around asking everybody if they was having a good time."

"We got to start out slow, just like with this place." Blackjack did a couple of deep-knee bends and swung his arms again. "I'm figuring just the two of us and a cook at first. Then, when things start to catch on and we're busy all the time, you move up front, and I retire to a booth by the door."

"OK. I can handle that." Giving his image one more glance, Little Nick stuck a toothpick in his mouth and rolled it from one corner to the other. "So, you really think there's going to be no more Prohibition?"

"I think we'll be out of business by the end of the year. That's when they're voting on the amendment."

"I'm going to miss the speak."

"Not me," Blackjack said. He leaned back in his chair, fingers interlaced behind his head. "I'm looking forward to taking it easy. Sure, the dough is good, but I got some socked away. I'm tired of dealing with all the dames coming in and hustling for work and the bums who follow them in here. I'm tired of counting money that ain't mine. I'm tired of roughing people up."

"Me, too, Blackjack. It ain't so much fun anymore." Little Nick removed the toothpick, studied it, and shook his head. He rubbed his knuckles. "That Lois Brown job, it just didn't seem right."

"Tell me about it," Blackjack said, studying the ceiling. "I'm tired of the rackets. I think it'd be nice to run a clean joint, wholesome-like, you know? A place where you can bring your wife and the family, eat high-quality grub, have a drink or two if you want, and go home feeling good about the whole thing. Class, Little Nick. What I'm talking about is class."

"Yeah, boss," Little Nick said dreamily. "Class."

—

THREE DAYS AFTER GAYLORD AND GINNY WERE MARRIED IN HER FRONT hall, Nell went with them to see the Evans clan off at the train station. Luther insisted that he needed to get back to the farm. He'd had enough of Memphis to last him for a good while, no two ways about it.

"Mr. Evans, is there something you need on the farm that I can help with?" Gaylord said. He put his hand inside his jacket to get his wallet.

"You take good care of our Ginny, son, and that's enough," Luther said. He pushed away the money the boy offered. "You don't have to take all the rest of us to raise. I ain't so old and broke down that I can't look after my family."

"I know that, sir, but you're all my family now, too. I want to help any way I can. It won't be much at first, of course, but I hope you'll let me do something."

"Daddy's been saying he needs a new mule," Ginny said. "Old Zeb is mighty gray in the muzzle, and Sal isn't much younger. Why don't we get you a mule, Daddy?"

Ginny looked from her father to her new husband and back again. Gaylord held out his hand to Luther, who shook it and slapped him on the back.

"Thank you, son."

"And do you mind if we call the baby Gaylord after you?" Kate said. "He can't go on without a name forever."

"Yes, ma'am." Gaylord grinned. "I'd be proud if you did."

The conductor called out, "All aboard." Waving, the Evanses piled onto the train. Ginny waved back until the caboose was out of sight and a little longer for good measure.

—

BACK AT THE HOUSE, NELL FOUND HATTIE IN THE KITCHEN, SNIFFLING over the pile of breakfast dishes.

"Hattie, what are you crying about?" Nell said.

"Nothing." Hattie wiped her eyes on her sleeve. "It's just that the house is going to feel mighty empty without all those children running around."

"It does seem quiet as a tomb now, doesn't it?"

"I always hoped you would have a house full yourself."

"Of children? You ought to be glad I didn't. Not with Ellis Marchand. Lord knows I am."

"It's not too late, you know."

"Well, there is the awkward business of not having a husband. I'm not ready to ask for that kind of notoriety yet."

"Dr. Calendar is a fine man." Hattie glanced at Nell sideways. "Handsome as a picture, too."

Rolling her eyes, Nell flopped down at the table. "Don't you start, too, Hattie. I don't ever want to get married again. Once was more than enough. Besides, Joseph Calendar is my friend. I don't want to ruin it by trying to make him more than that. And I don't think he wants a wife any more than I want a husband. He told me himself that he can't afford to be in love."

"Then you haven't got eyes in your head. I have never seen a man look at a woman with more wanting than how he looks at you. You give him the high sign, and he'll be on his knees at your feet."

"Hush, Hattie. The last thing I want to do is have him at my feet. We're fine just the way we are."

Hattie pulled out a chair and sat, too. "I'm not the only one thinks it would be a good idea. Miss Bess has got him all picked out for you."

"Well, you and Miss Bess can just mind your own business." Nell tossed her gloves at Hattie. "If you want this house to fill up with children, then you're going to have to supply them yourself. That's not a job I'm about to take on. There are too many other things I want to do."

"You going to keep on telling fortunes?"

"Long as I don't have any more visions."

"Uh-huh." Hattie went back to the sink full of dishes. "The thing about the Lord is He answers your prayers, but He doesn't always answer the way you want. I think you're going to have to take your visions any way He sends them and just hope you can figure them out."

CHAPTER 48

Beside the fireplace in Nell's sitting room, Joseph Calendar stood swirling brandy in the glass in his hand. The firelight picked out gold glints in his hair, and Nell found herself admiring his profile. She sipped her own brandy.

"I've known Franklin Bryant all my life, and I never on earth would have believed him capable of any of those things."

"Most people believe they're strong until they're truly tested. Even metal will bend at its weakest point."

"I think Ellis crumbled the minute Miss Bess gave birth to him. I don't know how I could have married such a man."

"There must have been something there, at least in the beginning. Some fine qualities that attracted you." Calendar came to sit beside her. "Be gentle with yourself, Nell. Whatever his sins, they had nothing to do with you."

"Thank you for that, Joseph." She squeezed his hand and released it quickly.

"You're sure you don't want to inquire more into his death? Doesn't that feel like unfinished business?"

His eyes were solemn. She knew that if she asked, he wouldn't rest until they knew the truth about what had happened to Ellis. That was enough for her.

"I'm sure. Even if he did kill Ellis, Franklin has been punished enough to suit me. I don't want Gaylord finding out his daddy was a murderer, too. All I want is to put this whole thing behind me. Let the dead stay buried."

"Then it is finished."

A log settled on the fire, sending a tongue of flame blazing up the chimney. They watched it burn.

"Thank you for everything you've done," Nell said. "I'm not sure I could have gotten through any of it if it weren't for you."

"What will you do now?"

"Go on telling fortunes. You know, it dawned on me that I really enjoy it, and I believe I'm offering a service to the people of Memphis. It's a little like being a minister."

He smiled an enigmatic smile. "Perhaps we could join forces. With my powers of observation and your visionary abilities, we could accomplish great things."

"That, I'm not ready to do." Nell leaned her head against sofa and smiled back at him. "I think I prefer to go on as I was before. And I'm counting my lucky stars that I'm not having visions any more. I was beginning to think that it had something to do with you."

"Nell, I believe your gift is yours to command or deny now. It's up to you."

Nell made a face but said nothing. They sipped their brandy in peace for a while.

"Joseph, you know just about everything there is to know about me, but you're a mystery. You never speak of your family or say much about your past. You never say anything at all about yourself."

"There's not much to tell. I was born poor, but I found my way out into the world. Through the guidance of wise teachers, I learned the work that I do now. I have been fortunate in my calling."

"After studying in London and Vienna, why did you come to Memphis when you could have gone anywhere else in the world? When Ellis died, I thought I wanted to put as much of the world between me and this place as possible. I was going to start with Paris and see every country I could before I decided if I ever wanted to come back here."

Calendar swirled the brandy in his glass again and studied its depths.

When he looked at her, he seemed almost guarded for a moment. Then he smiled, and it was gone.

"Something called me here. The world is wide and filled with wonders. I wanted to explore them all. I've seen things and been places that most people only dream of, and, yet, there was so much more to investigate. I had no plans to come to Memphis or even to return to the United States, but something seemed to draw me here. The minute I stepped off the train, I knew I was home. I knew that whatever it was that I had searched for all my life was here."

"Have you found it? The thing you were searching for?"

"Perhaps. It's too soon to tell."

THE END

ACKNOWLEDGMENTS

I am grateful to the wonderful folks who started the annual National Novel Writing Challenge, during which I blasted through the first draft. Without the companionship of Catherine Morris, Sherry Thomas, and Tracy Wolff for writing dates, I might not have finished it.

Thank you to Wendy Dittmer and Jason LaTurner for offering me the perfect writer's getaway while I revised that first very rough NaNoWriMo draft.

When I was trying to articulate what this story is about, Emily McKay helped me boil it down to a concise pitch. Deanna Carlyle, Rochelle Staab, and Gabrielle Luthy each read the manuscript at one stage or another, and their encouragement gave me the faith to continue. Thank you all.

About the Author

The author of award-winning novels and screenplays, Jane Sevier began her career as a feature writer. She covered fields as varied as artificial intelligence, the arts, the environment, and international affairs and traveled on assignment to exotic locales as diverse as Ecuador, Sri Lanka, and Texarkana, Texas. Several of her feature stories garnered national and regional awards. Jane loves travel and has lived in Nashville, Dallas, Paris, Washington, D.C., and Austin. An 8th-generation Tennessean, she will always be a true child of the South, no matter where she hangs her hat. Visit her at www.janesevier.com.

Made in the USA
Lexington, KY
30 August 2015